MW00475987

A
TOR
DOUBLE

ACTION
WESTERN

**Look for Tor Double Action Westerns
from these authors**

MAX BRAND
ZANE GREY
LEWIS B. PATTEN
WAYNE D. OVERHOLSER
CLAY FISHER
FRANK BONHAM
OWEN WISTER
STEVE FRAZEE
HARRY SINCLAIR DRAGO
JOHN PRESCOTT*
WILL HENRY*
L. C. TUTTLE*

*coming soon

Harry Sinclair Drago

LONE WOLF OF DRYGULCH TRAIL

MORE PRECIOUS THAN GOLD

TOR

A TOM DOHERTY ASSOCIATES BOOK
NEW YORK

LONE WOLF OF DRYGULCH TRAIL

Copyright 1936 by Periodical House, Inc. First published in *Sure-Fire Western*.

MORE PRECIOUS THAN GOLD

Copyright 1926 by The Frank A. Munsey Co.; copyright © renewed 1954 by Harry Sinclair Drago.

Compilation copyright © 1990 by Tor Books.

A Tor Book
Published by Tom Doherty Associates, Inc.
49 West 24th Street
New York, N.Y. 10010

Cover art by Ballestar

ISBN: 0-812-50542-5

First edition: November 1990

Printed in the United States of America

0 9 8 7 6 5 4 3 2 1

LONE WOLF OF DRYGULCH TRAIL

CHAPTER 1
Dead Man's Message

IN THE WHITE-HOT BITTER NOON, A SOLITARY HORSEMAN PICKED his way across the broken, lava-strewn plains of the Snake River Desert. A low ridge loomed ahead, and he made for it.

Summer and winter, winds forever fan those barren wastelands. Today was no exception; the desert zephyr kicking up little dust-devils that danced mockingly across the alkali flats. The rider went on unmindful of them, but his big, rangy black gelding eyed them suspiciously, and lowering its head, began to snort violently as the biting dust settled in its nostrils.

"All right, old-timer; just take it easy," the man urged. "We'll be out of this stuff directly. Accordin' to the map I've got in my head, that's Shoshone Butte over there to the north-west. Reckon we'll find ourselves right on top of their little old railroad before long."

He found himself in strange country—which had been the rule with him of late—but it imposed no great handicap, for he was a desert man and able to orient himself with uncanny accuracy.

From the crest of the ridge a rolling gray sea of stunted sage-brush stretched away to the horizon in all directions. Below him a line of telegraph poles marched toward the blue blur to the north that was the Salmon River Range.

"That'll be the railroad," he mused, his eyes focused on the stubby poles which looked no bigger than match sticks against the immensity of the desert, "and that huddle of buildin's will just about be Castro."

Unconsciously his mouth tightened as he gazed at the distant town, and his laughing blue eyes were suddenly cold and hard.

"This may be the place," he murmured grimly. "If it ain't, we'll just keep movin' along. Some day we'll just naturally have to pick up the trail we've been tryin' to find all these months. Until we do, we ain't got no other business on our minds, old-timer."

He was a young man—still in his twenties—but there was something about his bronzed, square-jawed fighting face that labeled him a person of experience. Certainly the manner in which he carried his forty-fives, belt hung low, the holsters strapped down to his chaps in the way of men who expect to have instant need of their guns, suggested that he could fill his hand in a hurry.

He was Laramie Johnson. The name smacked of Wyoming, and with good reason, for his home was in the Wind River Valley. But it was in northern Arizona, in that wide strip of country between the Mogollons and the Mazatzals, where, as the chief agent of the Tonto Basin Cattlemen's Association, that he had won no little measure of fame for the courageous and relentless war he had waged against organized rustling. When he had first said a man could not rustle cattle in the Basin and live, no one believed he could make the words good.

But he had. And therein lay the bitter irony that had changed the course of his life and turned the nectar of success to gall and wormwood; for while he was breaking up rustling in the Tonto, the Hole-in-the-Wall gang, the most vicious band of outlaws Wyoming had ever known, was plundering Wind River Valley, boldly running off stock and snuffing out the lives of those who dared to oppose them.

Kit Johnson, his younger brother, a boy of nineteen, had fallen before their guns. The news had been weeks in reaching Laramie. It had shaken him as nothing had ever done, for in losing Kit he lost about everything he had in the world.

For two years he had stubbornly refused to permit the boy to join him in the Tonto, thinking only to keep him out of danger. Unable to forgive himself for the decision, he had returned to Wyoming at once, to take up the cold trail of the killers.

In the meantime, the outlaws had been routed in a running battle that had lasted three days. With feeling so high against them, the gang had disintegrated and left the Hole-in-the-Wall for parts unknown. But Kit had scrawled a message on an empty cartridge box before he died. Of the four men who had cut him down, he had recognized one as Ike Mundy, the leader of the Hole-in-the-Wall gang. The others were strangers. One of them, however, had two fingers missing from his right hand.

Without any other clues to guide him, Laramie had begun his manhunt. It had taken him across Wyoming and Montana, through the Bitter Root Mountains and now into Idaho.

He had hung on tenaciously, refusing to admit defeat; but after months of searching he was still without the faintest clue as to the whereabouts of the four men whom he sought. But there was always tomorrow, and always another town.

As the big black came down off the ridge the going got better. Of its own volition, the gelding broke into a distance-devouring lope. Laramie's lips curled into a smile.

"Just remembered that we didn't have any breakfast, eh?" he queried. "Well, shake it up if you want to; but I sure hope we'll find somethin' more than a meal waitin' for us when we hit Castro. It's all new country north of here; no wire, no law, no nothing—and no questions asked." Suddenly his blue eyes were hard again. "That would appeal to the hombres who got Kit."

It was enough to inspire fresh hope in him. Presently he could see the steel rails glistening in the sun. Castro took definite form, bald and unlovely in the way of desert cowtowns, without a single tree to soften the ugliness of the score or more buildings that comprised it.

The hotel stood at the end of the street nearest the depot. Two men sat on the porch, chairs tilted back under the wooden awning. Without seeming to, they scrutinized him sharply as he rode up and nodded their heads in answer to the impersonal nod of greeting he gave them.

A crudely lettered sign announced that there was a feed-barn in back of the hotel. It made the question he had been about to ask unnecessary, and he turned into the alley that led to the rear. As he passed the corner of the building the two men exchanged a glance.

"Stranger," the taller of the two volunteered. He was a big man with piercing black eyes and hawk-like nose. "Notice the way he carries his guns, Judge?"

"Yeh, I noticed three or four things about him," the other answered. He was Heck Small, the justice of the peace; a heavy-set little man with a thatch of white hair and the round, pink cheeks of a child. "That big horse he's ridin' is wearin' a brand I never saw before. Where do you suppose he's from, Trace?"

"I wouldn't know," Trace replied. "He's kinda advertisin' the fact that he's tough, ain't he, ridin' into a strange town with his guns tied down to his chaps?" His lips curled into a contemptuous grin.

"That may be the general effect he's aimin' at," Heck agreed. "But don't get the idea this gent is a tinhorn. There's somethin' about the cut of him that makes me think he'd finish anythin' he started."

"Well," Trace exclaimed, "he seems to have taken your eye, Judge." Whether he intended it or not, there was a note of derision in the big fellow's tone. "He may be the man for you at that. At least he looks like a gunfighter."

Heck's white mustache bristled indignantly. "Hunh!" he snorted crustily. "You're gettin' to be quite a mind-reader, ain't yuh? How come you know what I'm thinkin'?"

"Aw shucks, Judge," Trace laughed immodestly, "an hour after I got in yesterday I heard that you and Washburn and the leadin' lights of Castro was lookin' for someone who could take the kink out of this town."

"Well, I reckon that's our business," Heck exclaimed testily.

"Sure! I'm not sayin' she ain't a mite wild and woolly—"

"A mite, eh?" The Judge had difficulty containing himself. "She's a hissin', spittin', curly wolf—that's what she is! A good dose of law and order might sweat some of the hell out of her. It's got so that every time a bunch of you punchers hit town you figger you've got the right to shoot out the windows and lights and stampede law-abidin' folks off the street. That's got to stop!"

"Well, I wouldn't get too serious about it," Trace advised. "A man spends his money in a town and he ought to have the right to let off steam a little. I—" He broke off abruptly and fixed his eyes on Heck. There was something cold and sinister in their icy depths. "There ain't nothin' personal in your remarks—is there, Judge? I had a little trouble here early this spring—"

"No—no, I wasn't pickin' you out specially. Burley always ran a crooked game. Nobody shed any tears over his demise. As a matter of fact, Trace, the neatness and dispatch with which you handled yourself in that little affair has led certain parties to believe we might go a long ways and do worse than appoint you town marshal."

"What? Pin a star on me?" The big man shook his head and said no. He was pleased nevertheless. "Not for me, Judge! I'll just keep on drawin' my wages from the Fryin'-pan. It's a good outfit, and me and Corbett hit it off okay."

Hughie Stone, the proprietor of the hotel, stuck his bald head out of the door. "Well, that damn Chink has finally got his 'taters cooked; I guess you boys can eat. This gent that just rode in is havin' dinner too. I'll set you all down together."

Heck caught Trace's eye as they stepped inside. "Just remember that anythin' I said to you was strictly private."

Trace nodded. "I get you, Judge."

A moment or two after they were seated, Laramie joined them. He had paused to refresh himself at the washstand in the rear. Hughie took their orders. They were the only diners.

Laramie was prepared to eat his meal without the aid of conversation, being obviously a stranger. Heck had other plans.

"I'm Heck Small, the justice of the peace," he volunteered. "This is Trace Morrell, of the Fryin'-pan outfit."

"Johnson is my name," Laramie said, acknowledging the introduction.

"Howdy," Morrell murmured in turn. "Saw you ride in a minute ago. Don't remember seein' you hereabouts before."

"No, first time," Laramie admitted, masking whatever surprise he felt at this unexpected affability and interest in himself. For reasons of his own he had no desire to discourage it. He turned to Heck.

"I suppose you're one of the old-timers here."

"Yeh," the Judge admitted, "I sorta grew up with the place. I used to brag that in one way or another I knew every man in this part of Idaho. Course now the railroad's bringin' in new people. But we see most everybody here in Castro, sooner or later."

Laramie decided to cultivate Heck's acquaintance. He glanced up to discover Morrell studying him furtively. Trace's manner was friendly enough, but under it Laramie sensed a vague hostility.

Hughie brought in their dinner. He set a platter of hot biscuits down in front of Laramie. "Just pass 'em around," he said; "I'll bring in some more when they're gone."

Laramie offered them to the Judge. Heck helped himself generously.

"You won't find the food bad at all if you've got any appetite," he declared

"Looks good and smells good," Laramie agreed, passing the platter to Trace. The big fellow reached to take it. The index and middle fingers were missing from the hand he put out. Laramie felt the blood pound in his arteries, but not an eyelid quivered as he waited for Morrell to help himself. "Better take another one," he urged.

Conversation died as they ate. Laramie was hungry, but food had lost its savor for him. Hate flooded his heart as he stole a glance at the man seated across the table. "I wonder," he thought, "—after all these months. A mutilated right hand. . . . two fingers missin'."

It tallied with the only definite clue he had. But once in Wyoming, and again in the Judith Basin, in Montana, he had encountered men with hands that answered that description. In both instances hope had soared high in him, only to be dashed as subsequent investigation proved that the suspected men could not possibly have had anything to do with the slaying of Kit.

"I won't make the mistake of takin' anythin for granted this time," he promised himself. "Maybe this hawk-nosed gent is as innocent as the other two. I'll just give him the benefit of the doubt until I find out otherwise."

He had as little liking for Morrell as Trace had for him. It was easy to believe it sprang from a mutual distrust.

"But he hasn't any reason to be suspicious of me, whether he's the man I'm lookin' for or not. That sneerin' mouth of his turned me against him, and maybe my face soured him."

It was not important. His task now was to win Morrell's confidence, and he was prepared to go to any length to accomplish it. At the same time he proposed to learn what he could from Heck. Certainly, Morrell and the Judge appeared to be on very friendly terms.

To his surprise, he caught the Judge scrutinizing him intently. Heck jerked his eyes away and Laramie pretended not to have noticed. Trace was still busily engaged with his dinner.

"Judge, can I pass you somethin'?" Laramie asked.

"No—no, I ate my fill," Heck declared. Then, in what seemed to be just an attempt to dissemble any embarrassment he felt at having been caught so flat-footed, "That long-legged black you're ridin', Johnson, seems quite a horse."

"He is, for a fact," Laramie acknowledged. "He's from way down in the Navajo country—"

"Is that so?" Heck's surprise was genuine. "You—mean you're from Arizona?"

The question was not one to be asked with impunity of a stranger; but the Judge found Johnson so much to his liking that he risked it.

"Yeh, that's my old stampin' ground," Laramie admitted readily.

"Well, what do you know about that!" Heck exclaimed. He half turned to Morrell. "Trace, here, hails from down thataway too."

"Is that a fact?" Laramie queried with a show of neighborly interest. "I'm certainly glad to meet up with a man from my home range."

He favored Trace with a smile. Morrell, however, did not appear overwhelmed with delight at the news that they were both from Arizona. He speared a potato expertly and mashed it in the gravy on his plate.

The absorbed attention with which Trace performed the simple operation appeared studied to Laramie. "He don't seem none too happy about this," he thought. He realized if Morrell had ever run wild with the Hole-in-the-Wall gang that the first thing he would have done on reaching a new country would have been to disclaim any knowledge of Wyoming and let it be known that he hailed from some region remote from his old haunts. It was the invariable rule when the law had a grudge against a man.

"She's a grand old state—and a big one," Trace got out, smacking his lips noisily and pushing his empty plate aside. "What section you from, Johnson?"

The question was put very adroitly. It increased Laramie's respect for Morrell.

"Around Coconino," he lied, his eyes guileless. He felt he knew enough about the plateau to make out a plausible tale if it became necessary. As he expected, however, he saw a look of relief flit across Trace's face.

"Coconino, eh?" Morrell showed his teeth in a patronizing grin. "I'm from further south. . . . Tonto Basin—"

Laramie stirred still another spoonful of sugar into his coffee. No betraying gleam of satisfaction brightened his eye. "Fine country down there," he said. "Always wanted to have a look at it. Reckon when I got the itch to ramble I'd have done better for myself if I had headed thataway—"

"Oh, I don't know," the Judge put in. "Idaho is comin' mighty fast right now. Plenty good jobs—"

"I guess we've both wished ourselves back there," Laramie went on, ignoring Heck's interruption.

"Sure," Trace agreed. He rolled a cigarette deftly and lit it. "I never should have pulled away. But that itch you was speakin' of got me too. Had a good job and was even runnin' a few head of my own on the side—"

"There's a lot of that done in Arizona. I've worked for men who'd let you do it. What outfit was you ridin' for?"

Laramie's question sounded innocent enough but he thought Morrell had to think for a moment before he could remember.

"The old Box A—quite an outfit."

"Yeh, I remember hearin' you speak about it," the Judge recalled.

"No doubt I did," Trace grinned. "I've always got a lot to say."

"This is one time you said too much," Laramie thought as he pushed back his chair. "You never saw the Tonto. I knew every registered brand in the Basin—and we never had a Box A on the books."

CHAPTER 2
A Tough Star-Toter

THEY FOUND HUGHIE BEHIND THE DESK AS THEY STEPPED OUT of the dining room into the office. Laramie paid for his dinner.

"Better fix me up with a room," he told him. "I may be here a day or two."

The Castro House did not boast a register, but the proprietor wrote Laramie's name on a slip of paper and hung it on a hook.

"Well, I'll set up the cigars if you gentlemen have time to set down and enjoy a good smoke," Heck offered.

Laramie was quite willing. Morrell accepted too. The Judge tossed a silver half-dollar on the counter.

"Give us three of them Dry Climate Specials," he ordered. Giving Laramie a wink, he added for Hughie's benefit: "Ain't nothin' special about 'em 'cept the price."

With their cigars going, they repaired to the porch. Castro still dozed, the noontime quiet broken only by the sounds of laughter issuing from the saloon next door. Three wiry little broncs stood at the hitchrack in front of the saloon, their heads down, eyes half closed and tails lazily swishing flies.

"When do you expect your outfit to hit town?" Heck asked Trace.

"Well, I figured they'd be in by now. They must be takin' it easy. I hope they ain't too late." There was a note of anxiety in his tone of a sudden.

"What do you mean by that?" the Judge inquired.

"Oh, I had a little argument over to the station this mornin'. The agent didn't want to let us have those cars he's got on the sidin'. He claims the Bar 44 arranged for 'em. But they ain't expected before tomorrow. No reason why we can't get loaded and be in the clear before that Mormon outfit gets in. Freight is freight, and first come, first served is a damn good rule. He can have plenty cars here by daylight."

"Well, that don't sound like much to argufy over," Heck declared. "Certainly won't take Corbett long to get what beef he's got aboard the cars."

"Oh, I don't know," Morrell demurred. "We're shippin' upwards of thousand head."

"My heavens, you don't mean it!" Heck's tone was frankly ind-credulous. "Why, it don't seem no time ago that Bliss Corbett didn't have much more than a fryin'-pan to his name. Sounds like you boys ain't askin' too many questions of the stuff you've been brandin'."

It was said in fun, and Morrell joined in the Judge's laughter. Laramie, however, began to wonder if the name Bliss Corbett was not just an alias for Ike Mundy and if the Frying-pan would not prove to be just a new label for the Hole-in-the-Wall gang.

"We're still a driftin' outfit, with a chuck wagon for a ranch house, but we ain't doin' bad at all," Trace remarked with the air of one who feels he can safely afford to belittle his own accomplishments.

"I should think not," the Judge sighed. "Kinda takes my breath away. Bliss must feel pretty proud of himself, ridin' in here to ship for the first time at the head of a bunch like that. You sure will need cars."

"We'll get 'em." Trace twirled his cigar with his lips. "Don't worry about that."

Heck puffed thoughtfully for a moment. "And still you boys talk about Arizona," he protested. "What's the matter with Idaho? Can you match anythin' like that? A free-range country for me every time!" He turned to Laramie. "You're a stranger here, Johnson, but you can understand what it means for a man to go from scratch to riches in five years, or less."

"I sure can," Laramie declared, pretending to be properly impressed. "Corbett must be a cowman."

"He's proved that," the Judge went on. "Why, when he started, he scratched a livin' for his stuff off of desert range that you wouldn't think could keep the hide on a coyote. It used to be pretty hard to keep track of him, he moved around so much, grazin' stock wherever he could find grass and hold on to it. I reckon you've got stuff spread around from the Lost River Mountains to Grande Ronde Coulee, ain't you, Trace?"

"Just about," Morrell grinned.

Laramie told himself it was an easy matter to rustle cattle in Wyoming and plant them on desert range in Idaho. "A herd multiplies in a hurry thataways," he thought.

"We're gettin' big enough to have somethin' to say about this country north and west of here," Trace volunteered. "Bliss fig-gers he ain't backin' up for anyone from now on—and I reckon that includes the Mormons."

"So that's the way the wind blows, eh?" Heck queried. He

pulled down the corners of his mouth. "Bliss will find he's got a fight on his hands if he tries to crowd old Isaiah Marr! Isaiah has carved out a kingdom for himself, and between those six strappin' sons of his and his grandsons and what not he's got it pretty well nailed down. Bliss better watch his step."

The warning was wasted on Trace. "We know what we want—whether it's railroad cars or water—and we figger to get it. Folks have been walkin' wide of the Bar 44 so long that it sorta takes some their breath away when you talk about standin' up and fightin' for your rights. We want water, and we're goin' to get it."

"You may find there's easier ways of gettin' it than movin' in on old Isaiah," Heck remarked pointedly. "He knows how to protect his rights."

"Rights? Hell, there ain't no rights, Judge!" Trace whipped out. "You know as well as I do that no court has recognized water rights. Grab it if you need it and hold on to it if you can—that's the law! We ain't askin' for nothin' better."

The Judge puffed his cigar furiously as he communed with himself.

"If you're feelin' thataway," he jerked out, "I hope your bunch gets out of town before the Marrs show up. If Snap Marr is in charge of the Bar 44 beef there'll be trouble—and we've had enough of that here. You sound to me as though you was askin' for a fight, Trace."

"No, we ain't askin' for one—and we ain't walkin' away from one," Morrell answered bluntly.

Laramie found himself strangely interested, even though this promise of trouble did not appear to concern him.

"That's war talk," the Judge stated, "providin' Bliss backs it up."

"Corbett an old friend of yours?" Laramie asked.

"You might say so. There's been times when I've lost sight of him for a year or two; but he always bobs up. I been seein' him pretty regular for the last ten months. Some men can't put two dollars together without routin' you out of bed to let you know about it. Not Corbett! Doggone him, he's the closest mouthed man I ever knew!

"He never gave me any reason at all to suspect that he was doin' well enough to think of crossin' swords with old Isaiah." He addressed himself to Trace. "You tell Bliss I want to see him as soon as he gets his stuff in the corrals."

Heck's saying he often lost sight of Corbett for months on end fitted in perfectly with what Laramie was thinking, as did the fact that the owner of the Frying-pan had evidently reappeared in Castro about ten months back. He had one more question to ask, and he found an opportunity to insert it into the conversation presently.

"Corbett sounds like he might be a good boss," he said, moving toward his point with characteristic indirection. "How long have you been workin' for him, Morrell?"

"Gettin' on toward a year this trip. You lookin' for a job, Johnson?"

So, Morrell had been among the missing too, and had returned about ten months back! The pieces of the puzzle seemed to slip into place almost too easily.

"No hurry about a job," Laramie drawled. "I thought I might speak to Corbett though—"

"Better have a look around first," the Judge advised. "You may find somethin' that will look better. If you're goin' to be here a day or two, I'll acquaint you with some friends of mine. There might somethin' turn up right here in town."

Laramie had no reason to suspect what was running through Heck's mind. He was not unappreciative of the Judge's expressed interest in him. He found the old man a likable, patently honest individual. But the Frying-pan had become a subject of absorbing interest and he was anxious to see how Morrell took his bid for a job.

"Town would hardly appeal to me, Judge," he said. "I've got to have a little elbow room." He glanced at Morrell. Trace had whittled a match to a point and was busily picking his teeth with it. "Do you think there's any chance of my catchin' on?" he persisted.

"Well, the slack season's just ahead." Trace tossed away his improvised toothpick. His manner was frankly discouraging. "Bliss does his own hirin' and firin', but with all respect to you, Johnson, a stranger wouldn't be much good to us."

It was exactly the attitude Laramie had expected him to express. He was more convinced than ever that he had just about reached the end of the trail he had been following for months.

Two men stepped out of the saloon next door. Their intentions appeared friendly enough, but they had their six-guns in their hands. One of them hailed Heck.

"Hi, Judge!" he called out. "Suppose you climb offen that

porch and referee this argyment. Shorty, here, claims he can outshoot me, and I'm bettin' the drinks for the crowd he can't.''

Half a dozen loungers had come to the saloon door to watch the fun.

"Say, Gid, you boys look pretty well in the bag to be waverin' your hardware around like that," Heck warned. "Somebody's apt to get busted here."

"Not unless he walks out on that sign up there," Gid declared. He turned to his companion. "There's your target, Shorty!" The old sign that hung in front of the hotel had served a similar purpose many times. Lead and weather had all but effaced the letters.

"That letter O in Castro, eh?" Shorty inquired.

"That's her, brother!" the other agreed. He raised his gun.

"Wait a minute, Gid!" Heck cried "Give us a chance to get in the clear here!"

Laramie and Trace followed him to a point of vantage to the rear of the marksmen.

"Here she goes!" Gid called out. He blinked his eyes groggily at the sign. The long barrel of his Colt began to weave back and forth, as though he were shooting at a moving target.

"Go on, shoot!" Shorty urged. His step was unsteady. "What you wavin' that gun for? You want me to hold that target down for yuh?"

"Don't rush me—don't rush me," Gid grumbled. "I got her dead center now—"

He fired from the hip. Stone sober, he could not have bettered his performance, for in rapid succession he put five slugs squarely inside the letter O.

Shorty had a try at it and came in a bad second.

"Hear me howl!" Gid roared. "I'm just a shootin' fool!" He turned around to catch a sneer on Morrell's lips. His good humor was gone instantly. "What are you grinnin' about, Morrell?" he whipped out fiercely. "I know you've had some reputation around here since you handed your respects to Burley, but if you want any of my game, step up! For ten dollars you can't fade me!"

"Sober, I'd take you up," Trace answered coolly.

"Drunk or sober you can't fade me!" Gid got out defiantly.

"All right, you're on!" Morrell fished two five-dollar gold pieces out of his pocket and handed them to Heck. "You hold the money, Judge. I can always use ten dollars."

The crowd had received reinforcements until it numbered a score or more.

Trace permitted Gid to name the target. He indicated an empty tomato can lying in the road beyond the hotel.

"Empty a gun at it," Morrell invited.

The best Gid could do was to hit it once. Morrell clipped it three times out of five. "Your money, Trace," the Judge exclaimed. Trace did not reach to take it.

"This is a free-for-all," he said, his glance roaming over the crowed and coming to rest on Laramie. "Anybody else want any of it, for all or part of the twenty?"

Laramie hesitated only a moment. He knew there was a challenge here that had nothing to do with the few dollars at stake. "If we can find a couple cans, I'll take whirl at it," he said.

"For how much?" Trace asked. He felt very sure of winning.

"I'll shoot the twenty," Laramie laughed.

Somebody got a can and threw it into the road. Morrell fared even better than his first attempt, hitting the mark four times out of five tries.

Another can was tossed out for Laramie. The Judge was watching him intently. He wanted to see him draw. A little grunt of delight was wrung from him as he saw Laramie's hands flash downward. They slapped the holsters with a resounding whack. The guns he wore were Colt .45's with the dogs filed off. He had the hammers back before the guns left the leather. His arms came up and he began to fire. There was no pause for sighting. It was done swiftly, but unhurriedly; one movement from the draw to the first shot.

He scored a hit. The can began to roll. His second shot made it dance faster. Without apparent effort, he put three more slugs into it. The crowd gaped in astonishment. Then, for good measure, Laramie opened up with his second gun, and without a break sent five more bullets into the battered can. It went tumbling down the road.

"Ten shots and not a miss!" Heck cried. "I call that shootin'!"

"Pretty good," Trace admitted, hiding whatever disappointment he felt behind a forbidding grin. "It's your money, Johnson."

The crowd broke up. Laramie blew the smoke from his guns and reloaded. Trace and the Judge walked over to examine the can.

"I told you there wasn't any foolishness about this gent,"

Heck reminded Morrell. "Wait till this news gets around town! There'll be a committee waitin' on Johnson, beggin' him to take charge of Castro. I never saw a man quicker on the draw, nor neater shootin'."

"He didn't have anyone crowdin' him," Trace scoffed. "That sometimes makes an awful difference."

"No need to take it thataway," he chided Morrell. "He was just too good for you, Trace. As for crowdin' him—I'd hate to be the man to try it."

Morrell shrugged his shoulders contemptuously and said nothing.

Laramie was waiting for them when they returned to the hotel porch.

Trace had stopped on the steps. A dustcloud on the desert to the north had caught his eye. It moved slowly toward town.

"Here they come," he announced. "Pretty near on schedule. I gotta be leavin' you."

The big fellow entered the hotel. His horse was in the barn at the rear. He came out of the alley a minute later and rode away with a flourish.

"Looks like there might be a little excitement in town to-night," Laramie suggested.

"Plenty!" the Judge answered laconically. "Step here a moment, Johnson. Ain't that another cloud of dust off there to northwest?"

"Why, yes. Movin' right along too."

"Yeh, just what I thought!" Heck exclaimed excitedly. "Sure as you're alive it's the Bar 44! I bet Bourne got word to old Isaiah some way. There'll be hell to pay now, especially if Snap Marr is in charge of that beef herd! Ain't no Mormon about him. Snap's just a drinkin', fightin' devil when he's in town."

"Accordin' to what I've gathered, this Corbett person ain't no slouch either when it comes to fightin'," Laramie observed.

"Not for a minute he ain't! Once he gets his stuff in them corrals he won't move out for hell or high water 'till he's got every critter loaded! It'll be a miracle if there ain't some blood spilled over this."

It soon became apparent to them that Corbett and his men were aware of the other drive.

"They see each other, sure enough," Laramie stated. "They're makin' a race to it."

"Yeh, but it can only end one way. Bliss will beat 'em in. The Marrs are closin' up, but they're too far behind to ever catch him. It looks like they'll have to hold their stuff on the flats outside of town for twenty-four hours and lug water to it.'' The Judge sighed heavily. "It's bound to lead to gun-play, and nothin' can stop it."

"The right man could stop it. What's the matter with your town marshal?"

"Ain't nothin' wrong with him, 'cept he's been dead for two weeks," the Judge muttered glumly. "The damn fool tried to disarm a bad greaser by askin' him for his guns. Valmores handed 'em to him all right, but he gave 'em the double roll and we've been without a marshal ever since. . . . That gets this conversation right down to the point I've been aimin' for ever since I laid eyes on you, Johnson."

It pulled Laramie up sharply. "I don't get you, Judge—"

"Well, suppose we just step across the street to my office. We can talk without bein' disturbed. I'll guarantee not to take up much of your time."

"Lead the way," Laramie laughed. "You sound awful serious of a sudden."

"Reckon I never was more so," Heck informed him. It was only a few steps to his office. He closed the door and faced Laramie. "I ain't goin' to waste words," he promised. "As I said to you just now, you took my eye the moment I saw you. What I've seen of you since has convinced me I wa'n't mistaken about you. And I ain't referrin' to your performance with a six-gun. Johnson, as the chairman of the town board I want to appoint you marshal of Castro."

Laramie's eyes warmed into a smile. "So that's the job you figured I might land in town, eh?" he queried.

"Exactly! I know you can give us law and order. I hadn't figgered you'd have a fight like this on your doorstep before I got around to askin' you. It'll take a man with nerve and judgment to stop it. I'll pay you the compliment of sayin' I know you can do it. There won't be any difficulty over the money end of it!"

It was in Laramie's mind to refuse with thanks. He could not see how Castro's problems concerned him. "That certainly is a compliment," he murmured, dropping into a chair, "but I'm afraid I'll have to say no. I suppose when I said the right man could stop this trouble you figured I had myself in mind."

"Well, didn't you—for a fact, now?" Heck demanded doggedly.

"Maybe I did at that," Laramie had to admit. "I didn't figure you'd be puttin' it up to me like this."

"Well, I am puttin' it up to you, and not just because of the money there's in it. The Marrs have always been friends of mine; so has Bliss Corbett. I can't expect it to mean anythin' to you if they wipe each other out—"

Laramie pulled himself up sharply. Here was an angle he had not considered. With suspicion become almost a certainty that Morrell was one of the men who had killed Kit, and that Bliss Corbett would prove to be another, how could he stand by and see them snuffed out in a cowboy feud?

"No," he told himself, "I don't propose to lose 'em that-away." He jerked himself to his feet and flung the door open. The distant bawling of cattle reached him. The Frying-pan herd was less than half a mile from town.

Laramie turned from the door to face the old man. His mouth was unaccountably grim.

"Better give me a star, Judge," he said. "I'm takin' the job."

The marshal and justice of the peace shared the same building, only a wooden partition separating their offices. A small building in the rear had been made over into an improvised jail. When Laramie had been sworn in, Heck handed him the keys to the place.

"You're in charge now," the Judge said. "I ain't goin' to begin by tryin' to offer you any advice. It'll take the wisdom of a Solomon to keep Corbett and Marrs from clawin' each other to pieces. The best I'm expectin' you to do is to keep 'em from goin' for their guns. You can work that out any way you please. In the meantime, I'll step down the street and acquaint the other members of the board with what I've done. I wish you luck, Johnson."

"I'll likely need it," Laramie thought.

He locked the door and headed for the feed-barn in back of the hotel. The Frying-pan had almost reached town by now. Through the dust he could see the bellowing steers, heads lowered, horns flashing as they thundered along. Above the din rose the shrill, impatient cries of Corbett's cowboys as they hazed the cattle.

Laramie threw his saddle on the big black.

"What's your name?" he asked the sleepy young Mexican who had charge of the barn.

"Joe," the boy replied.

"Well, Joe, you take my war bag into the hotel. Tell Hughie to have it put in my room."

He mounted quickly and pressed his knees into the gelding. The animal leaped away as though he had raked it with his spurs.

On reaching the street, Laramie headed for the corrals beyond the depot. He could see Morrell sitting in his saddle, holding excited conversation with a man in shirt sleeves, whom he correctly surmised to be Pete Bourne, the railroad agent. Bourne was a formidable Irishman, with plenty of fight in him.

"You can't have these cars, Morrell!" he exclaimed fiercely as Laramie rode up. "I've sealed every one of them! You break the seals and you'll be prosecuted!"

The two men flashed a glance at him. The agent was frankly surprised to see the badge of authority pinned on Laramie's vest. It failed to startle Morrell.

"So Heck sold you the job, eh?" the big fellow sneered.

"He didn't sell me anythin'," Laramie countered. "I went into this with my eyes wide open."

"Yeh? Maybe you're bitin' off somethin' you can't chew. You're a stranger, Johnson, and I'm tellin' you if you're smart you'll stay out of this."

"I may be a stranger," Laramie murmured calmly, "but I'm sure enough the marshal of this town now. Don't you make any mistake about that."

His manner impressed the agent. Bourne introduced himself. "I'm holding these corrals for the Bar 44," he said. "Two weeks ago they arranged for those empties I've got on the siding. Now this outfit shows up without a word and thinks it's going to grab the corrals and cars. I'd like to know where you stand, Johnson. I've sealed those cars—"

"If you have, they'll stay sealed," Laramie informed him. "If it becomes necessary, I'll call on the Federal authorities to back me up in that. Enterin' a sealed railway car ain't no ordinary case of unlawful entry."

"Why, you—" Morrell raged.

"Wait a minute," Laramie warned. "Better let me finish." He turned back to the agent. "Bourne—I understand the Bar 44 was not due here before tomorrow. Wasn't that the arrangement you made?"

"I don't know where your got your information," Bourne answered. "You've got it straight anyhow. What did you think I was going to do? Wait until they got in before I wired for cars?"

"I'm not thinkin' about the cars just now," Laramie informed him. "You've got some corrals here, and they happen to lie within the town limits. I figure that puts it up to me to see there ain't no disturbin' of the peace. I take it these corrals was built by the railroad company to be used by any person who has livestock to ship. They're empty at the moment, and accordin' to your own statement you didn't promise anyone they'd have the right to use 'em before tomorrow mornin'.

"The Fryin'-pan outfit is here now. They've got beef to ship. Can't be any question about their right to use these corrals—until tomorrow mornin'."

"They can't get 'em!" Bourne stormed furiously.

"They'll come pretty close to gettin' 'em," Laramie murmured with disconcerting assurance. "This railroad has no right under law to refuse freight when it happens to be livestock. Has your division superintendent given you authority to refuse it?"

"I got to refuse what I can't handle," Bourne snapped.

"But you could get more cars." Laramie did not raise his voice. "Blackfoot is only sixty miles away. You could have cars here by late afternoon."

"Course he could!" Morrell ground out, agreeably surprised at the stand Laramie was taking.

"And what would I do with them?" Bourne demanded. "I've got only one siding, and it's full now!"

"Well, how you handle the cars is up to you," Laramie told him. "It seems to me the easy thing to do would be to trade loaded cars for empties. Course that's only an idea—"

"Just what I thought you had in your mind!" Bourne bristled wrathfully. "You can't come that on me, Johnson! My responsibility is to the company and to no one else!"

Laramie measured him with his eyes. A stubborn determination to do what he thought was his duty was written in every line of Bourne's florid face. The Frying-pan herd was pounding across the tracks by now.

"You're askin' for trouble, Bourne," Laramie jerked out.

"I'm standing on my rights, you mean! The Bar 44 is the biggest shipper we've got. Do you think I'm going to let another outfit come in here and browbeat me into letting them use their cars while they have to hold their stuff on the flats overnight?'' Bourne's indignation ran away with him. ''It's your duty to back me up!''

''Not when you're wrong.'' Laramie's tone was suddenly as sharply edged as a knife. ''You were within your rights when you sealed those cars, and I'll guarantee you no one tampers with 'em; but you're dead wrong in refusin' these folks the right to use the corrals.'' He swung around in his saddle. ''Better get those gates open, Morrell!'' he advised. ''Your bunch is almost here!''

''I can't open 'em!'' Trace answered. ''They're locked!''

''Unlock 'em!'' Laramie ordered.

''I'm damned if I will!'' the agent shouted. ''The key is in my safe, and there she stays!''

''All right, I'll take the responsibility of openin' the gates,'' Laramie informed him. He edged the black up to the corral and shot the lock off.

''You're destroying company property!'' Bourne yelled.

''We'll be mighty lucky if that's all that is destroyed here,'' Laramie told himself. He helped Morrell push the gates back.

Trace was well satisfied with the situation. He felt that once they were in possession of the corrals it would be up to Corbett to see that they got the cars.

A second or two later the Frying-pan steers were pouring past them. A level-eyed man, white with dust, rode up. There was an air of authority about him. He nodded to Morrell. A yearling broke away. He went after it and hazed the steer back into the herd.

''Who is he?'' Laramie asked Trace.

''Corbett,'' Morrell answered. ''Reminds me of you in some ways, Johnson.''

''Yeh?'' Laramie murmured tonelessly. His mouth was hard as he turned away. He could not hide his disappointment. Certainly the man with level-set eyes was not Ike Mundy.

''I sure was all wrong about him,'' he mused bitterly. ''I knew this thing was workin' out too easy. I shouldn't have got my hopes up.''

To complete his chagrin, he found himself drawn to Corbett, something about the man appealing strongly to him. By the cut of his jaw it was easy to believe he was a fighter.

''But he's a square-shooter, if I know anythin' about men,''

Laramie told himself. "I'll bet my roll he never ran an iron on another man's stock."

A steer crashed into the gate. It almost upset Morrell. His cursing broke in on Laramie's musing.

"What about him?" he asked himself. "If Morrell is the man I think he is, what's he doin' with this outfit? Maybe I'm wrong about him too."

Bliss Corbett had seven men in his string. They were all lean, hard-riding buckaroos; desert men, every one of them. Their rigging was shiny from hard wear, their chaps patched. One of them, a dark-skinned man with hair blacker than midnight, wore a feather in his hatband, Indian fashion.

"A breed, all right," Laramie decided. He had never seen him before, nor any of the others. "Except for Morrell, there's nothin' about this bunch to make me think I've got anywhere. But I'm sure not goin' to lose sight of him until I know I'm dead wrong. I started a play here and I'll see it through."

CHAPTER 3
Snap Marr — Triggerman

LARAMIE MOVED BACK OUT OF THE DUST. THE FRYING-PAN MEN knew their business. Only once or twice did Corbett have to shout an order. He and Morrell were helping to work the cattle into the corrals. Trace kept up a running fire of conversation with him, acquainting him with the situation, Laramie surmised.

The men began to close in and soon had the herd corralled.

"Shut the gates, Frenchy!" Corbett yelled at the man who wore the feather in his hatband. "Give him a hand, Trace!"

Between them, the two men closed the heavy gates and dropped the bar into place. Immediately, Corbett wheeled his horse and rode up to Laramie. Bourne, in the meantime, had returned to the depot.

"I'm obliged to you, Johnson, for the way you handled this mix-up," Corbett said, raising his voice to make himself heard above the din. "This stuff is pretty wild, but we can load it in a few hours if we get the cars. Bourne is just bein' pig-headed about this business. We could be in the clear by sundown if he'd listen to reason."

"That'll work two ways, won't it?" Laramie demanded. "If you'll pull your stuff out of the corrals, I'll see that the Bar 44 is in the clear by sundown."

"Not a chance! We're stayin' right where we are!"

"You're stayin' there until tomorrow mornin'—no later," Laramie informed him. "If you can talk Bourne or this other outfit into lettin' you use the cars that are here, okay. Don't try to grab 'em. I'll stop you if you do."

Corbett's mouth tightened as he hesitated over his answer. Suddenly he decided against making any answer at all, for through the dust he saw a rider racing toward the corrals. He came on at a free-swinging gallop, and even at a distance there was an air of fury about him.

Laramie caught sight of him a moment later. "Who'll this be?" he asked Corbett.

"Snap Marr!" Corbett edged his horse closer. "You keep your eye on this gent, Johnson. He's strictly hair-trigger. He can start somethin' here he'll never live to finish."

Laramie nodded. "I'll manage to keep an eye on both of you," he drawled.

The Frying-pan men had deployed advantageously, their mouths tense and eyes keenly alert as they waited. Every one of them was armed.

"Snap Marr is either a brave man or a damn fool," Laramie thought, "ridin' in alone to face a bunch like this."

The Barr 44 herd was still half a mile out when Snap Marr brought his bald-faced roan to a slithering stop at the corral gates. He was taller even than Laramie with a tremendous breadth of shoulders. Desert winds had tanned his skin to the color of old saddle leather. Nature had cast his countenance in a coarse, forbidding mould. Even in repose, his was a cruel face. Now, breathing fire, eyes flaming, there was something murderous about it.

"Hunh," he grunted as he caught sight of the star Laramie was wearing. He gave the new marshal an appraising and frankly hostile glance. If he arrived at any conclusion it was not reflected in his snapping eyes. "So you're the marshal here now."

"Yeh, I am. Johnson, by name—"

Snap tried to stare him down, and failed. "You stand for some pretty raw stuff, don't you?" he blazed, his eyes narrowing to pin points.

"Not too raw," Laramie remarked with chilling emphasis.

"Well, you'll save yourself a lot of trouble if you keep out of this, Johnson," Snap raged. "These corrals belong to us, and we're gettin' 'em!" He whirled on Corbett. "You get those gates open and start pullin' your stuff out!"

Corbett shook his head. "No, we're stayin' right where we are—"

"You think you are!" Snap thundered. "I'm tellin' you to get movin'! We're comin' after you if you don't!"

"Come a-smokin' when you come!" Corbett rasped defiantly. He was as angry as Snap.

"That's exactly the way we'll come! You've been askin' for a showdown for six months. You can have it right here!"

"No, there won't be any showdown here, unless you force me to one," Laramie cut in. "I'm maintainin' the peace in this town. The first man who draws a gun around these corrals is a dead man." It was said quietly, but there was a note of unflinching determination in his voice that was not without effect on both men. "If I have to, I'll deputize every man in Castro to back me up. You can pass that word along to your men—both of you."

"That's great, ain't it?" Snap sneered. "You let this bunch take possession of the corrals when you knew damn well they had no right to 'em. Now you begin yappin' about keepin' the peace. Well, you're too late with that talk. If you'd been on the square you'd have kept 'em out of here, and we could have settled this without your put in. I'm tellin' you it's *goin'* to be settled!"

They wrangled for another ten minutes without getting anywhere. Laramie refused to lose patience with Snap. He realized that there was no chance of avoiding hostilities unless he could effect a compromise of some sort.

"That's good, tellin' me the cars belong to us!" Snap jeered. "What can I do with 'em? Do you think I can load wild, desert stuff without a chute?"

"You'll have the chute in the mornin'," Laramie promised him.

"He'll have it after we get loaded!" Corbett whipped out. "A man with stock to ship ain't trespassin' in occupyin' a railroad corral. There wasn't any unlawful entry, Johnson; you opened the gates for us."

"I'll open 'em for you tomorrow mornin' too," Laramie assured him.

"No, you won't! I'll go before Heck Small and get a writ that'll stop you! The railroad can worry about gettin' me cars. I'll just lay back and wait."

Laramie had good reason to believe Bliss could do it. He began to breathe easier as a consequence, for here was a stalemate as perfect in its way as Bourne's sealing the empties on the siding. He felt he had an ace in the hole now.

"You can try that if you care to," he said to Corbett. "If you do, I'll advise Marr to agree to pay demurrage charges on his cars and keep 'em standin' on that sidin' until you wish you'd never seen these corrals."

"By hell, I'll do it!" Snap cried. "They won't dare to move 'em! If you load ahead of me, Corbett, you won't do it in Castro!"

The Bar 44 herd had come on. Laramie saw that Snap had at least a dozen men with him. One of them rode up now. He proved to be Nephi Marr, one of Snap's brothers. He was several years younger than Snap, but almost his equal in stature. Their size was the only marked resemblance between them.

"Shall we come on, Snap?" Nephi asked. There was grim determination in his eyes, but none of the bluster about him that characterized his brother.

"Better hold 'em up for a spell," Snap told him. "Any place beyond the tracks will do. I'll be back directly."

"We'll be waitin' for yuh," Nephi said. He turned his horse and loped away after staring defiantly at Corbett.

"I'm goin' to see Bourne," Snap declared. "This conversation ain't gettin' me anywhere."

"Maybe it will be just as well if we all see him," Laramie suggested. "We'll find him in the depot, I reckon. I don't know what good it will do. If you want to get anywhere, Marr, you and Corbett have got to meet each other halfway. This thing can be worked out like anythin' else if you'll compromise a little—"

"I'll see myself in hell before I'll do anythin' of the sort!" Snap growled.

Bourne had been watching them through the window. He had declared himself and he did not propose to back up an inch. It was not necessary for him to leave his chair to keep them in sight as they rode up to the station platform.

Snap was the first man through the door. He did not hold

Bourne responsible for the difficulty which confronted him. As the Judge suspected, it was Bourne who had got word to the Bar 44 drive.

The argument was taken up with renewed fury, Bourne lining up squarely with Snap. Threats of violence and reprisal were hurled back and forth.

Laramie was satisfied to sit back and listen. He felt he held the winning cards, but he did not intend to play them until their clashing wills cooled.

There was a train schedule on the wall. He perused it with interest as Corbett and Snap continued to defy each other.

"Why keep this up?" he asked at last. "You know you're wastin' your time. You've got the corrals, Corbett, and Marr has got the cars. One without the other won't do you any good. But maybe you'd better hang onto 'em. You can stand each other off for days. That'll be profitable, of course," he added with fitting sarcasm, "especially if beef drops a cent or two a pound in the meantime, as it's very likely to do at this time of the year."

Snap cursed to himself. Bliss had nothing to say. Laramie took it as a very hopeful sign.

"I've just been looking over the train schedule while you've been rantin' at each other," he went on. "There was a mixed train leavin' Blackfoot for the north at three o'clock. On account of the local freight it carries it ain't due here until after seven. You could have got some cars thataway and been in position to use 'em. You've talked yourselves out of that chance."

"I've got all the cars I need right here," Snap grumbled.

Laramie thought he caught a note of indecision in his tone. "Sure you have," he agreed. "But they ain't worth nothin' to you. On the other hand, I reckon Corbett would give most anythin' to get 'em."

"You mean pay him a premium for them?" Bliss queried. "Not a chance! Why should I?"

His willingness to argue the question told Laramie he was wavering.

"I didn't mean money exactly," he said. "The afternoon is half gone, but if you could get those cars, I imagine you'd agree to work this evenin' and get started again by daylight so you could be through by six-thirty tomorrow mornin'. There's a train south at that time that could roll 'em away. At 7:20 there's a through freight due from Blackfoot. The Bar 44 could begin loadin' a few minutes after they got into the corrals."

"I don't know," Bliss murmured. "My boys are dog weary—"

"But you'd agree to do it—"

"Well—yes, I would—"

"But I won't!" Snap turned to leave. "I'm keepin' what's mine!"

"Nobody can blame you for that," Laramie agreed heartily. "You ain't runnin' cattle for the fun of it. Of course you won't put any fat on your steers if you have to hold 'em three or four days. If it was only for tonight, I reckon the agents would let you water 'em at that tank down the tracks."

"Yes, I could do that," Bourne volunteered.

Isaiah Marr's name had not been brought into the conversation, but Snap was forcibly reminded of his father every time Laramie brought up the question of profit. In fact, Snap found himself between two fires, for a profit was what his father would have out of the spring shipping, come high, come low.

"You'd have your stuff rollin' out of Castro by noon," Laramie reminded him. "That was as good as you figured on doin'."

It was true enough. Forced to decide between braving his father's wrath and backing down to Corbett, Snap could not decide what to do. But along with his bluster and swagger, there was a certain degree of cunning in him. It came to his aid now. To eat crow would be bitter medicine for him to swallow; but the idea that had flashed in his brain led him to believe he could keep part of the unpalatable bird for Bliss Corbett to digest before the last play had been made.

"Maybe we'd have our stuff rollin' tomorrow—and maybe we wouldn't," he got out as fiercely as ever. There was a cagy light in his eyes however. "You'd have my cars, Corbett, but what guarantee would I have that you'd be loaded by six-thirty?"

"I'll give you my word on it," Bliss said.

Snap shook his head. "Your word don't mean that much to me."

"You don't have to worry about Corbett keepin' his word," Laramie spoke up, believing the moment had come for them to get together. He was aware of some subtle change in Snap, but he did not question it. "I promise you he'll do as he says he will."

Again Snap shook his head. "I'm still sayin' no! If you want my cars, Corbett, put up five hundred dollars with Pete. If you ain't in the clear by six-thirty tomorrow mornin', the money belongs to me." He started for the door. "I don't expect you to put up it up. I know you ain't got any idea of playin' fair. You handed me a raw deal today, but you ain't givin' me another one in the mornin'!"

"Wait a minute!" Bliss commanded. "My word has always been my bond. But I'll call your bluff! Here's the five hundred— I'll stop in for it tomorrow, Bourne!"

Laramie caught the gleam of satisfaction that flashed in Snap's eyes. Suspicion crystallized in his mind as he followed him to the hitchrack.

"I don't pretend to know what you've got on the fire," he said to Snap, "but don't you do anythin' that'll make it impossible for him to be in the clear on time. Just remember I warned you, *muchacho*."

Snap laughed and climbed into his saddle. "You're a suspicious gent, ain't you? But quite a fixer at that." His mouth hardened suddenly. "Since you're handin' out warnin's—let me give you one. If you're interested in makin' your job permanent— keep out of my way!"

In the way of all prosperous cowtowns, Castro did not begin to hum until after nightfall, that portion of its population which existed without visible means of support—and it was not an inconsiderable percentage—being of the night-blooming variety. Others too—drifting cowboys, freighters, ranchers, cattle buyers—who had not been in evidence during the day, appeared miraculously as the lamps began to glow.

But long before the rattle of chips and the cries of the faro dealers started to resound in Castro's dozen or more emporiums of chance and conviviality, the new marshal had won the respect, if not the good-will, of its cosmopolitan population. The star-studded night was pleasantly warm, and inside the open doors of the Castro Mercantile Company's store, Nat Washburn, the proprietor, Doc Samuels and the Judge were congratulating themselves on the happy chance that had brought Laramie Johnson to town.

"Why, the way he handled that situation this afternoon was about as neat as anythin' I've ever seen," Heck declared. "Played 'em off against each other! It was a ticklish job, I'm tellin' you! I was all set for a massacre—"

"Danger ain't over yet," Washburn murmured gloomily. He stroked his long jaw thoughtfully. "Corbett's bunch is still workin'. They'll finish up on time. That won't be the rub. Johnson made Snap crawl—and Snap ain't the kind to let it go at that.''

"Why, he didn't neither make him crawl!" the Judge exclaimed sharply.

"Snap thinks he did—and that's just about the same thing. He's drinkin' pretty heavy and talkin' a-plenty. If he gets likkered up enough, he'll start somethin'.''

"Yes, he's just tinhorn enough to do it," said Doc. In addition to being the local physician, Samuels loaned money at eight percent and owned the buildings that housed several of Castro's saloons. He was reputed to be the wealthiest man in town. "Snap couldn't have his way this afternoon, but he didn't come off so bad at that. He'd be doing himself more good if he stayed with his cattle, instead of coming into town with half his men to get tanked up.''

"I agree with you," Heck murmured. "Who'd he bring in with him?"

"His brother Zack, Brad Nash, Reb Taney—I don't know; half a dozen anyhow.''

"And left Nephi to do the work." The Judge shook his head disgustedly. "Must be some consolation to Isaiah to know he's got only one black sheep in his flock. I wish the old man was here. I understand he's on his way in.''

Laramie was patrolling the main street. He happened to pass the store at that moment. He nodded to the three men and walked on. He had removed his chaps, but he had strapped his holsters down to his breeches.

His manner was tense and alert, for the apparent peacefulness of the early evening had not deceived him. Under cover a tremendous excitement gripped the town, and he sensed it every time he peered into a saloon, the boisterous laughter dying away to a murmur at his approach.

He had been up one side of the street and down the other a dozen times or more in the last hour. As he walked toward the hotel now he could see a campfire out on the flats where the Bar 44 was bedding down for the night. Their wagon had arrived hours back. The firelight revealed several men lounging about it.

A fire burned over at the corrals too. It flared up every few seconds as some one tossed a piece of sage on the embers. Work was done for the night, Corbett having finally called a halt. Although it was well after nine o'clock, he and his men were just finishing supper. Laramie could hear the Frying-pan cook rattling his pots.

"I suppose they're beginnin' to wonder what sort of money is used in this town," he said to himself. "They'll be in directly to find out, and that won't help matters any."

Snap and his men—they were all related to him in one way or another—were holding forth in the Silver Dollar, next door to the hotel. Laramie had looked in on them once or twice to find Snap leaning his back against the bar and telling the world in general that the man didn't live who could make him crawl.

Marr had drawn about him not only men who had ridden in with him, but a number of cronies from town as well. Their allegiance had become more outspoken as he continued to foot the bill. Whisky brave, they had about agreed that the Frying-pan outfit should be wiped off the map, and the new town marshal along with it, when Laramie pushed back the swinging doors and walked into the saloon.

The snarling, muttering crowd froze to sullen, defiant attention, ready to back up Snap, no matter what he proposed.

Laramie looked them over as he stepped up to the bar. He knew the moment was charged with dynamite that could be set off with a word. There was no hint of it in his calm, unruffled manner.

Snap leered at him contemptuously. "Well, if it ain't the marshal," he sneered. "I thought maybe you'd left town, Johnson—"

The insinuation was too plain to be misunderstood. Laramie met it with a laugh.

"No," he said. "I ain't been run out of town yet—though I hear there's been some talk to that effect." His tone was velvety but it rubbed the smirk from Snap's mouth. He suspected that Snap was not as drunk as he pretended. "Just keep on wishin', Marr; the night's still young."

Snap stared into the cold, icy-blue depths of Laramie's eyes. He found something there that made him cautious, and he was content to say: "You're right for once." Turning away, he struck the bar a resounding thump with his fist and called for another round of drinks.

Laramie waited, determined to give him an opportunity to say whatever was on his mind. The crowd waited too, faces stained with hatred.

Snap flicked a glance at him, his eyes venomous. The seconds ticked away and the silence deepened. He started to say something, but he changed his mind before the words reached his lips. A look of deep cunning settling on his face, he dashed off his drink and turned his back to Laramie. "Drink hearty, boys!" he invited.

The crowd was obviously disappointed.

Laramie sauntered out, watching Snap in the mirror that hung over the doors. His step was deliberate, and he appeared unperturbed. Secretly, he was sorely perplexed. Not for a second did he believe the issue between Snap and himself had been decided; but Snap had backed down, when a word from him would have precipitated hostilities, with the advantage all on his side.

"He sure must have a play of some sort up his sleeve to hold off thataway," Laramie told himself. "He wanted to come after me, and I reckon he would if he'd been ready to show his hand."

He continued on to the hotel. No one was about as he climbed the stairs to his room on the second floor. Hughie had given him a corner room. He did not strike a light. Through the open windows he could command a view of the street and particularly of the entrance to the Silver Dollar.

He sat there in the dark for ten minutes or more. Bliss Corbett and some of the Frying-pan men appeared from the direction of the corrals, their spur chains jingling as they walked down the plank sidewalk. He saw them glance into the Silver Dollar as they passed. They went on without stopping and entered the Golden Rule Bar, farther down the street. Morrell was not with them.

Laramie took it for granted that Trace was one of two or three men remaining in charge of the Frying-pan steers. He saw nothing strange in the arrangement, inasmuch as Morrell had already had two days in town, to say nothing of having been spared the hard work of the drive.

"Corbett's usin' his head, keepin' a man or two on guard," he mused. "Smart of him too, taggin' along with this bunch that's just come into town."

He was glad that Morrell was not one of them. He did not want anything to happen to Trace. "I've taken a lot on my shoulders just to keep him healthy until I can prove up on him."

He got to his feet a few minutes later and was about to leave the room when he saw Snap come to the door of the Silver Dollar and peer cautiously up and down the street. Evidently satisfied that he was not being watched, he slipped out of the saloon and hurried down the alley beside the hotel.

Snap's roan still stood at the hitchrack.

"There's only a barn back there. If he ain't lookin' for his horse, what is he lookin' for?" Laramie asked himself.

He stepped out into the hall. A window at the rear looked out on the barn; but a wall lamp cast its rays so that anyone standing at the window must be seen from below. Avoiding it, he went down the stairs and made his way through the darkened dining room.

The dining room windows were closed, and filmed with dust. In a moment or two, however, he located Snap. He was standing well within the shadow of the barn, conversing with someone.

Laramie could not see their faces nor catch what they were saying, although Snap's manner indicated that it was to the point. The two men parted as he watched, and Snap turned back into the alley. He had taken only a step or two when he half turned and said loudly enough for Laramie to overhear: "Remember— I want it tomorrow!"

His tone left no doubt of his intention to get whatever it was that he wanted tomorrow. He passed close to the window where Laramie stood, and his step was steady as though he were stone sober.

The other man turned the corner of the barn, and keeping in the shadows, quickly crossed the open lot in back of the Silver Dollar. For a moment the light from the rear window of the saloon outlined him. He was a big man, and although his back was to Laramie, the latter thought he recognized him.

"I could have sworn it was Morrell!" he breathed incredulously. He waited for Snap to reach the street before he opened the back door of the hotel and ran across the yard. He was too late. Whoever the man was, he had disappeared.

Laramie did not know what to make of it. The two men had had their heads together about something, and they had not met by accident. If one of them was Morrell, what did it mean? What reason could he have for meeting Snap secretly? The most plausible answer was that it had something to do with possession of the corrals.

"But that don't make sense," he murmured. "If Morrell had wanted to sell out on Corbett he wouldn't have put up the fight he did with Bourne. I know he wasn't bluffin' about that."

That Snap and Trace could have made any arrangement since the two outfits had arrived in Castro was equally unbelievable.

"They couldn't have got together," Laramie argued. "Snap hasn't been near the corrals, and Morrell hasn't been out of them until fifteen minutes ago." He was almost ready to believe he had been mistaken in thinking he had recognized the big fellow. "No, I couldn't have been wrong," he decided; "I can't prove it, but it was Morrell all right!"

CHAPTER 4
A Sidewinder Strikes

LARAMIE STEPPED BACK INTO THE DINING ROOM AND MADE HIS way to the office. When he was convinced that Snap was not watching from the door of the saloon, he crossed the road and headed for the corrals, intent on discovering whether Morrell was there or not.

"If he is, I'll admit I was wrong," he murmured. "Certainly the man I saw talkin' to Snap hasn't had time to circle around and get there ahead of me."

He found two Frying-pan men perched on the corral fence. They were gazing enviously at Castro's glowing lights, bright with their promise of pleasures long denied.

Morrell was not one of them.

A few minutes later, he walked into the Golden Rule. The saloon was crowded. Frenchy Le Brun, the half-breed, and another Frying-pan man were playing roulette. Corbett, Morrell and the others stood at the bar, flanked on either side by friends who had rallied to their support even as Snap had drawn reinforcements from his acquaintances.

Trace had his glass raised when he caught sight of Laramie. He said something under his breath to Bliss and then turned to beckon the marshal to step up.

"Come on, have a drink with us, Johnson!" he exclaimed with rough cordiality, raising his voice so that it carried to the street. "You're among friends. Move over there, Brent, and make a little room."

"Don't bother," Laramie advised, exchanging a nod with Corbett. "I'm not even smokin' tonight." He suspected that

Trace's noisy protestation of friendship had been voiced with some definite purpose in mind; possibly in the hope that it would be promptly brought to Snap's attention, for he surmised they might well be playing a game of cross purposes.

"Well, suit yourself," Trace said, not a bit abashed by Laramie's refusal of his invitation. "I reckon it's a busy night for you at that."

"Not for me alone," Laramie answered lightly. He saw Trace's mouth tighten and knew the big fellow was asking himself if the remark had reference in any way to his activities.

For a moment they peered deep into each other's eyes. Laramie's bland, tell-nothing smile was too much for Morrell to solve. He reached for his glass.

"Work never hurt nobody," he declared virtuously. "That goes for all of us." It was an abject retreat. Corbett, unwittingly, came to his rescue.

"You used your head this afternoon, Johnson," he said, "and shot square with both sides. When a man plays fair with me, I don't forget it. We'll be in the clear in the mornin', with time to spare. I reckon Snap Marr knows it by now, the way he's runnin' at the mouth. He's filling the town full of talk that don't set so well with me."

"Nor with any of us!" Oddie Dill, the Frying-pan cook, growled. He was a hatchet-faced little man who had been sharpening his temper for years on the cowboys of one outfit or another. "I'm ready to make him eat his words."

"So am I!" Brent Taylor rasped. He was a red-headed buckaroo who had been riding for the Frying-pan from the time Corbett first registered the brand. "And the sooner the better!"

The others agreed with him, swearing vengeance. Morrell joined in rather reluctantly, Laramie thought.

"I reckon you know what's been said, Johnson," Bliss remarked gravely.

"I've heard some of it," Laramie admitted. "I figure that most of it can be put down for just the barroom chatter of a disgruntled bunch. I wouldn't take it too seriously. Talk's awfully cheap."

Le Brun and Sante Fé Williams left the roulette table and edged into the crowd at the bar. The attention of every man in the saloon was focused on Corbett and the marshal by now.

"It's the cheapest thing in the world, but you can get too much of it," Bliss remarked gruffly. "You can take Marr's talk any way you want. If you're willin' to let him call you a blackleg and get away with it, that's your business. When he says I run an iron on stuff that don't belong to me—that's *my* business!''

"Has he said it?" Laramie asked.

"He's as good as said it. He made the crack that you couldn't tell by lookin' my yearlin's in the eye whether they was Mormons or Presbyterians.''

Laramie could not repress a laugh.

"That's funny to you, eh?" Corbett scowled.

"Yeh, and it ought to be to you,'' Laramie answered, his smile fading.

"Well, believe me, it ain't! There's never been anythin' but hard feelin' between the Marrs and me. More than once they've handed me the wrong end of the stick, and I've had to take it and like it; but drunk or sober I've never got down to callin' 'em rustlers.

"I'll pay Isaiah Marr the compliment of sayin' I don't believe he ever rustled a steer in his life. I believe he's man enough to say the same about me. Evidently that doesn't go with Snap. He's half said I'm a rustler. Now he can back down or say it so there'll be no mistakin' what he means!'' Corbett's face was white under its tan. "I hope somebody here carries that word to him.''

"I reckon there'll be somebody sure to oblige you,'' Laramie observed. He knew Corbett was not bluffing. "As I told you this afternoon, I'm interested only in maintainin' the peace. If you feel you can't get along without a showdown with Snap Marr, that's your pleasure. But don't have it within the town limits of Castro, because I'll sure have to stop it, Corbett, and that'll end this little love feast we've been havin'. You said somethin' a moment ago about my givin' you a square deal and you're not forgettin' it. I reckon you didn't mean that.''

Bliss drew himself up stiffly. "You had my word on it, didn't you?''

"All right, I'll take you at your word. If you meant it, you can prove it by gettin' your men back to the corrals and callin' this a night.''

It won a surly no from Corbett's men and those who were prepared to stand with them. Bliss shook his head.

"You can't ask me to walk out like that,'' he murmured stonily. "There's angles to this quarrel that you don't begin to understand, Johnson. It goes back a long way—''

"Don't misunderstand me," Laramie interrupted. "I don't intend to crowd into any man's quarrel. You and Marr can step out on the desert with your men and blast away at each other as long as you can crook a finger around a trigger, and there won't be a peep out of me. But you can't do it in town—leastwise I'll do my best to stop you. If you're as wise as I think you are, Corbett, you'll go back to the corrals. It might be smart in more ways than one."

Corbett's followers urged him to say no, but something in Laramie's tone made Bliss feel a warning was being conveyed to him that had nothing to do with their argument. "Have you got some reason for sayin' that, Johnson?" he inquired.

Without seeming to, Laramie watched Morrell. The big fellow's face remained a wooden mask, as though whatever answer might be made had no bearing on any secret plans of his. It went a long way toward convincing Laramie that whatever Trace and Snap had been discussing it had nothing to do with making it impossible for the Frying-pan to be done at the corrals on time.

"Well, I don't know anythin' definite, if that's what you mean," he answered Bliss. "You've got five hundred dollars up that can be forfeited. If it was my money I'd be a little anxious about it."

Corbett's mouth twisted into a grim smile. "That's a mighty clever argument," he said, believing it to be only a ruse on Laramie's part to sway him. "I'm sure obliged to you for worryin' about my money. But I'm stayin' right here so that ornery skunk will know just where to find me. I'm goin' to see that he has a chance to back down or fill his hand tonight!"

"All right," Laramie muttered coolly, "have it your way." He knew it was idle to argue further with Bliss. "But before you call my hand, Corbett, remember this—if there's anybody in Castro bluffin' tonight it sure ain't me!"

He turned without another word and walked out. Crossing the street, he found Heck in his office, feet perched upon his desk.

"You're just the man I'm lookin' for," Laramie greeted him. The Judge pulled down his shaggy brows and glanced at him sharply.

"Say, you look like a man with somethin' on his mind," he declared. "What's up?"

"Judge, there's goin' to be a gunfight here in a few minutes that'll be a stem-winder, once she starts."

Heck jerked himself to his feet. "What makes you say that?" he demanded brusquely.

Laramie repeated what had just passed between Corbett and himself. "I'm tellin' you there's fifty men ready to line up on one side or the other at the crack of a gun."

The Judge sucked in his breath nervously and began to pace the floor, his pink cheeks paling with admitted anxiety. "Maybe Bliss will change his mind about this," he dared to suggest. His tone said he knew better.

"Not this time," Laramie answered bluntly. "That gent ain't foolin' one little bit. And don't you make the mistake of thinkin' that Marr's bunch ain't plenty dangerous."

Across the way in the Silver Dollar a pool ball or a bottle shattered a window. The glass fell with a shivery sound. Drunken laughter followed from within.

"Gettin' playful now," Heck glowered.

Laramie made no comment. When he turned from the window a moment later, he had reached a decision. "Judge, there's just one thing for me to do."

"What's that?" Heck rifled at him.

"I'm goin' to ask both sides to turn in their guns."

"What?" the Judge gasped. Shaking his head, he dropped into a chair. "I don't believe you can get away with it, Johnson—"

"It's a chance—the only one I've got," Laramie ground out doggedly. "Will the town board back me up?"

Heck considered the matter for a moment. "Well, I said I'd back you up, and I will! What do you want me to do?"

"Just get a basket and follow me. We'll step into the Silver Dollar first. We ain't got a minute to waste now."

The bar was an L-shaped affair, with the short end of it paralleling the street. Laramie and Heck stepped up to the short end, and the latter placed his basket on the bar. By this arrangement, they faced Snap and his friends and had their backs to the door.

The Bar 44 cohorts glared at them in charged, hostile silence for a moment. Snap found his tongue then.

"There you are!" he roared. "Bust a window and yuh can't tell what the wind will blow in!"

The others expressed themselves more pointedly.

"Boys," Laramie exclaimed, "I'm askin' Corbett's bunch and you to turn in your guns—"

The crowd growled him down. He could get no further for the moment.

"Come and take my gun if you want it!" Brad Nash, one of Marr's brothers-in-law, dared him. He looked small, standing beside Snap, but he was really a dark-browed six-footer. His beady, repulsive eyes were treacherous.

Laramie did not offer to answer him. He was watching Snap, waiting for the vicious outburst he felt must come any moment. There was an ominous glitter in Marr's eyes; but seconds passed without bringing a word from him. Surprise gave way to suspicion in Laramie. A movement beyond Snap caught his attention. He saw Brad Nash nudge the man next to him. The other nodded, and their hands dropped to their guns.

"Better change your minds about that!" Laramie advised. "Standin' the way you are, it'll be just like stringin' fish if I open up on you."

There was a dreadful insistence in his tone that made Brad and the other man reconsider their play. They put their hands back on the bar and looked to Snap for their cue.

Even now Snap Marr had nothing to say. He filled his glass to the brim and stared into its amber depths. It was suddenly still again.

"You can have your guns in the mornin'," the Judge observed, his voice strained. "Don't seem to be any other way of keepin' the peace—"

Snap did not bother to glance at him.

"I reckon this is between you and me," he said to Laramie. "What's the other side got to say about turnin' in their guns?"

"I'm not worryin' about what Corbett will have to say," Laramie informed him. "The Frying-pan will give up its guns or get out of town."

Snap thought it over for a moment or two.

"All right," he said. "We'll meet you halfway."

The crowd was stunned by his decision. Four or five started to demur. He silenced them. There was a crafty light in his eyes. "We'll give up our guns, boys," he grinned. "This is an out for somebody; that's what it is. Somebody was gettin' awful nervous. You know it wasn't us."

Laramie dissembled his surprise at winning so easily. He knew that in some way he had played into Snap's hands.

"Just drop 'em in the basket," he ordered. The crowd obliged reluctantly. "Don't make the mistake of lettin' any of your friends slip you their guns later on," he warned. "You can't tote a shootin'-iron in Castro tonight and get away with it."

He and the Judge left directly.

"It took my breath away," Heck sighed. "I was all set for trouble. What do you make of it, Johnson?"

"I don't know," Laramie answered soberly. "Marr either has a trick up his sleeve or he was lookin' for a chance to back down. We won't have such an easy time of it with this other bunch."

"I'm afraid not," Heck agreed. "Trace is apt to put up a fight, for one. . . . Keep your eye on him."

Laramie nodded. They had arrived at the Golden Rule.

"Better let me step in first," he suggested. "The contents of that basket don't leave much to the imagination. Let me speak my piece before they get a flash at it."

His step was brisk as he walked in. The men seemed a bit surprised at seeing him back so soon. When he stepped behind the bar, they froze to attention. Laramie spoke to the proprietor. The latter nodded.

"All right over there!" he called out. "Just hold the wheel and your chips quiet for a moment. The marshal wants to say somethin'."

Laramie addressed himself to Bliss.

"You're the boss of this outfit, Corbett, so I'll do my talkin' to you. I don't like to ride herd on any man, but when a situation gets tough the only thing I can do is to get tough with it. I've just asked the Bar 44 crowd to turn in their guns—and they obliged. Now I'll have to ask you to do the same."

The Judge entered and plumped his basket on the bar. This visible evidence of the fact that Snap and his friends had given up their guns amazed the crowd almost as much as Laramie's request that they follow suit.

"Well, I'll be damned!" Trace gasped. "What do you know about that?"

Laramie was watching him closely, believing that Morrell rather than Corbett would give him the most trouble. But as with Snap, the expected outburst did not materialize. On the other hand, Bliss met him with flaming defiance in his eyes.

"Johnson, you can't take my gun away from me," he declared with marked dignity. A chorus of sullen approval greeted his stand. Morrell joined in, but his enthusiasm sounded lukewarm to Laramie, who thought he saw Trace exchange a furtive glance with Frenchy Le Brun. The breed's face remained an inscrutable copper-colored mask.

"I didn't have any thought of *takin'* your gun away from you," Laramie informed Bliss. "I'm just askin' you to turn it in. And I'm askin' you last, because I thought that was a little courtesy you'd appreciate. I ain't leanin' one way or the other, but I'll admit I figured if Marr met me halfway I could count on fair play from you."

Corbett's face purpled. "Daggone it," he protested irascibly, "you're puttin' me in a hole, ain't you? Can't you do anythin' else but toss my words in my teeth?"

"I reckon we'd better oblige him." Trace ventured to laugh, and Frenchy joined in. It broke the tension. Corbett could only shake his head.

"You win, Johnson," he groaned. He pulled out his gun. "You're pretty smooth. . . . What'll you have us do with 'em?"

"Just drop 'em in the basket," Laramie advised. "They'll be waitin' for you in the mornin'."

Heck hoisted the basket to his shoulder and started out.

"Better watch your step, Judge!" Morrell called out. "Justice will sure take a ride if you stub your toe with that load of dynamite."

Trace laughed heartily at his own jest. The crowd grinned.

"No danger of that," Heck retorted. "I've staggered home with loads that was harder to handle than this one—and they wa'n't on my shoulder either."

"My mistake," Trace chuckled. "I plumb forgot that you always travel right side up."

The laughter was general as Heck disappeared through the doors. Laramie came out from behind the bar and faced Corbett.

"I'm obliged to you, Corbett," he said. "I know you'll see that your boys don't make the mistake of showin' up with borrowed guns later this evenin'."

"You've got my word for it," Bliss answered. "Just be sure the other side doesn't make a mistake of that sort."

"I will," Laramie assured him with emphasis.

Heck was waiting for him when he reached the office. The Judge shook his head incredulously. "I can't believe it even now, Johnson," he sighed. "It beats anythin' I ever heard tell of. You hardly had to raise your voice. These men are strangers to you; but I know them. I can appreciate what you did."

"I'm afraid it wasn't very much."

"Oh, yes it was!" Heck insisted. "It took nerve and brains. It was just the way you did it that made it seem easy."

"Better not praise me too much." Laramie tilted his chair to a comfortable angle and settled back, a frown of preoccupation furrowing his forehead. He communed with himself for a few moments. "I can't put my finger on it, Judge, but there's somethin' movin' under the surface here that I don't savvy at all."

"Meanin' what?" Heck queried anxiously.

"That it wasn't in the cards for both sides to lay down to me—and that's what they did." Heck tried to protest, but Laramie waved him down. "I know Corbett gave me a little argument," he continued. "If his men had backed him up the way I figured they'd do, I would have been stopped right there."

"You referrin' to Morrell?"

"I ain't referrin' to no one else. He seems to be top man with Corbett. It was from him and Snap that I expected trouble, the two of 'em bein' a pair of fire-eatin' hombres, accordin' to the record. You saw what happened. One of 'em shows his teeth and gives in; the other says yes with a laugh. You figure that out for me if you can, Judge."

"Why bother about it?" Heck protested. "You did what you set out to do, and that's good enough for me. I may have missed a trick, but my guess is that you've convinced those boys that they don't want any of your game. If you—" He stopped abruptly and stiffened to attention. "What's that?" he demanded.

They listened intently for a moment. The dull rumble of pounding hoofs reached them. It swelled into a roar even as they listened. Laramie leaped for the door and threw it open. A mad bellowing greeted him. Rushing down the street from the direction of the corrals came an avalanche of stampeding steers, sweeping everything before them. One charged into the post that supported one end of the wooden awning in front of the hotel. The blow ripped the post to splinters. The awning buckled and crashed to the sidewalk with a thud. A moment later, the frightened herd swept past Laramie.

"There's your answer, Judge!" he whipped out. "The Fryin'-pan steers have been turned out of the corrals! Snap has sure called my hand—"

"It's a good thing we've got their guns," Heck muttered.

"You stay with 'em," Laramie commanded. "Lock the door and turn out the light. If they try to break in on you, drop the first man who steps through this door! I won't be far away!"

CHAPTER 5
Empty Holsters

BETWEEN THE MARSHAL'S OFFICE AND THE CASTRO MERCANtile Company's Store, at least a score and a half of horses stood at the hitchracks, reins dangling. Snorting and squealing with fear, they reared and fled before the onslaught of flashing horns. The few ponies that were tied broke loose and followed them.

The town was in an uproar by now. Corbett and his men rushed to the doors of the Golden Rule and recklessly tried to force their way out as they saw it was their own steers that filled the street. Morrell edged along the front of the saloon for a few feet, only to be forced back.

"The fools," Laramie groaned, "they'll never get out thisaway!" He cupped his hands to his mouth and shouted for them to use the back door and circle around behind the buildings. They had left their horses at the corrals. Without them they were powerless to stem the stampede.

"Go around!" he yelled again. "You'll save time thataway!"

He could not make himself heard; but Corbett evidently realized the hopelessness of trying to get across the street, for he waved his men back and dashed into the saloon with them.

"They'll be lucky if they find their horses waitin'," Laramie told himself. Whoever had driven the herd out of the corrals would hardly have failed to turn the Fry-pan ponies adrift too. "I suppose they figure I knew somethin' about this, askin' them to turn in their guns a few minutes before this happened."

He dismissed the thought for the present. If the steers were not turned before they got out of town, Corbett would be the rest of the night rounding them up. Laramie believed there was still a chance to head them off. Between the little buildings, which housed his office, and the Owl Saloon, next door, there was an opening ten feet wide, which ran back to a row of cabins in the rear. Three or four horses had been trapped there in their flight. Who owned them was not important for the moment.

Laramie leaped for the opening and made it safely. The saloon had a side door. He flung it back on its hinges.

"Come on, men, give me a hand!" he cried. "We can round this bunch up if we hurry!"

A dozen men rushed out.

"There's only three or four horses in here," Laramie exclaimed. "I'm borrowin' them. We'll go out by the rear and swing around so we can get ahead of that bunch."

The horses were frightened, but with a dozen men to handle them it was only a moment or two before Laramie and three others dashed away, skirting the cabins and riding for the western limits of the town. A block beyond Nat Washburn's store they flashed past the head of the herd and swung back to the street, fifty yards in advance of the front rank of stampeding cattle.

Laramie found himself astride a snuffy little buckskin that seemed to know what was expected of it. The three men who rode with him were experienced hands. Shouting, waving their sombreros, they succeeded in turning the steers into a cross street. The maneuver checked the herd's mad rush.

Several other riders appeared to lend a hand.

"Some of you get ahead of 'em again!" Laramie shouted. "Try to get 'em movin' toward the corrals!"

With a fair measure of luck and some help from the Frying-pan men, he believed the steers would soon be back in the shipping pens. Instead of ending the incident, trouble could be expected immediately. He now understood perfectly Snap's readiness to meet him halfway when he had asked him to turn in his guns.

"He sure figured this stampede would be a lot more serious than it's turnin' out to be," he thought hurriedly, "and allowed he'd have his men all armed with borrowed guns long before the Fryin'-pan would be ready to come after him."

The main thoroughfare was clear now. He felt he had men enough helping him to warrant his racing back to the corrals to make sure the gates were open. Pulling the little buckskin into a hard gallop, he flashed up the street.

The saloons had disgorged a throng of excited men. One ran out and shouted for him to stop. He was the owner of the horse. Laramie beckoned for him to follow, and raced on to the corrals.

As he rode up he saw three or four men gathered about the Frying-pan wagon. One of them proved to be Corbett.

"Get those gates open!" Laramie cried. "We've got 'em turned; they'll be here in a minute!"

Brent Taylor and Santa Fé arrived at that moment. They had recovered the horses. Corbett flung himself into the saddle and spurred up to Laramie. He was killing mad.

"What do you mean, you got 'em turned?" he whipped out.

"Just that," Laramie answered. "Here they come now!"

Sight of his beef herd being hazed back to the corrals left Corbett speechless for a moment. "I'll be damned," he got out breathlessly. "I sure figured they was all over hell by now—"

"No, we caught 'em in time," Laramie informed him hurriedly. "Better get ready for 'em! I'll give you a hand."

"Don't trouble yourself!" Morrell blazed viciously as he leaped for the gates. He had just hurried over from the wagon.

Laramie was not looking for gratitude, especially from him. But the gates had to be opened quickly and he did not hang back. Without dismounting, he reached down and caught one. Backing his pony, he swung the gate open and got in the clear.

It was neatly done. Morrell said nothing further.

"Come on, boys! Send 'em along!" Corbett shouted.

The steers seemed anxious to get into the corrals and away from their tormentors. It took only a few minutes.

"Well, there they are again," Corbett sighed heavily as Morrell dropped the bars in place. "I'll see that they stay there this time." He turned appreciatively to the men who had answered Laramie's call. "Certainly the drinks are on me for this, boys. Don't know how to thank you—"

"Better thank Johnson," one of them said. "He took the bull by the horns, so to speak—" He started to supply the details.

"You needn't bother about my part of it," Laramie spoke up. He turned to Bliss. "I'd like to know what took place here. What happened to the two men who were lookin' after your stuff? They were sittin' here on the fence, stone sober, when I saw them last, less than an hour ago."

"That's where they were sittin' when they heard somethin' over by the chutes that sounded suspicious," Bliss got out gruffly. He was not disposed to have any more conversation than absolutely necessary with the marshal. "They couldn't find anythin' wrong when they got there, so they started back. It's pretty dark there. First thing they knew, three men jumped 'em; took their guns and then tapped 'em on the head. I reckon you know the rest."

"Did you recognize the three men?"

"What the hell, Johnson!" Corbett exploded. "Why talk of

recognizin' 'em? I know and you know who they were without seein' 'em! There's only one skunk in Castro low-down enough to pull anythin' like this! I don't care whether Snap Marr was one of the three who came over here and knocked my men out or not; this thing was his doin'—and I'm layin' it up to him!''

"It was Marr, all right," Laramie agreed soberly. "And it's about as ornery a trick as I ever heard of one cowman pullin' on another. But I've got to have evidence before I can arrest him—''

"Don't you bother about arrestin' him!" Bliss clipped the words off short. "I don't want to appear an ingrate, Johnson. You apparently saved me a night's work and my five hundred dollars; but that don't stop me from feelin' that you knew somethin' was in the wind. You even hinted as much to me. I'm tellin' you to your face, if you knew when you asked me to turn in my guns that this was comin' up, you took a damned unfair advantage of me.''

A crowd of at least twenty men had gathered about them, all Fry-pan partisans, including even the man whose horse Laramie had borrowed so hurriedly.

"I'm obliged to you for the 'if' you use," Laramie answered Corbett. "Believe me, I was all set for trouble when I asked you and Marr to give me your guns. I wouldn't have done it otherwise. When I tried to tell you to stay close to the corrals, I was usin' my imagination, and didn't stretch it any to figure some attempt might be made to turn your stuff out. But you can take it from me that I didn't *know* what was goin' to happen, or I would have been here tryin' to stop it.''

"So you missed a trick, eh?" Morrell jeered. "That's quite a comedown for you, ain't it, havin' to admit you was wrong about somethin'?''

Three or four in the crowd echoed his sentiment. The others, including Corbett, glared at him and said nothing. They realized he stood in the way of their vengeance, and they were in no mood to brook further interference from him.

Laramie felt the sullen determination in their eyes. It warned him that hostilities could not be averted for long now. The thoughts tightened his mouth as he singled out Morrell.

"I'm often wrong," he told him. "Then again, there's some things that don't fool me a bit, Morrell. You'll understand that when you get to know me better.''

The others missed the mocking innuendo in his words, but

Trace caught it promptly. With a scornful grunt he tried to dissemble whatever vague anxiety it inspired. It did not deceive Laramie.

"I don't want to tip my hand," he cautioned himself, "but I sure aim to slow him up."

Frenchy Le Brun and another Frying-pan man rode in, driving three steers ahead of them, the net result of scouring the town for strays.

"This is all of 'em," Frenchy called out.

"All right, shove 'em in!" Bliss ordered. "We're about ready to tend to other matters, I reckon." He asked seven or eight men in the crowd to stand guard at the corrals. They agreed readily. "The rest of us are goin' back up the street."

"They're apt to raid us again," Morrell muttered. "Mebbe I'd better stay here, Bliss—"

Laramie wanted to laugh in his face.

"I want you with me," Corbett said. "Pete will take charge of things here."

"There's plenty Bar 44 cattle out there on the flats," a man reminded him. "The Marrs might appreciate a dose of their own medicine."

"No, sir!" Corbett exclaimed emphatically. "I know I'm dealin' with a skunk, but that don't mean I'll get down to his level."

Laramie started to leave, anxious to reach the Silver Dollar ahead of them. Bliss called him back.

"Johnson—are you goin' to be man enough to return us our guns?"

"You can't have 'em tonight," Laramie answered flatly.

Corbett held his temper with an effort. "Do you call that fair play? You know as well as I do what's become of the two guns that was taken off my men here. And that bunch didn't stop there. They're armed to the teeth by now!"

"I want to see a gun in their hands," Laramie got out tensely. "If there's some heads broken here tonight over this business, I ain't goin' to get very excited about it; but the man who shows up with a shootin' iron in his fist will sure have to answer to me."

"Have it your way," Corbett got out hoarsely. "I'm warnin' you now—don't expect me to hold to my word. And don't add to your mistakes by gettin' in our way."

"I don't know what your way is goin' to be; but you'll find me doin' my duty." With that, Laramie left them.

As he approached his office, sounds of hilarity issuing from the Silver Dollar told him that Snap and his friends were still there in force. He listened a moment and then called on Heck to admit him.

"I was wonderin' what had happened to you," the Judge exclaimed. He was full of questions. Laramie acquainted him with the situation.

"Anybody try to break in on you, Judge?"

"Not a soul—"

"Well, you just stay here. No tellin' what the next few minutes will bring."

"But Lord a'mighty, Johnson, you ain't goin' into that saloon single-handed, be yuh? You won't have a chance, man, when those two crowds come together!"

"It wouldn't help me any to swear in deputies now," Laramie murmured. "It's too late for that. I'll just have to play it my own way. I know I can't prevent a fight, but if I can stop it short of gunfire, I'll be satisfied."

Heck nodded gravely. "They're roarin' drunk across the street, and likely enough most of them *are* totin' guns. Let 'em have it if they cut down on you. I don't expect you to wait for them to fire first."

Laramie opened the door an inch or two and peered out cautiously. His eyes narrowed instantly.

"Corbett and his bunch are comin' now," he got out hurriedly. "They're crossin' to the Silver Dollar. I'm goin' to crowd in ahead of 'em. You lock this door as I step out."

Fourteen strong, with Corbett in the lead, the Frying-pan men and their allies came on at a swinging, determined stride, glancing neither to right nor left.

Laramie glanced at their holsters. They were empty. Not a gun was showing; but there were suspicious-looking bulges under their shirts that convinced him they were armed. A step or two ahead of them, he walked into the saloon.

Every eye in the place was riveted on the doors, proof enough that Snap had been warned that Corbett and his crowd were coming. He and his men stood at the bar, but they had arranged themselves along the rear end of it so that no one could jump them without giving notice of such intention.

Eyes alert, Laramie walked over to the short end of the bar where he had stood with Heck. The hilarity continued, much of it at his expense; but he suspected it was forced. A moment later, with a blow that almost knocked the swinging doors off their hinges, Corbett leaped into the barroom, with his men rushing in after him.

Suddenly it was still, drunken laughter dying away to a hushed whisper and the profanity and vituperation of the moment just gone no more than an empty echo. In a twinkling the air had become charged with an oppressive, electric tension that held both sides motionless as well as speechless.

Someone upset a glass. It broke the spell. Words rushed to Corbett's tongue.

"There's a skunk in here by the name of Snap Marr," he charged. His voice had a dreadful whine. "Let him step out! We're here to pay our respects to him and the rest of you pole-cats!"

Snarling ferociously, Snap tossed two of his men out of the way and stepped forth to face Corbett, his puffed, pasty-looking face working nervously.

"I'll make you eat that!" he bellowed. "You ain't sneakin' up any canyon now—grabbin' another man's water and grass and everythin' else in sight! I got you out in the open at last, where I been tryin' to get you! Now you white-livered whelp, fill your hand!"

His hand flashed to his shirt. It was a signal for a dozen others to do likewise, Corbett among them. Before they could get their guns out, Laramie leaped behind the bar.

"I got you covered!" he droned. "I'll drop the man who draws a gun!" His tone left no doubt that he would do as he threatened. "This argument will have to be settled without gun-play."

Both sides hesitated, the decision hanging in the balance for a moment. Finally hands that had been groping for guns began to reappear; and they came out empty. Snap was the last to give in. He edged nearer the bar, and with catlike swiftness reached out for an empty whisky bottle and sent it hurtling through the air at Corbett. It passed over Bliss' head to crash into the mirror above the doors.

As the shattered glass fell, both sides made a concerted rush at each other, fists thudding as they found their mark. Anything that was movable became a weapon. Santa Fé picked up a pool cue, and swinging it about his head, rushed at Snap. Suddenly the cue went flying out of his hands to wreak havoc among the glasses stacked on the backbar. Snap caught him and lifting him bodily, flung him halfway across the room.

Reb Taney and another Bar 44 man dashed at Corbett. He met them toe to toe. Morrell came to his aid; but instead of lashing out at the common foe, Trace tried to smother Reb in his arms. It was not taken as a friendly overture by Reb, who backed away and promptly closed Morrell's right eye.

Laramie observed the incident. "Evidently Snap neglected to tell his men that Morrell, under cover, is a brother in good standin'," he thought.

Corbett disposed of the other man and tried to reach Snap. Brad Nash brought him up short before he could take a second step. They were of a size, but in years the advantage was all with the Bar 44 man, who boasted of his prowess as a rough-and-tumble fighter.

Nash immediately tried to trip Corbett. To get a man down and kick him into insensibility was perfectly permissible in a fight of this kind. Bliss slipped and would have gone down if Oddie Dill had not caught him. Undismayed, Brad flung himself at both of them. The fight went out of him abruptly, however. Someone hurled a pool ball at him. It struck him between the eyes and he went down like a felled ox.

Others went down, only to get up cursing and grunting, mouths bleeding and the clothes half torn off them, and fight on, trading punches right and left.

A head taller than any man in the room, his great strength unmatched, Snap Marr was in his glory. In twos and threes the Frying-pan men assailed him. Every atom of strength they possessed was in the blows they landed on his jaw. They shook Snap; but he weathered them and struck back, lashing out like an enraged desert lion with his huge paws.

It was riot run wild. The Silver Dollar was a wreck. Not a window remained whole, nor a lamp chimney. The hanging oil-lamps, blackened, smoking dangerously, illumined the saloon with a ghastly light.

Laramie did not attempt to interfere. Short of gunplay, he was willing to let the fight burn itself out, knowing it would clear the atmosphere for weeks to come.

As Laramie watched now, four men rushed Snap. He slammed one to the floor and was in a fair way of doing as much for another when Corbett brought his hand up from his knees and landed a terrific blow to the jaw. Snap was caught off balance. It lifted him to his toes. As his head went back, Brent Taylor's fist crashed into his chin.

Snap threw out his arms and tried in vain to save himself as he fell. Down he went.

He was up almost instantly. With a bull-like rush he bore down on Bliss.

"I'll get you now, you damn rustler!" he screeched.

Corbett gave him a clip on the ear. It didn't even shake Snap. Grinning hideously, he came on. The owner of the Frying-pan was no match for him, and he knew it. His fist flashed. It struck Corbett high on the cheek. Only the fact that Bliss was going away from the blow when it landed saved him.

Snap's left shot out to do what his right had failed to accomplish. Again Corbett escaped him. Beside himself, Snap lowered his head to butt him. Before he could charge, an interruption came at the door that halted him in his tracks. A white-bearded giant, fully Snap's equal in size, had pushed his way into the saloon.

"Stop!" the newcomer roared. There was authority in his voice. He might have been a prophet, a fighting prophet, come to admonish his flock. He was old, but he had the strength of a grizzly in his loins. Tossing men out of his way, irrespective of which side they fought on, he pushed his way through the crowd until he stood between Snap and Corbett. Although Laramie had never seen him before, he knew the man was Isaiah Marr.

"No more of this!" the old Mormon cried out. He flung Snap back and faced his men. "Don't let me see another blow struck here! You can't draw wages from me if you do!" Even in his anger there was an unassailable dignity about him that laid violent hands on every man in the saloon.

He searched them out in turn with his outraged eyes. Snap tried to answer. Isaiah rubbed the words from his son's lips with a transfixing glance.

"Drunk!" he charged with withering contempt. "Dragging the good name you bear across a barroom floor! Was it for this I sent you here?"

Again Snap would have spoken; but his father cut him off.

"I've heard the facts!" he ground out. "They can't be denied!" He turned to face Corbett. "There's been bad blood between us for years," he continued. "I do not draw the line at fighting you; but it's never been my way to do my fighting in a saloon or transact my business in the middle of the night. I've never needed the cover of darkness to help me out, Corbett! You know it, man! I do not believe you had any right to the corrals; but right or wrong, I'll have no part of a sulking boy's game of stampeding another man's steers. If there's been any damage done, I'll pay for it.''

Snap was so amazed he fell back a step, gasping for breath. The other Bar 44 men were hardly less dismayed. As for Corbett, he was so embittered that he was suspicious of every word the Mormon uttered.

"Don't talk to me of damages," he muttered fiercely, telling himself he liked Isaiah's intervention as little as Snap did; "you can't do me any favors. That part of it's forgotten, but I ain't forgettin' that the name of rustler was given me here tonight. That's somethin' you can't square. I'll be the one to do that.''

The old man did not try to hide his surprise. "We've been losing a number of calves," he said, "but I never thought to accuse you of it—"

"Then where does your son get his talk from? He didn't find it in a whisky bottle. It was in his mind when he rode into town. You come in with your amens and psalm singin'—and it don't mean a damn thing to me. I've brought my outfit a long way since the days when I could be chased off of good grass just because you happen to have seen it first. I've come along right under your nose; and that's what is behind this talk.''

"I'll say we're worried!" Snap jeered. "We must be when Isaiah Marr will make his son crawl—somethin' you nor any other man in this town could do!" He flashed a poisonous glance at Laramie. "The Marrs used to stand together—"

"Stop!" Isaiah thundered. "It's I who have been shamed, not you! Would you forget your religion completely and show me further disrespect by defying me?''

"My religion don't bother me; I got more important things on my mind." The blasphemy left the Mormon aghast. As he fumbled for words with which to express his horror, Snap said: "Don't try to frown me down and quote scripture to me. There's a time for it, and it ain't now. If you don't understand what Corbett's tryin' to say to you—I do!" He addressed himself to Bliss. "So you're gettin' ready to move in on us, eh? That's your threat, ain't it?''

"I'm runnin' cattle, and I'm goin' to find grass and water for 'em," Corbett flung back at him.

"And you've got a damned good idea where you're goin' to look for it!"

"I sure have!" Corbett admitted unhesitatingly.

"Try it!" Snap dared him. "We'll know what to do about it!"

Iron-faced, Isaiah Marr stared from one to the other, the saloon brawl and his altercation with Snap forgotten. Unconsciously, his mighty shoulders hunched and his great hands tightened until the knuckles were white. For thirty years and more he had defended his borders against encroaching cowmen and Indian raiders. What he claimed for his own, no other white man had claimed before him, for he had pioneered the wilderness in establishing himself on the Snake River Plains.

He had seen the country settled; towns built; railroads put down. And his troubles had multiplied with their coming, for there were many to covet what was his by right of conquest.

"I have always protected what is mine, and I will continue to do so," he said simply, his tone passionless. "You are angry tonight, Corbett, and threats and hot words fly to a man's tongue when he is beside himself with rage. I can't believe you meant what you said. If you did—it means war to the hilt between us."

"That's what I intend it to mean!" Bliss answered. "For the first time in your life you'll find an outfit facin' you that won't run! You've always had the idea you had some God-given right to grab all the grass and water in sight, far beyond your needs. You got away with it because no one dared to dispute you. Well, that's all over! I need range—and I'm goin' to get it! And I'm goin' to get it the same way you got it!"

He motioned for his men to leave. He started to turn away himself, when he paused to fix his eyes on Snap.

"Rustler, eh?" he ground out. "Well, I've been losin' calves too—plenty of 'em and if it'll make you feel any better, I've got a pretty good idea where they're goin'!"

"You rat!" Snap screamed. "You asked for it and you can have it!" His hand darted inside his shirt. It caught the crowd off guard.

Laramie was watching him. There was no time to call a halt. He fired as Snap's hand came out clutching his .45. The gun went spinning through the air. Blood spurted from Marr's hand.

"Take it easy!" Laramie cried. "I warned you once not to

show a gun. You get your crowd out of here now, Corbett; you Bar 44 men stand back.''

He walked up to Snap. Isaiah faced him. They fenced with their eyes. It was steel meeting steel.

"What do you propose to do now, marshal?"

"I propose to do my duty. I'm arrestin' this man."

"Will that be necessary if I give you my word he'll leave town at once for our camp on the flats and stay there until morning?"

"I'm sorry; I'll have to lock him up," Laramie answered. "Do you mind handin' me that gun, Morrell?" Trace picked up the blue-barreled Colt and gave it to him. Laramie waited for Corbett and his followers to leave. They turned and walked out. "Come on," he said to Snap.

The Bar 44 men were muttering angrily among themselves.

"You're overplayin' your hand, Johnson," Brad Nash exclaimed. "You'll find it out!"

"Let him have his way," Snap said, patronizingly. "I'll go along with him."

He started for the door with Laramie a step behind him. The Bar 44 men were ready to interfere. Isaiah waved them back.

"I'll take care of this," he told them. "Corbett may be running the marshal, but he is not running this town."

CHAPTER 6
A Coyote is Trapped

THE NIGHT BEGAN TO QUIET DOWN SURPRISINGLY WITH SNAP Marr locked up. Doc Samuels had been summoned to dress the injured hand. When the doctor had finished, he and Laramie stepped into the marshal's office. The Judge awaited them.

"He's sure makin' plenty of noise," Heck muttered. "Best thing could have happened to this town—lockin' him up." He was thoroughly acquainted by now with what had taken place in the Silver Dollar.

Laramie swung back in his chair and gazed at the ceiling with a deep preoccupation. "Marr says he won't be in here long."

"He'll be here until he comes up before me tomorrow mornin'," Heck exclaimed crustily. "Let him talk—"

"It may be more than talk," Doc declared soberly. "I line up with you a hundred per cent, Heck, but Isaiah Marr won't let any son of his languish in jail overnight if he can help it. Take my word for it, he'll put the screws on certain members of the town board. Don't be surprised if some of them do a little backsliding."

"Washburn, eh? And Coates and Porter—" Heck expressed his contempt eloquently. "They better not try to buttonhole me! I'll call a few gents in this town by their right name!"

"I'm of the same mind as you," Samuels remarked. He started out only to stop in the doorway. "Guess I'll stay," he murmured. "Here comes Washburn and the rest of them now."

"What, comin' *here*?" Heck demanded belligerently.

Doc did not have to answer. Washburn strode in before the words were cold on the Judge's lips. Coates and Porter, the other two members of the board, were only a step behind them. They were all very solemn.

"Glad to find both of you here," Washburn announced, jerking his head an inch or two in a nod to Heck and Samuels. "You too, Johnson." He gave Laramie a wintry smile. "The three of us have been talking things over. There seems to be some question about the wisdom of what's been done, and now that things have quieted down—"

"Wait a minute!" the Judge cut in. "Just wait a minute there, Nat! By any chance are you comin' here to ask that Snap be turned free?"

"Well, yes,—if that's the way you want it put," Washburn answered. "And I don't propose to be stared down about it. Whatever reason Johnson had for locking Snap up is gone now; the town has quieted down. To keep him in jail overnight is just rubbin' it in. Isaiah Marr is not only the leadin' cowman in this country but a man of his word. You can depend on him to see there'll be no more trouble. He feels pretty bad about this."

"And we can't afford to bear down too hard. He'll take his business to some other town," Anse Porter declared gloomily. His saddlery and harness business was one of Castro's leading institutions.

Laramie smiled inscrutably and said nothing. The Judge, however, appeared to be on the verge of apoplexy.

"Why, you ornery, rubber-kneed hypocrites!" he exploded, leaping to his feet and looking them over from head to toes. "The idea! I swear they ain't backbone enough in the pack of you to make a jackrabbit hold his head up! What in 'ternal hell do you mean, throwin' down a man that's done for you what Johnson has tonight?"

He leveled an accusing finger at Washburn. "It's you, Nat! You're responsible for this! Isaiah Marr went to you right off, and you scuttled the ship, didn't you?"

"It won't do you any good to abuse me," Washburn snapped. "We're just thinkin' ahead a bit. We don't propose to have the Mormons think we're pickin' on them. They're comin' into this country right along, and it's been my experience they bring good hard dollars along with 'em. We don't propose to do anythin' that will discourage 'em against comin'.''

"Sounds to me, Nat, as though you were crawling out from under," Samuels remarked. "Or maybe all your chatter about law and order doesn't mean a thing when your pocketbook is being hit."

"He'll get law and order!" Heck screeched. "I know what your game is, Nat, marchin' in here with Coates and Porter. You've got special meetin' of the board written all over you. Well, you can outvote me, but I'm damned if you can outsmart me! I'll just beat you to the punch, Nathaniel!" He turned to Laramie. "You trot your prisoner out here; I'll hear his case right now!"

"You can't do that!" Washburn railed. "It ain't legal!"

"I'll take a chance that it'll be legal enough," the Judge informed him. "Bring him out, Johnson."

Laramie shook his head, thoroughly disgusted.

"No, Judge, I won't do that," he said. "You backed me up like a man, but I ain't goin' to force your hand. It does get under my skin, though, to have men run out on me like this."

"You've said enough, Johnson," Washburn warned. "I don't propose to listen to any abuse from you—"

"You'll listen; make no mistake about that," Laramie remarked ominously. "You may be small enough to walk under a rattler's belly without bending your shoulders, but you'll stand tied when I speak to you. I made two mistakes this evenin'— one in believin' you really wanted law enforcement and the other in not dropping Snap Marr in his tracks when he flashed a gun. But no matter! I'm not your man any longer!" He tossed his badge of office on the desk. "You get yourselves another marshal—"

"Oh, don't be hasty," Heck pleaded. "I know a man never got shabbier treatment; but we need you, Johnson—"

"No, I'm through, Judge," Laramie insisted. "This outfit would short change me in one way or another, and you know it! Snap Marr has threatened to get me for what happened tonight. I'll be around where the gettin' will be easy. If he comes after me, packin' a gun, I'm promisin' you there'll be one member of the Marr family who'll never do any more tradin' here in Castro."

Laramie repaired to his room at the hotel and went to bed, if not to sleep. In his mind's eye the evening passed before him. In many ways he was glad that his tenure of office as the marshal of Castro had terminated so abruptly. It had never been his intention to remain there for long. His purpose had been to avert a bloody gunfight in which Trace Morrell might be wiped out. He had accomplished it.

The night passed without further disturbance. In the morning, Laramie was finishing breakfast when Bliss and Morrell walked into the hotel office. Through the open dining room door he could see them seated at a table in the office, busy with some figures. The last of the Frying-pan steers were aboard the cars and the Bar 44 herd was going into the shipping-pens. Snap was in charge, having been given his freedom a few minutes after Laramie had turned in his shield.

"Mornin', Johnson," Bliss called out as Laramie entered the office. "Hear you got a pretty raw deal."

"Well, I thought it was a little raw," Laramie smiled. "I see you got in the clear, all right."

"Yeh, thanks to you," Corbett grinned.

"How come? I figured you and your bunch thought I was bearin' down pretty hard."

"Reckon we did; but I've thought things over. You were in a tough spot, Johnson. I'm obliged to you for shootin' that six-gun out of Snap Marr's fist. He'd have downed me but for you."

Laramie purchased and lit one of Hughie's Dry Climate Specials.

"Snap was lucky," he murmured as he got his cigar going. "He'll never know how close he come to fillin' his hand for the last time. Men don't pull that sort of stuff and live, down in our country—do they, Morrell?"

"No," Trace answered without looking up from the tally-sheets he held in his hands. "Where you headin' for now, Johnson?"

"Most any place," Laramie answered lightly. "Got to find myself a job punchin' cattle or somethin'."

Corbett put down his pencil. "You don't have to look any further," he exclaimed heartily. "The way you rounded up those steers last night makes me think you can handle stock just about as well as you can men. You're ridin' for the Fryin'-pan from now on, if you say the word. I'll pay you top wages."

Trace said nothing, but he scowled at the sheets in his hand.

"Reckon you've hired a man," Laramie answered. "When are you pullin' out?"

"Oh, in the cool of the afternoon. Want me to advance you some money? It'll be some time before you see town again."

"No, I've got a few dollars and a day's wages comin'," Laramie answered with a grin. "I'm goin' to step out and try to collect. I'll have my roll on the wagon in plenty time."

He found the Judge in his office, ready to hold court but with no cases in sight. Heck was still wrathy. They talked half an hour before Laramie told him he was now riding for the Frying-pan.

"That'll be a nice piece of news for the Marrs," the Judge

exclaimed. "When they hear it they'll swear you were stringin' along with Bliss from the start."

"You know better," Laramie reminded him.

"Yeh, I know a lot of things, but knowledge ain't no virtue in this town," Heck got out caustically. "I better step down the street and get your pay before Washburn hears you've thrown in with Corbett. You just sit here."

Laramie closed the door. Seated at Heck's desk, he could observe through the window what went on across the street. It was in his mind to keep an eye on Morrell. He had not forgotten Snap's admonition to Trace that he wanted something tomorrow. He hoped to discover what that something was.

Morrell walked up and down the street half a dozen times, stopping once at the post office and another time at the Golden Rule. The other Frying-pan men were idling about town, but he kept to himself and always he returned to the hotel. Laramie began to feel that it was there he expected to meet Snap.

The Judge came back shortly with the money. Laramie let him talk on indefinitely. He knew the Bar 44 must be almost through at the corrals. Ten minutes later he saw Snap heading for the hotel. Trace sat out in front, talking to Hughie.

Laramie hurried across the street and took a chair beside Morrell. A moment or two later, Snap appeared. He went in and climbed the stairs to the second floor. No sign passed between the two men, but Snap was hardly out of sight before Trace recalled that he had left his razor in the room he had occupied.

"Go up and get it," Hughie advised. "I saw it there this morning."

Laramie suspected that Morrell had planted the razor so he would have a valid excuse for going upstairs. He gave Trace a moment's start and then followed him. Morrell had hurried, for when he reached the stairs, the big fellow was not to be seen.

Laramie went on up. As he reached the second floor, he was surprised to find Snap facing him. Marr glared at him venomously and walked on down, muttering viciously.

Laramie continued on to his own room. He left his door ajar. Presently, Trace stepped out of a room down the hall and descended the stairs.

"Well, I don't know any more now than I did before," Laramie had to admit. "Certainly didn't take them long, whatever it was."

Through the window he could see Snap walking toward the depot. The work at the corrals had been finished.

"It was money that passed between them," Laramie told himself. "They weren't up here long enough for it to have been anythin' else."

He was still turning the thought over in his mind when a door across the way opened and Isaiah Marr came out. Laramie didn't know what to think. Was it possible that the old Mormon was a party to the mysterious business between Morrell and Snap? He found it hard to believe.

The only answer he could arrive at was one that put a steely glitter in his blue eyes. "If that's the case," he muttered, "Morrell is sure enough the gent I'm lookin' for!"

"You'll get onto this country in no time, Johnson." The speaker was Bliss Corbett. The Frying-pan outfit was two days out of Castro, moving along slowly so as not to outdistance their wagon. "It ain't all desert. You'll find natural barriers here to keep your stuff from driftin', just as you do down in Arizona.

"Those blue hills over there to the northeast are really the Lost River Mountains. I've got some stuff over there, on Squaw Creek. They'll graze up as high as the lava rims by late summer, but by the time snow flies, they'll be back on the creek."

"Good range?"

"No, nothin' to speak of," Morrell put in. The conversation had been a three-way affair for miles. "Be good sheep country some day."

"I reckon that's so," Corbett agreed thoughtfully. "You see those big ragged black peaks over there, far to the northwest? Sawtooth Range. Sheep in there right now, and doin' well, I understand. It's never bothered me any; we don't get over anywheres near that far. You can see that these Salmon River foothills and the Lost River Mountains make a sort of half-circle ahead of us. It's always been a natural deadline with me.

"My range is spread out too much as it is. Summer and winter I'm payin' wages to a dozen or more men. That's expensive, Johnson. But what can I do?—a little grass here and some more forty, fifty, even sixty miles away. But even with a big outfit I'm losin' stuff all the time. Wolves and mountain lion pull down a few; but there's a bigger leak than that."

"It's rustlers, of course," Laramie ventured, the conversation having suddenly become of absorbing interest to him. "Somebody sifting down through those mountains and raidin' you."

"That's what I tell him," Morrell seconded, "but Bliss won't have it thataway."

"And you know why," Corbett exclaimed. "Most natural thing in the world for a man to jump to the same conclusion you did, Johnson. With all that broken country to the north, you'd figure right off that was where your stuff was goin'. I figured so myself; but we've ridden that country lookin' for rustlers till we were ragged, and we never picked up a sign that said we were on the right trail. You heard what I said to Snap Marr the other night, so you know what I'm thinkin'."

"Do you mean the Bar 44?" Laramie asked carelessly. "What makes you so sure the Bar 44 is the well-known nigger in the woodpile?"

"If you knew this country you'd understand why," Corbett answered rather sharply. "There's only two ways our stuff could be goin'; if it ain't north then it's sure to the west—and that puts it up squarely to Isaiah Marr!"

Laramie shook his head. "I can't believe it. I've known a lot of Mormons in my time—good, bad and indifferent—and I'd pretty near have to catch the old man in the act before I'd believe he would run an iron on stuff that didn't belong to him."

"Now that's just about what I said, ain't it, Bliss?" Trace demanded with an air of triumph. "Isaiah is a range hog who won't give an inch; he's done his damnedest to run us out; but I'm stringin' along with Laramie on this point. Old Isaiah ain't rustlin' our calves and yearlin's."

Laramie masked his surprise at hearing himself addressed so familiarly. The other Frying-pan men had welcomed him into the outfit, but this was the first sign of good-will from Trace. He questioned its sincerity, as he did the big fellow's purpose in insisting that the rustling had no connection with the Bar 44.

"Don't let the old man's sanctimonious air fool you," Corbett grumbled. "And don't forget that Mormon bunch does a lot that Isaiah Marr never hears about until it is an accomplished fact. Anyhow, I'm going to keep my eyes open."

The first hint of evening was in the air when the Grande Ronde finally lay stretched out before them. Laramie found it a little breath-taking, even after Arizona. In the truest sense it was no coulée at all, but a great pocket, miles wide, scooped out of the desert. The walls descended precipitately for several hundred feet.

The floor of the coulée was carpeted with grass. In the distance, a fringe of green trees held a promise of unfailing water.

"Well, this is the home range," Bliss said to Laramie.

It took them another hour to make the descent and reach the trees. Two brush corrals and a sod shanty were all the evidence that the Frying-pan had been in possession of the coulée for years.

"There's Uncle Elmer!" Santa Fé called out as he caught sight of a man seated on an upturned box outside the shanty.

"So it is," Corbett acknowledged. "Reckon he and Shorty have been back here several days. Chadron ought to be in too. This is the rest of our outfit, Johnson. They've been combin' the country north and east of here, brandin' what stuff we missed and tryin' to check on how much stuff we've got runnin' wild. I'm sure anxious to hear what old Elmer has got to say."

Uncle Elmer was old and weather-beaten. A thousand little lines had been carved by the wind on his leathery cheeks. He sat as stolidly as an Indian as they rode in, giving no sign at all that he saw them.

The other two men, Steve Chadron and Shorty Sefrancis, appeared from the direction of the corrals and called out a greeting.

"I'm sure glad to see you all," said Steve, "especially you, Oddie. I got a hankerin' to put some store grub inside of me. I been livin' on roots and grass for two days. I'm damned if I could go the slumgullion Uncle Elmer has been dishin' out."

"You sure said a mouthful, brother!" Shorty averred. "I've et after squaws whose cookin' I preferred to his. I don't care what he puts in the pot it comes out tastin' like jerked wildcat."

"Don't pull my leg thataway," Oddie barked at them. He had been growling at everything for so many years that it no longer fooled anyone. "If you want to eat tonight, get them hosses unhooked and break up some stuff for a fire."

Laramie exchanged a nod with the two men, and after turning the big black into the corral with the other horses, walked over to the shanty with Corbett. He surmised that Shorty and Steve would soon know all about him, or rather as much as Oddie and the others knew. Any thought he had entertained that he would find Ike Mundy in the Frying-pan camp was gone now. Uncle

Elmer, Steve and Shorty did not fit the descriptions of the men he wanted.

"Well, Uncle, how long you been back?" Corbett asked the old man.

"Three days." Uncle Elmer squinted his eyes at Laramie in a frank appraisal. "A new member of the family, eh?"

"Yeh. Laramie Johnson by name," Corbett informed him. "This is Uncle Elmer Hosper, Johnson." He winked at Laramie. "Uncle was the first man ever took wages from me. He's got to be a cantankerous nuisance and I ought to have fired him long ago; but the fact of the matter is I couldn't run this outfit without him."

The old man laughed and then did an unprecedented thing for him: he shook Laramie's hand. "Brother, it's a pleasure to spread the robe and light the pipe for you, as our Injun friends put it."

"Well, Uncle Elmer, what's the good word?" Corbett asked.

"To make a long story short, it ain't good at all, Bliss," the old man answered, the smile dying out of his faded eyes. "If cow nature ain't changed all of a sudden it would appear that we've been gettin' a pretty raw deal from certain unknown parties. We worked everythin' from Squaw Creek to Antelope Springs—and we worked it hard—and the results was mighty discouragin'. We located some unbranded stuff—not as much as we figgered to find—and as for calves, we're way short."

"How many did you burn?" Corbett asked tensely.

Morrell, Le Brun and three or four others had joined them in time to hear the question.

"Less than two hundred head," Uncle Elmer answered Bliss.

"What? Why, it don't seem possible! We've got breeders enough up there to give us a crop of calves half again as big as that!"

"I know it," the old man agreed. "We didn't do so bad at the springs, but there ain't nothin' left in that Lost River country."

Corbett was so incensed that he could not contain himself. He turned to Morrell.

"Trace, you and Frenchy were over there six weeks ago. All the spring calves had been dropped by that time. When you got back you didn't seem to have any idea things were as bad as this."

"No, I didn't," Morrell declared. "Don't forget there wasn't a calf weaned then. No rustler who knows his business is goin' to bother with unweaned stuff. They just waited until the takin' was easy. I've always said we ought to watch those hills. Maybe this will convince you I was right. It ain't reasonable to suppose the Bar 44 got this bunch. You get a line on anythin', Uncle Elmer?''

"I can't say we did. There's a new outfit runnin' cattle beyond the lava beds—the Box Z. We got into their stuff and had a good look at it. Everythin' seemed to be in order; there wa'n't an over-branded critter in the bunch. There was some calves, but not too many.''

"I never heard of this Box Z crowd," Corbett said. "Who are they anyway?''

"I can't say as to that. They're all strangers to me," Uncle Elmer declared. "Apparently it's just a small, driftin' outfit.''

"Did you talk to 'em?" Bliss inquired.

"I talked to one—a fellar named Harkins. Didn't get anythin' out of him.''

"Mighty funny a strange outfit should show up just when our stuff is bein' rustled," Santa Fé remarked pointedly. "Don't sound right to me.''

Laramie was of the same opinion; but he said nothing. The appearance of a third outfit fitted in perfectly with the idea that had been fermenting in his mind ever since he reached the conclusion that money had passed between Snap and Morrell. The next moment, however, he was surprised to hear Trace say:

"I'd like to ask that crowd a few questions. They'd talk to me or I'd know why. Must be some damn good reason why they're tryin' to scratch a livin' out of the lava beds.''

"Well, I'll give you plenty chance to talk to 'em," Bliss informed him. "I want you and Frenchy to pull out for the creek in the mornin'. You're to stay there until you hear from me. Better take grub enough along to last you a week. Uncle Elmer— you go back to the springs. Take two or three men with you. Santa Fé will be straw-boss here—'' Corbett broke off to pick up a stick. Squatting on his toes he made a diagram on the ground.

"See here, Santa Fé, what I want you to do," he continued. He had no need to ask for attention; the men were hanging on his words. He pointed to a mark he had made with his stick. "This is the creek over here; there is the springs. I want you to work north in between 'em, so if either Uncle Elmer or Trace wants you in a hurry they'll know where to find you. You'll have men enough so you can spread out and still keep a sharp eye on things. You'll—"

"What's the idea?" Morrell interrupted. "Are we goin' after this new outfit?" Laramie thought he sounded very much concerned.

"I'll tell you in a minute what's on my mind," Corbett answered him. "Just let me finish." He used his stick to illustrate his point again. "You can see you'll be workin' on just about a straight line, from east to west. That's what I want. If our stuff seems inclined to drift north, turn 'em back. In other words, you'll be in between 'em and the hills all the time. If anybody gets at 'em, they'll have to slip by you to do it. Do I make myself plain?"

The three men whom he addressed signified that they understood him perfectly.

"Give this Box Z crowd a mighty good lookin' over. If you find anythin' suspicious—run it down. If you catch them redhanded, well—you know what to do." He turned to Morrell. "Now, Trace, I'll answer you. I'm headin' west in the mornin'. I'm takin' Johnson with me. We're goin' to scout for new range. If we find it—" he slapped his knee to give emphasis to his words—"we're pullin' out of the Lost River country!"

The men expressed their surprise in various ways.

"Say, Bliss, that sounds like we're runnin', don't it?" Uncle Elmer demanded crossly. "What's come over you?"

"That's what I'd like to know," Morrell exclaimed, his eyes flashing. "Unknown parties rob us blind and now we get ready to pull out. I call that good! First time I ever knew the Fryin'-pan to back away from a showdown."

"Don't get me wrong," Corbett advised. "I'm not backin' away from anythin'. I've had it in my mind for over a year to pull out of Squaw Creek. This rustlin' hasn't anythin' to do with my decision. Our stuff has never done well there. Every dry year we've been hit pretty hard.

"I tell you, I'm lookin' ahead, boys. Another five or six years and this is goin' to be a fenced country. In less time than that you'll see the courts recognizin' water rights. Believe me, I'm preparin' for that day. I'm goin' to consolidate my range if I can and get in shape to hold down what I claim."

CHAPTER 7
Hot Lead Warning

I<small>T</small> PROVOKED ENDLESS ARGUMENT. THEY WERE STILL AT IT when Oddie called them to supper. Laramie had had little to say. Left to decide for himself he would have chosen to go to Squaw Creek with Morrell and Le Brun, rather than head west with Bliss.

Before turning in for the night, preparations were completed for an early start. Bliss handed Laramie a .30-.30 rifle.

"I noticed you had a saddle scabbard," he remarked. "Better slip this into it; it may come in handy. We ain't goin' to bother with a pack animal. Whatever we take we'll carry on our saddles."

"Sure," Laramie agreed. "Grub won't bother us. We can always knock over a sage-hen or two. If we're goin' to find grass we'll have to find water."

"Oh, we may have a dry camp or two. No difficulty about that though."

Trace had come up to them. "Got any idea where you'll strike for first?"

The question sounded innocent enough, but Laramie was not disposed to arm Morrell with information that might be passed on in some mysterious fashion to Snap Marr. "Oh, we'll just follow the grass, as the Navajos put it, and let it lead us into the green pastures," he remarked before Bliss could answer.

It was said with a laugh, but Corbett glanced at him shrewdly, sensing that he had deliberately turned Morrell's question.

"Yeh, that's about it," he agreed, satisfied to follow Laramie's lead. "We'll try to be awful hard to find."

Later, when he was alone with Laramie, he referred to the matter.

"Why were you so cagy with Trace?" he asked.

"No reason at all except that when you're ridin' into hostile country it's just as well if your friends don't know where you are; they couldn't help you, and they might drop a word, without intendin' to, that would hurt you."

"That's bein' plenty cautious," Corbett chuckled, "but I

daresay you're right." He wound his watch and glanced at the time. "I suppose Brent and Pete are rollin' through Wyomin' with our steers by now. Well, it's been a long day for all of us." He yawned. "Four o'clock will get around in a hurry. We better turn in."

Laramie rolled up in his blanket, but he did not fall asleep at once. It was obvious to him by now that whatever Morrell's game was, the big fellow did not want the Frying-pan cattle pulled off their present range.

"And it ain't because he figures the Bar 44 may lose some grass if we move west," he told himself. "He's got a better reason than that. He was quick to accuse this Box Z outfit— almost too quick, in fact. For all his talk they may be friends of his. If they ain't, he's connected with some one north of here, and he don't want that arrangement interfered with. If the Box Z is a rustlin' outfit it may well be Mundy and the very crowd I'm lookin' for."

As Bliss had said, four o'clock came quickly. In the purple morning haze they rode for miles, with hardly a word passing between them. Off in the malpais a coyote trotted out on a ledge and bayed a welcome to the new-born day. In all the immensity about them nothing else moved.

"We'll bear north a little as we go along," Corbett advised. "That broken-faced peak can be our guide-post for today. It'll be well along toward evenin' before the country begins to change at all. We'll be out of the lava then an' you'll find some bunch grass in among the sage."

At noon they halted to eat a piece of jerky and smoke a cigarette.

"You can head into these hills and find some grass in a dozen places," Corbett remarked. "But you know how it is; water in the spring and not a trickle left by August. That would work out all right for me if I could locate some water nearby that I could count on the year around. Of course, Isaiah Marr lays claim to everythin' he's ever had his eyes on, just as I said. Why, he'd have an army to hold down what he says is his. But if we can find somethin' that cattle haven't been on of late that'll do the trick for me, we're movin' in!"

Laramie approved his stand as eminently fair.

The country began to change in the late afternoon as Corbett had predicted. They turned into the hills, crossed several low ranges and returned to the desert without finding anything to interest them. That night they made a dry camp. They were well within the enemy's country now.

The second day was well along before they found themselves standing on the brink of a depression in the desert that was very much like the Grande Ronde Coulée. It was not as deep, but certainly as large. The grass was green.

"Limestone Tanks," Corbett stated. "I've often heard of it." They were looking down on the tops of willows and cottonwoods. "Plenty water! The Marrs used to be here in force."

"Don't see a critter down there now," Laramie remarked as he studied the basin.

"No, neither do I. Shows you what range Isaiah must have to turn his back on anythin' as good as this. We'll follow the rim around for a mile or two and see what we can see."

An hour passed as they reconnoitered the tanks.

"Nothin' down there at all," Corbett announced. "We can ride in." The tracks they discovered were old.

"No cattle been in here this year," Laramie declared. "Maybe longer than that."

The springs that gave the place its name bubbled forth from a limestone dike. There was a steady flow, the water running off for two or three hundred yards into a shallow pool.

"You can appreciate what these tanks would mean to me, can't you?" Bliss inquired. "As the crow flies we ain't over twenty-two or three miles from Antelope Springs."

Laramie had never seen him so elated. "How far do you suppose we are from the Bar 44 home range now?" he inquired.

"I don't know definitely. I've always taken it for granted that Limestone Tanks was about halfway between the Grande Ronde and Marr's range. It's up to us to make sure of that."

"Strange they haven't sent a few men in here," Laramie murmured thoughtfully. "They must realize that with the Fryin'-pan settled here, halfway to 'em, we'll be twice as dangerous."

"Reckon we've just moved a little too fast for 'em," Bliss chuckled. "They'll be here, but with luck we'll be ready for 'em. I'll nail this water down so no man will ever get it away from me. I'll build a house here and make the tanks our headquarters. Heretofore, I've been as bad as the rest in tryin' to rip a fortune out of this country without doin' anythin' to develop water. I'm goin' to change my tune when I move in here."

They camped at the tanks. In the morning, they separated; Corbett starting off to make a ten-mile circle to the south, and

Laramie swinging around to the north. Whoever returned to the tanks first was to wait there for the other.

The sun swung high as Laramie crossed a series of ridges, each steeper than the last, until he could look back and trace the route he had come. Ahead of him, to the north, the hills continued to swell away into the Salmon River Range. To the west, he caught sight of a deep canyon that cut a mighty slice out of the desert. The rimrocks were black and frowning.

"Ought to be water there," he concluded. "Like as not there's a creek flowing down that canyon. Must be some run-off from these mountains."

He took it for granted that if a flowing stream traversed the canyon he would find the Bar 44 in possession.

"A man layin' out in those rimrocks with a high-powered rifle could pick me off pretty easy," he mused aloud. "Most likely what he'd do too."

He realized there was some virtue to riding up boldly where a man whose movements were suspicious would have no chance at all if the Marrs were posted on the rim.

To his surprise, he went on until he was not more than a hundred yards from the canyon without anyone calling a halt. He pulled up and slid out of his saddle.

Leaving his horse, he walked off to the right for twenty feet so that the animal would be out of any line of fire directed at him. Behind a clump of sage, he dropped to his knees and proceeded to crawl ahead. He covered perhaps fifty yards without anything happening. It convinced him he was not being watched.

He found himself looking down on a garden spot. A tiny creek glistened in the sunlight that filtered through the aspens and willows. He saw now that the great fissure he had seen from the hills was really a series of box canyons. The one spread out below him was not very large.

He studied it intently for minutes. Not a steer was to be seen.

"Can't understand that," he said to himself. "There don't seem to be no way of gettin' from this canyon to the next; but shucks, it's only two or three miles; if the Marrs ain't usin' it they must have a garden of Eden somewhere."

In the end, he decided to go down to the creek and have a look around. The walls fell away sheer to the canyon floor; but he returned to his horse and followed the rimrocks until he found a way down.

"Bein' used, all right, by looks of this trail," he decided. "I may be gettin' myself into one awful jackpot, goin' in here."

Twenty minutes later, he found himself at the creek. The soft ground was badly cut up. A glance gave him the answer.

"Sheep," he muttered. "That's what they're usin' this for. A man must have range to throw away when he can afford to feed bluejoint to sheep."

He got down to slake his thirst. The big black moved up also and dipped his muzzle into the water. Lying prone, his hands spread out in the water to support his shoulders, Laramie heard a piece of brush snap in the willows behind him. He froze to attention. It was impossible for him to spring to his feet or twist or turn so that he could get his guns out hurriedly. For the moment, he was helpless, and he could only listen, hoping he had been mistaken or that it was only a bobcat. He had just about decided that such was the case when someone called out:

"I've got you covered! You can get to your feet now, and don't reach for your guns! I'll shoot if you do!"

Cursing himself for having been caught so flatfooted, he straightened up and turned to find a rifle pointed at him. His surprise was complete as he saw a girl of twenty step out of the willows.

"Stranger—what brings you here?" she demanded bluntly.

"This is pretty good," Laramie thought, "bein' stuck up in this fashion by a girl." He felt worse than foolish.

The grin that wreathed his lips faded as he realized her deadly earnestness. The sunlight awakened golden glints in her hair. Her eyes were as blue and unafraid as his own. The short, homespun dress she wore could not conceal the beauty of her lithe, young body. She wore no stockings, but her feet were encased in heavily beaded buckskin moccasins. Life in the open had tanned her cheeks a rich brown.

"Well, I'm waiting for your answer," she prompted, her tone milder. She found him good to look upon. "If you came in only to water your horse, you're welcome to that."

"Ma'am, you sure surprised me," Laramie got out rather breathlessly. The curve of her throat fascinated him. "I figured I had this canyon to myself."

"You sure are a stranger," she smiled. As her eyes warmed, Laramie was aware of a deep, lustrous quality in their depths.

"Why do you say that?" he asked.

"Sure, everyone hereabouts knows this canyon belongs to Father Marr—"

Laramie's mouth tightened unconsciously. "Oh, I see," he murmured. "You're Isaiah Marr's daughter?"

The girl shook her head. "No," she told him, "I'm Ellen Garth." She said it proudly, as though the name alone should enlighten him. Understanding failed to dawn in Laramie's eyes. "My father was Major Philip Garth, the Indian fighter, who was killed by the Bannocks at Grande Ronde," she continued. "Father Isaiah was my own father's best friend—so I was brought here to live with the Marrs. What is your name?"

"Johnson—Laramie Johnson—"

He felt her surprise at hearing his name.

"Are you the man who shot Snap in Castro?" she demanded excitedly. "The marshal—"

"I—I was the marshal for a few hours," Laramie admitted grudgingly, fully aware of the barrier rising between them. He saw contempt curl her lips, and he believed it was for him. "It wasn't done wantonly, ma'am," he ran on. "I had to stop him—"

"I know—" she murmured, her eyes suddenly hard. "I reckon Snap got what he deserved. He's not like Nephi and the others—"

Her voice trailed off to a whisper, and Laramie could only wonder what lay behind her bitterness toward Snap.

He realized his life had changed in the last few minutes; that something precious had come into it. Ellen still held her rifle carelessly in her hands; but both of them seemed to have forgotten the part it had played in their strange introduction.

"Funny she isn't married—livin' with Mormons," he argued to himself. There leaped into his mind the fear that Snap Marr had found her as desirable as he. "Been crowdin' her," he brooded. "Reckon that explains the situation." He could imagine Snap's way with a girl.

Their eyes met and held for a moment. Laramie was about to speak when an old Indian appeared a few yards up the creek. The Piute's attitude was anything but friendly.

"I see you're well protected here," Laramie smiled.

"Just old Stony and two or three squaws," Ellen answered absent-mindedly. "They look after the sheep—"

"Yeh, I see there's sheep in here. I didn't know Isaiah Marr was a sheepman."

"This flock is all we have—just enough to give us wool for our homespun." She spoke to the Indian, and he disappeared up the creek.

"You aren't afraid of me?" Laramie asked lightly.

"Why should I be? I can handle a gun, and a smoke signal would bring help in a hurry, if I had need of it. Why do you stare at me so?" she asked suddenly.

"Ma'am, I didn't mean to embarrass you," Laramie murmured apologetically. "You're so pretty I can't help lookin' at you—"

"Well, you have the trick of saying nice things, haven't you?" She started to laugh, only to check herself abruptly. She fell back a step, as hostile now as old Stony. "I asked you what business you had here, and you didn't answer, but I remember now what Father Marr said. You're a Frying-pan man, aren't you? You came here to spy on us!"

"Oh, please, don't put it that way," Laramie entreated. "It's true I'm workin' for Bliss Corbett, but as for spyin'—"

"You are looking for grass and water, aren't you? So what is the difference? You know this range belongs to the Bar 44; that you haven't any right here! Get out of here now!" She raised the rifle to her shoulder.

"Ma'am—I can't go like this," Laramie insisted, his voice husky with emotion. "You know I don't mean you any harm. Can't we forget that I'm on one side of this argument and you on the other? Can't we be friends?"

For a second indecision touched her eyes.

"Father Marr's enemies are mine!" she cried. "Get on your horse and ride!"

"All right, I'll go. But you'll sure see me again, sometime, ma'am!"

Without glancing back, he sent the big black up the steep climb to the rim.

Just before he reached the head of the trail leading out of the canyon, Laramie slipped from his saddle and covered the last few yards on foot, moving with extreme caution. Being so near the Bar 44 house, he felt he would be fortunate indeed if he did not encounter some of the Marrs.

It meant that he was reasonably safe, but his face did not lose its tense expression. He was thinking of Ellen Garth, and his train of thought brought him no peace of mind. Meeting her had complicated matters for him.

Laramie took it for granted that Ellen would promptly acquaint old Isaiah with the fact that he had been in the box canyon.

Keeping a safe distance between himself and the rimrocks, he circled south of the box canyon and found the trail the Marrs used in traveling back and forth.

He got some idea of the immensity of the second canyon even before he was able to look down on the Bar 44 stronghold. He could see it stretching away in the distance, narrowing to a portal that evidently led into a third canyon.

In another ten minutes, Zion Canyon—so named by Isaiah Marr—spread its wonders below him. Gazing at it with a cowman's eyes, he could appreciate it for the paradise it was.

"No wonder he doesn't use Limestone Tanks," he exclaimed, awed no little by the sight that met his eyes. "He's got everythin' here that a cattleman ever dreamed of wantin'. If they ain't more than two or three entrances to it, a handful of men could defend it against an army."

The Bar 44 houses were not to be seen, but cattle were everywhere.

As Laramie estimated it, the distance between Zion and the Tanks was not over twelve miles. That the Marrs would ever permit Corbett to establish himself there without putting up a bitter fight was incredible.

When Laramie left the canyon he headed due east, thinking to cut across his own trail and follow it back to Limestone Tanks. He had covered two-thirds of the distance when he found a wide dry-wash before him. He remembered having crossed it that morning, but where he had crossed it was narrower.

"I'm too far south by half to three-quarters of a mile," he told himself, turning north to follow the bank.

A moment or two later, he saw the big black prick up its ears and sniff suspiciously. It got his immediate attention. Moving cautiously up to the bank, he saw three men riding toward him. They rode abreast, a few yards separating them, their eyes on the ground, evidently looking for tracks. They were near enough for him to recognize Snap Marr, Brad Nash and Reb Taney.

Laramie fell back at once, convinced that they had not seen him.

"They've found my trail, sure enough, and they're followin'

the arroyo, hopin' they'll be able to cut me off,'' he decided quickly.

When he had put what he considered a safe distance between himself and the bank, he gave the gelding its head and set a course that would permit him to circle around to the north of the three men.

He drew away rapidly and was just about to congratulate himself on having avoided them so easily, when he heard a horse whinny in the wash. He knew they would investigate it at once. Touching the gelding with the spurs, he raced away, but it was only a moment before Snap Marr dashed up the bank.

Glancing back over his shoulder, Laramie saw him signal to his companions, indicating for them to turn back up the arroyo and head him off. He then took up the chase himself, quirting his horse and raking it with the spurs.

''He's stayin' close to the bank,'' Laramie muttered, glancing back again. ''Knows I've got to cross the arroyo to get east.''

Seconds were precious now, and he endeavored to make the most of them, the gelding responding with a fresh burst of speed. He had no time to glance back. The sharp *zing-g-g* of a bullet whining over his head was the first warning he had that Snap had begun to use his rifle. A second shot kicked up a puff of dust a few yards short of him.

''Gettin' the range,'' Laramie ground out. A third shot was dangerously close. ''I'll have to chance gettin' across now,'' he decided.

The big black went off the bank without losing its footing and was quickly out of the deep sand. Laramie risked a glance down the arroyo. He saw Brad Nash and the other rider fanning their mounts. On catching sight of him, they opened up with their rifles immediately.

''A lot of noise but not much damage in that sort of shootin','' Laramie muttered grimly.

Snap appeared on the bank and joined in the fusillade. In a few moments, however, Laramie was out of range. They fired another volley at him as he climbed the eastern bank, then rode away.

When Laramie reached the tanks he saw at a glance that several horses had used the trail in the hours he had been gone.

''Snap,'' he decided. ''They know we've been in here.''

He studied the tracks for a few minutes and was unable to

find any sign that Bliss had returned. Caution prompted him to wait there, rather than go down to the water and give the Bar 44 men opportunity to ambush him.

An hour passed before he sighted Corbett. There was nothing about the manner in which he rode to suggest that he had encountered difficulty of any sort.

"Gettin' a little worried about you," he said as Bliss drew up beside him. "I've been here quite a spell. Have any trouble?"

"No, didn't see a soul," Bliss answered. "By the looks of the dried sweat on that horse of yours, you've been runnin' him. You find yourself in a jam?"

"I'll say I did," Laramie grinned. "Had plenty lead tossed at me." He gave him a detailed account of what had happened since they parted, save that he said nothing about Ellen Garth.

"Huh," Bliss grunted as he turned the news over in his mind. "Do you suppose they were here?"

"They were. Look at the tracks; you can see for yourself. I reckon we'll find a reception committee waitin' for us when we get back here."

"Maybe," Bliss murmured stonily. "They know that ordinarily it would take me over a week to move in; I'm goin' to shave two or three days off that; so we may surprise 'em at that, Johnson."

An hour later they were riding east. Bliss began to unfold his plans.

"I'll be headin' north for Antelope," he declared. "I'm goin' to move everythin' I've got there down here, and drive the Squaw Creek stuff to Antelope. That'll save some time. I want you to go to Grande Ronde and find Santa Fé. Explain to him what I'm doin' and tell him he's to take his boys to Squaw Creek and help Trace and Frenchy to get the stuff movin' toward the springs. You can all lend a hand. It shouldn't take you long."

"Who'll be givin' the orders?" Laramie asked.

"Maybe you better take charge; I'll have a chance to talk this over thoroughly before we separate. When you get the stuff movin' through open country, I want you, Santa Fé, Trace, and Frenchy to come ahead to the springs. Shorty, Steve and Little Billy will finish the drive. They'll be short-handed, but they can do it. By the time you reach Antelope, we'll be on our way; you'll overtake us easy enough. That will bring me into the tanks with men enough to put up an argument."

Laramie asked about the wagon.

"Oddie better head for the springs as soon as you reach camp," Bliss answered. "Have him leave enough grub behind to last a man for a couple of weeks. For a day or two there won't be a soul at Grande Ronde; it's a chance I've got to take. As soon as you get in touch with us I'll send Uncle Elmer back to the coulée."

It was an ambitious undertaking. Counting Oddie Dill, who was a warrior of no mean ability, Corbett had less than a dozen men to carry it through.

In scouting the tanks they had traveled many miles, drifting in and out of the hills to the north. Late in the afternoon they found themselves back in country that Corbett knew. They were continuing on, with little to say, when Laramie reined in the gelding sharply.

"What is it?" Corbett asked.

"A cow trail," Laramie answered. "Cattle been across here—and recently too!"

A hasty examination proved him correct.

"What do you make of that?" Bliss queried. "Must have been quite a little bunch—twenty to thirty head. They were movin' north."

"Could it have been any of your stuff?"

"No, not so far west."

"Reckon that leaves only one answer," Laramie declared. "You heard old Isaiah say he was losin' stock. It's my guess it was his steers that made this trail. Seein' they were bein' driven north makes it look like the same bunch that's gettin' your stuff is helpin' itself to the Bar 44 yearlin's."

"It does for a fact," Bliss had to admit. "Only in my case they ain't drivin' the stuff across open country. If they try anythin' as raw as that on me I'll tie a knot in their tails in a hurry."

They went on for another hour.

"I'll be leavin' you here," Corbett said. "We're about due south of Antelope."

In the early evening Laramie rode into the coulée. The wagon was there. From Oddie he learned that Santa Fé and the others were expected in that night. It was well along toward midnight when they arrived. They did not pretend to hide the excitement his news evoked. He had to give them a detailed account of his brush with the Marrs.

Laramie told them what Corbett wanted done.

"What's the program now?" Santa Fé asked. It made no difference to him that Laramie had superceded him as straw-boss.

"You need some sleep," Laramie stated. "At four o'clock we'll roll out of our blankets and head for Squaw Creek."

Santa Fé led the way to the creek. It was a long, hard ride. By pushing their horses they made it in ten hours. It was evening, however, before they located Morrell and Le Brun.

The two men were surprised to see Laramie. When they learned what was afoot, and that he was in charge, their eyes narrowed apprehensively.

"Well, you're comin' along pretty fast, ain't you?" Trace queried sarcastically. "At this rate, you'll own the brand in a couple of weeks."

"You know—the old story of the new broom," Laramie grinned. "How did you find things here? As bad as Uncle Elmer reported 'em?"

"A damn sight worse," Morrell declared sullenly. "Countin' everythin' there ain't over eight hundred head of stock on the creek wearin' our brand."

"What?" Santa Fé bellowed. "Why, that means there ain't nothin' but cows, bulls and some two-year-olds left!"

"That's what it means," Morrell reiterated. "You won't find a dozen yearlin's. They've all been cut out and run off."

He proceeded to curse the rustlers. Laramie said nothing and contented himself with watching him and Frenchy. On the way to the creek he had asked Santa Fé if Trace and Le Brun usually rode together. The answer was yes: that they seemed to hit it off better with each other than with anyone else. Laramie felt he understood why that was so.

"You talk to this new outfit?" Santa Fé asked Morrell.

"Yeh, plenty!" Trace averred. "They claim they drifted down into this country through the Bitter Roots. They ain't got much stuff—all pretty runty."

"As I remember it," Laramie put in, "you were convinced that this Box Z outfit got our calves. Are you still of the same opinion?"

"I just been sayin' different, ain't I?" Morrell demanded sullenly. "We watched 'em for hours the other day; didn't see a thing that looked queer—did we, Frenchy?"

"No," Le Brun agreed. "I don't think it was them fellars. Maybe wolves—"

"Must be an army of them to pull down two hundred head in a week," Laramie remarked without interest.

"I'll say!" Santa Fé grumbled. "They might have got a dozen or so—"

"More than that," Frenchy got out sulkily. "One of those big buffalo grays can pull down a lot of stock." He turned to Morrell for verification. "You know that's so, Trace. You remember what they did to us one winter in Wyoming—"

Morrell started to nod agreement, but he caught Laramie's eyes on him and stopped abruptly, as though loath to commit himself. "That was years ago," he whipped out scoffingly. The glance he gave Le Brun was murderous. "Ain't so many wolves no more. This was rustlers, all right; no question about it."

They made camp, but Morrell had no more to say. A dozen times Laramie caught him watching him covertly.

"He's afraid he tipped his hand," he told himself, "and I reckon he did."

CHAPTER 8
Two-Legged Polecats

A DEEPLY RELIGIOUS MAN, ISAIAH MARR PROFESSED TO SEE God's hand in everything he accomplished. So it was with pride touched with humility that he often sat on the porch of his own house and gazed about him on the fruits of their mutual labors. He sat there this evening as the vermilion that splashed the rimrocks slowly faded to purple.

Smoke rose lazily from a dozen chimneys; the homes of his sons and daughters and grandchildren. A tinkling bell heralded the approach of the milch cows. A bare-footed boy drove them into the milking corral across the way. At the open smithy, just beyond the corral, his son Heber, next to Snap in years, banked his fire for the day.

It was a scene of utter peace. Always it was Isaiah's favorite moment of the day. This evening, however, a frown furrowed his broad forehead and his face was grave as he thoughtfully stroked his long white beard. On the steps at his feet sat Snap, Brad Nash and Reb Taney. They had ridden in an hour back with the story of their encounter with Laramie.

Father Marr had listened calmly, refusing to be stampeded by their excitement and alarm. His rights were about to be invaded, but he had yet to say what he proposed to do about it.

"I can't see what there is about this that needs thinkin' over," Snap grumbled impatiently. His right hand was still bandaged. "This thing is just as plain as the nose on your face. The Fryin'-pan's headed for Limestone Tanks. There ain't no doubt of that in your mind, is there?"

"No," Isaiah answered with great deliberation. "When Corbett warned me he was moving west, I foresaw that the tanks would figure in his plans."

"Twelve miles away!" Brad muttered fiercely. "Let 'em get in there and it won't be long before they'll be here for the real showdown!"

"You said it!" Snap agreed vehemently. "If we're goin' to stop 'em, let's stop 'em before they get started!"

"I'll have something to say as soon as the boys come in," Isaiah informed him. "No need of saying it twice; I want them all to hear it. And don't forget, Reb, it's a wise man who keeps his head."

"Here comes Zack and Brig now," Snap announced. "We can call Heber over and you speak out."

"No, I'll wait until Nephi and Moroni ride in," his father insisted. "Someone fording the creek. It'll likely be them."

His surmise proved correct, and a few minutes later, Nephi and his brother rode into the yard. Snap called to them. Heber was already on the porch.

Isaiah looked them over. It was seldom he found his sons gathered together like this. He felt that any father might have been proud of them. To all, except for Snap, his word had been always been law, and it was Snap alone, with his drinking and gambling, who had given him great concern.

"Why have you called us together, father?" Nephi asked. "Has it something to do with Corbett's threat?"

"It sure has!" Snap answered for his father. "We ran into Johnson today; he's spyin' on us. We picked up his trail this side of the tanks and tried to cut him off in the long arroyo."

"What happened? Didn't you sight him at all?" Moroni asked.

"Ran right into him!" Reb informed him. "He got away; but we sure was shootin' at him."

"Was Johnson alone?" Zack asked.

"No, he had somebody with him—Corbett no doubt. We saw

where they had been into the tanks. Now you all know what that means. But instead of doin' somethin' we sit here talkin'.'' He faced his father. "I'd sure admire to hear what you've got to say about it.''

"I shall speak at length,'' Isaiah announced, his face stern. He knew Snap's incendiary appeal to his brothers had prejudiced them against any course but violence. "I can see that what I am about to say will not be to your liking. However, it is my decision, and I have reached it after thinking this matter over for days, for I foresaw that it must come. What I have to say is this: if Corbett tries to move into the tanks, I will not oppose him.''

"What?'' Brad and Reb chorused. Young Zack and Brig were equally amazed. Snap was so beside himself he could not find his tongue for a moment.

"I knew it!'' he roared when he could speak. "I knew that was why you wouldn't give me an answer! You can't ask us to lay down like that! I don't know how the others feel, but Corbett ain't walkin' over me!''

"Hear me out!'' Isaiah commanded, his flashing eyes cowing Snap to silence. "Water and grass have always been precious to me. For years I rode myself to the bone looking for it and it is not in me to speak lightly of giving up a foot of good range. For years after I came here there was so little water in these canyons that we didn't dare to put the cattle on the grass until late summer.

"We used to range the desert in the spring until the snow water was gone. Then we moved into the foothills. By July, the only water left was here and at the tanks. It was precious. We had to sleep on our rifles to keep it. Some of you—you especially, Snap—are old enough to remember the last fight we had. You were only a half-grown boy, but you could work a gun even then.''

"Yeh, and I ain't forgot the trick of it,'' Snap rasped surlily. "We had to fight, and fight hard, or get pushed out. That's what we got to do now. A man won't fight for his rights won't have 'em long.''

"Oh, I'll fight for my rights, never fear for that,'' his father assured him. His tone was mild, but it was vibrant with confidence in his ability to protect his own. "I have often been called a range hog.'' He nodded to himself over the memories the words awakened. "It was undoubtedly true in the beginning. A man had to have range to spare, it was all so poor.

"But that belongs in the past—times have changed. We have developed water beyond our needs here in Zion and the south canyon. The tanks no longer mean anything to us. We have not ranged cattle there in two years, and it is unlikely we ever will again."

The words fell upon his sons' ears as the rankest heresy. Brad and Reb were no less aghast. From childhood they had been schooled to regard Limestone Tanks as one of the Bar 44's richest possessions. To be told that they were about to relinquish it without lifting a hand in its defense passed belief. Even Nephi lent his voice to the chorused protests. Snap's face was bloodless. He stopped his cursing to glare at his father.

"I'll say we'll never run stuff there again—not if we give Bliss Corbett a toehold! The tanks may come in mighty handy for us some day!"

"Leastwise grass an' water are worth money!" Zack got out belligerently. "They ain't somethin' you give away or let a man steal right under your eyes!"

"You are right, Zack," the old Mormon agreed; "the tanks are valuable. We have claimed them for years, but we can't prove title to them."

"Possession is title enough," Heber declared. "By what other right do we hold Zion and north and south canyons? We have been in possession of the tanks in the past. Before daylight we can be in there again. We can even build a shack so some of us can live there the year around."

"No doubt but what it can be done," said Isaiah. "But it will mean bloodshed—lives wiped out—and I will avoid that if I can. Remembering the blessings with which the Lord has showered me and mine it would ill behoove me to offer my sons and blood kin as a sacrifice to my greed. I know how you feel. At first I shared that feeling. But I overcame it. I was permitted to see my duty to you and the Almighty. Amen!"

"But father, there's no promise of peace in such a course." It was Nephi who spoke. "You know Bliss Corbett. He's a fighter, and he's ambitious. Do you think he will be content with the tanks? Not for long! Some day you will find him here, and the blood you would not see shed at the tanks will be spilled in Zion Canyon!"

"There's the truth, and no walkin' away from it!" Snap cried. "Nephi and I don't agree very often, but he's right for once! With the Fryin'-pan in the Grande Ronde they can't make us any trouble, but you're proposin' to give 'em a steppin'-stone that'll land 'em on our doorstep!

"Damn it! We'll plug those springs so they'll never flow again! In a year there won't be a blade of grass in that basin to tempt Corbett or any man."

"No, that I will not do!" Father Marr cried, aghast. "I am a desert man! The Almighty, in the goodness of His heart, has put water in these sandy wastes for man and beast, and he who destroys it is beyond the mercy of heaven. Come what will, I'll not have that on my conscience!"

The supper-bell rang as he finished. He waited until the echo died away before he got to his feet, indicating that the meeting had come to an end.

"Our destiny is here, in these canyons," he told them, "and we will defend them, with our lives if need be. In the meantime, we'll keep ourselves informed about what takes place at the tanks."

"There's just one thing will happen," Snap muttered: "The Fryin'-pan will move in—"

"When that happens the long arroyo will become the deadline between us," Isaiah announced. "Any of their men caught west of it will be trespassing." He was about to step into the house when he paused for a question. "Did any word come in from the south canyon this afternoon, Nephi?"

"Yes, I met Dan at the pass. Martin and he are still camped under the east rim where Snap left them two days ago. He said they'd been in the saddle most of the time."

"Well, what did they find?" Isaiah prompted. "Have rustlers been in the canyon again?"

"Dan wasn't sure, father, but he thinks another small bunch has been cut out—maybe twenty-five head."

"Well, that's not very pleasant news," Isaiah said worriedly. "Dan must have good reason for thinking another bunch is gone. This is something real to worry about, and I propose to put an end to it if we have to ride day and night. It's the first trouble of the sort we've ever had. In the past, rustlers found it too hard to run stuff out of the canyons to make it interesting for them."

"Somebody is sure doing it now," Nephi reminded him, "and we haven't been able to catch even a glimpse of them."

"I can't understand it," his father murmured gravely.

"Maybe you will after Corbett moves into the tanks," Snap remarked pointedly. It drew fire from Isaiah.

"Do you call that using your head?" he demanded angrily. "If Corbett is rustling our stuff then he's known for months that we have not been using the tanks. Why would he have waited until now to move up? Believe me, we'll have to look nearer home for our calves. They have not been going to the Grande Ronde. I want you to step in tonight. We'll discuss this business further."

Snap and Brad walked off together.

"What do you think he meant by sayin' he'd have to look nearer home for the rustlers?" Brad asked when they found themselves alone.

Snap shrugged his shoulders and said nothing.

"It don't set so well with me," Brad pursued nervously. "Sounds suspicious—like he had somethin' on his mind."

Snap's eyes flashed reprovingly. "You better keep your hat on," he growled. "It's only talk; it don't mean a thing."

"I hope you're right," Brad mumbled as they walked on. "What are you goin' to do about the tanks?"

Snap laughed grimly. "You know what I'm goin' to do about it! I may be one hell of a Mormon, but I ain't no fool!"

"Your father will know, Snap," Brad got out uneasily. "Won't be no way of coverin' that up."

"I ain't even goin' to try to cover it up! Won't be nothin' he can do about it after it's done. You set out a couple shovels where we can pick 'em up in the mornin'. I'll attend to the rest."

That evening, however, Father Marr ordered them to the south canyon with half a dozen others, and three days passed before they left the house to scout the country to the east. Once away from the ranch, they went directly to the tanks. They found they had the place to themselves.

"How long will it take us?" Brad asked, his eyes restless.

"Why do you ask?" Snap demanded.

"Why?" Brad whipped out. "You know damn well why! It would be just too bad if they trapped us in here."

"Well, they won't," Snap assured him. "They can't get here for days. Get the shovels and we'll drain this pool."

It did not take them long to destroy the basin that held the run-off from the springs. The released water spread out over the ground and disappeared quickly.

"We better drop a little dynamite in the tanks and get out of here," Brad suggested.

"No we won't!" Snap came back at him. "We're goin' to put

it deep enough so it will do the work. You start luggin' rock, so we can put weight enough above the charge to send the force of it down instead of up in the air.''

An hour passed before Snap was ready to light the fuse. The wanton vandalism of what he was about to do was lost on him. Even the excuse that the safety of the Bar 44 demanded it was a subterfuge. He knew he was doing something that would, in a measure, square his account against Corbett and Laramie, and he was filled with a fiendish pleasure.

"You better get back," he advised Brad; "I'm goin' to touch her off. I'll close this account for keeps. I'm only sorry I'm not blowin' Johnson and Corbett to hell along with it!''

He scurried to safety as the fuse sputtered. With a blast that shook the ground, the dynamite did its work. A ghoulish grin contorting his face, Snap peered at what was left of the tanks.

"Well, there you are!" he ground out. "Let 'em laugh that off! They made a dog of me in Castro, but I'm gettin' even with 'em, and I ain't through yet!''

"Come on, let's get out of here," Brad pleaded. "Nothin' more to do.''

Snap swaggered over to his horse, but he was secretly anxious to be off. In a few minutes they climbed to the desert. Brad stood up in his stirrups and shielded his eyes with the palm of his hand as he stared off to the east.

"What is it?" Snap demanded irritably.

"Take a look!" Brad commanded. "We didn't get out none too soon! It can't be nothin' but cattle kickin' up that much dust!''

"You're right," Snap muttered, "it's the Fryin'-pan! . . . I'd sure like to see their faces when they get their first good look at the tanks!''

Corbett rode out of the dust-cloud that enveloped the moving herd. His eyes were red rimmed. He and his men were saddle weary, but his plans had been carried out to the letter.

"All right, Johnson," he called to Laramie, "we'll ride ahead. Trace and Frenchy are movin' up too. We ain't over two miles from the tanks now. Time we knew what's waitin' for us.''

Laramie nodded. They were about to pull away when Santa Fé spurred up.

"Will you get word back to me or will I send the stuff right along?" he asked.

"Just keep 'em movin'," Bliss told him. "We're goin' into the tanks if we have to shoot our way in. What else can we do? No chance of holdin' these steers back after they get a sniff of water."

"All right! I'll throw 'em at you!" Sante Fé shouted. "Be ready for 'em!"

Corbett and Laramie were soon ahead of the herd. They saw Morrell and Frenchy waiting for them. Since leaving Squaw Creek, relations between Trace and Laramie had become so bitter that every man in the outfit was secretly wondering how long it would be before their quarrel moved out into the open.

"I don't know what put Trace on the prod," Corbett volunteered, "but I can't afford a fight between you now. He ought to have sense enough to know by this time that he's got no business crossin' swords with you. But he's a hot-head. It'll be a favor to me, Johnson, if you back away from him for a day or two until we know where we stand."

"That's all right with me," Laramie smiled. "I've backed down so often in the last two or three days that the boys all figure he's got the crawl on me. I guess once more won't make any difference."

They picked up Frenchy and Morrell and rode on until they were within several hundred yards of the tanks.

"The trail that leads in is off there to the left," Bliss said. "We'll go straight ahead until we reach the rimrocks. We'll be able to see then if there's anyone waitin' for us below. If there ain't no one in sight, we'll follow the rim over to the entrance."

"It's takin' a chance, ridin' up," Morrell argued.

"We'll be takin' nothin' but chances from now on," Corbett answered. "If there's anyone hiding out on the rim, they see us. Nothin' to be gained by tryin' to crawl up."

He led the way. Frenchy brought up the rear. The caution with which they approached the tanks was wasted.

"That was easy," Bliss grinned as he looked down on the basin.

Laramie was watching Frenchy and Trace, wondering if they had even seen the place before. The gasp of surprise it wrung from them convinced him they were gazing at it for the first time.

"Look at that grass!" Trace exclaimed. "I ain't seen nothin' so green in years!"

"I thought we'd be able to see the pool from here," Laramie remarked. "I'm sure we did the other day."

"We'll see it when we get down," Corbett said, studying the trail that led to the bottom. "See anythin' suspicious down there?"

"Not a thing," Morrell declared. Frenchy agreed with him. Corbett glanced at Laramie.

"How does it strike you, Johnson?"

"Looks all right."

In three or four minutes they were at the entrance. Laramie got down to study the dusty trail.

"Fresh tracks," he announced. "Mighty fresh; ain't a bit of dust sifted into 'em. I'd say two horses came up this trail less than an hour ago."

Corbett got down and examined the tracks carefully. "Tracks goin' in and out," he said.

"Yeh, same horses made 'em. They're all fresh."

"Well," Corbett muttered thoughtfully. "I don't know what to make of it right off. A man leavin' here an hour back sure must have seen our dust."

"Reckon that's true," Laramie agreed. "They pulled up here. You can see that." He followed the sign out into the desert for a few yards. "They didn't lose any time pullin' away, once they got started," he announced. "If it was the Marrs, and they're down there in force, they'd hardly be high-tailin' it away like that."

"That sounds reasonable," Bliss declared approvingly. "We'll take a chance. We'll string out goin' down. If a gun barks, slide out of your saddles in a hurry. If we reach the bottom without drawin' fire, we can take it for granted we got the jump on 'em. Ain't no other place they could stop us so easy as here."

Not even a jackrabbit contested the right of way with them.

"All that for nothin'," Bliss grinned, "but it's always better to be safe than sorry." He was jubilant. "Old Lady Luck is sure smilin' at us now. I never expected to—"

"Wait a minute!" Laramie interrupted, "There's somethin' wrong here."

"What do you mean?"

"Look at the pool—it's dry. That's why we couldn't see it from up above!"

"Good Lord!" Corbett groaned. "There ain't a drop of water in it!"

Without another word he spurred his horse across the basin. The others followed him. They came up with him as he rode in among the aspens. A glance was all it needed to tell them what had been done.

Corbett was speechless with horror.

"A garden spot turned back to desert—that's what this means," Laramie got out. "No flow at all left; not even a trickle."

"The rats!" Bliss groaned. His cup of milk and honey had turned to gall. "They wouldn't fight for it, so they destroy it! What sort of human skunks are these Marrs? I hope their tongues hang out and rot for doin' this! I've helped to string up rustlers, and felt sorry for 'em; I've even had a sneakin' sympathy for a murderin' coward; but the man who did this is lower than any thief or murderer who ever drew breath!"

"How do you know it can't be cleaned out?" Morrell asked.

"A chance in a hundred," Laramie declared.

"Or less!" Corbett raged. "We've got a herd of thirsty cattle comin' in here, bawlin' for water. They'll die of thirst before they get a drink out of these tanks. But I ain't through; this don't stop me! Isaiah Marr dodged a fight here, but I'll take one to him now that he won't run away from! We're goin' right on west!"

"You won't bring the herd in at all then?" Laramie asked.

"I'll hold 'em here tonight," Corbett answered. "At least there's grass here. But we'll go on! I haven't any choice about it; I've got to go on! I want you to pull out of here now, Johnson. Scout the sheep canyon you found. The Marrs will be layin' for us; most likely along that wash where Snap tried to bring you down. Find out where they're holed up. We've got to give 'em the slip and grab that canyon!"

Laramie stared at him incredulously. The audacity of the move was all he could find to recommend it. Suddenly thought of Ellen Garth flashed in his mind, and he was filled with fear for her. Even though she were there alone, with only old Stony and the squaws, he knew she would stand her ground and fight. She wouldn't have a chance. Corbett was desperate now, and once he got that far, he would not be balked, even though he had to do battle with a girl.

In the days that had passed since she ordered him out of the canyon, Laramie had never given over his intention to meet her again. In his vague plans he had not foreseen himself arriving with a band of armed men, come to run her out and do her bodily injury if she resisted them.

"Why the long face?" Corbett asked him. "You don't seem to like the idea at all."

"You're bitin' off a big mouthful," Laramie answered skeptically. "We thought we could surprise the Marrs. Fact is, we haven't taken a trick so far."

"All the more reason why we should take this one," Bliss snapped. "You told me there was only a few Indians in that canyon—"

"That was three or four days ago. I also told you they use smoke signals back and forth between the sheep canyon and Zion."

"We'll do our signalin' with gunpowder," Corbett blazed.

"Reckon we'll have to," Laramie murmured gloomily. "After what we found here it ain't in the cards to suppose the Marrs ain't ready for us."

"Say, what's the matter with you, Johnson?" Morrell sneered. "You don't seem to like that at all, as Bliss says. You losin' your nerve?"

"Lay off of that, Trace!" Corbett jerked out as he heard Laramie's jaws click together ominously. "We got fightin' enough to do without havin' any of it here!" He turned to Laramie. "Of course I know the Marrs are waitin' for us, but it's mighty likely they're a lot nearer to us than the canyon. If that's the case, you ought to be able to circle around 'em, if you swing far enough north.

"All I want you to find out is whether the canyon is under guard or not. I've got to have that information before I can go ahead. I respect your judgment, Johnson, but if there's any reason why you don't want to go, say so and I'll send Trace."

It forced a decision on Laramie. He had to go now, and not only because of the treatment he feared Ellen would receive at Morrell's hands. The secret understanding that existed between the big fellow and Snap Marr would, in itself, have been enough to sway him.

"I'm dead willin' to go," he drawled. "If I seemed to hang back, it was only because I know we can't take anythin' for granted from now on; we've reached the point where the trouble begins."

"No doubt of that," Bliss agreed. "The lid's apt to fly off

any moment now. I tell you what you do, Johnson; take Trace with you. The both of you go—''

"I'll make it alone all right," Laramie declared. "I can move faster—''

"The two of you go," Corbett insisted. "I want to be mighty sure one of you gets back. Better get movin' right away. And don't waste any time talkin' to Sante Fé if he hails you. I'll be along to tell him what's what."

Again Laramie felt his hand was being forced, for he could not demur without offering a reason. He gathered from the look on Morrell's face that he was none too happy over this turn of affairs. "Come on," he said to him, "let's ride."

The herd was within half a mile of the tanks by the time they reached the desert. Sante Fé shouted at them, but they hurried away without stopping.

"You know the country," Trace grumbled. "Suppose you lead the way."

Laramie nodded. "I'll keep an eye on you," he told himself. "It might be awful convenient to knock me off and blame it on the Marrs."

CHAPTER 9
A Gunman's Threat

AFTER LEAVING THE TANKS, LARAMIE AND MORRELL HEADED north for at least five miles before finally turning west in the general direction of the hidden canyon.

"Where's the arroyo Bliss spoke of?" Trace asked. It was the first time he had spoken in miles.

"Reckon we're well to the north of it," Laramie replied. "Nothin' but open country between us and the canyon now, except for a low ridge of sand hills. We'll cut through 'em and follow 'em almost to the rim."

They saved their horses as much as they could, not knowing when they might have to call on them for speed. Eventually they crossed the sand hills and followed them as Laramie had suggested. They had seen nothing to give them reason to believe their presence had been discovered.

Just before they reached the end of the ridge they pulled up.

On foot they climbed to the crest. They had a good view of the rimrocks. Minutes passed as they studied them.

"Don't seem to be anyone there," Morrell volunteered. "Do you go in on this side?"

"Yeh, off there to the left. We won't know whether it's safe to ride in until we try it. Suppose I go in alone."

There was nothing in his tone to hint that the suggestion had not been born on the spur of the moment, and yet, he felt Morrell's eyes suddenly had a knowing look.

"No need of your doin' that," the big fellow muttered. "We'll go in together."

"Fair enough," Laramie agreed, his voice cold and toneless.

They moved up to the rim with great stealth. They had advanced to within fifty yards of the entrance when Morrell stiffened abruptly.

"Somebody over there on rocks," he warned under his breath. "Right where we go down."

Laramie looked and saw old Stony, the Piute, stretched out, apparently asleep in the sun. He had built up a pile of green sage a few feet from where he lay. Its purpose was plain.

"Already to signal for help," Morrell whispered. He slid out of his saddle. "You cover me, Johnson; he may have a gun."

Morrell's advance was noiseless, but just before he reached the Indian, the Piute sat up, blinking his eyes owlishly. Before he could get to his feet, Trace pounced on him. Stony was too old to put up much resistance.

"Come on, get up!" Morrell growled at him, and when the Indian did not move fast enough, he used his boot on him.

"No need of that," Laramie said. "Let me talk to him." He walked up to the old Indian. "Chief—you here alone, eh? No men in the canyon?"

The Piute's face remained a wooden, copper-colored mask. Laramie repeated the questions and got no answer.

"I'll make him talk!" Morrell promised, raising his quirt.

"Wait!" Laramie exclaimed. "I've got a better idea. We'll herd him down the trail ahead of us. If there's only Indians in here it'll stop 'em from takin' a potshot at us."

The wisdom of it was apparent to Morrell. They encountered no one on the way down, and when they reached the bottom Laramie suggested they tie up the prisoner and reconnoiter the canyon. He was to take the east wall and Morrell the west.

"All right," Trace agreed readily. Again his eyes wore a knowing look. "I'll meet you right here."

The Piute was quickly trussed up and they separated.

"He's suspicious," Laramie muttered to himself as they drew apart. "I'll be lucky to miss havin' my hand called."

It was his thought to find Ellen as quickly as possible and warn her to get out at once. The tiny stream hugged the east wall, and he hoped to find her along it. That accomplished, he would cut across the canyon and overtake Morrell. In some way he hoped to maneuver their return so that Trace would see nothing of her.

He soon lost sight of the big fellow and he went on, not knowing that Morrell had turned back and was following him. Laramie's reluctance to undertake the trip at first, and then his offer to enter the canyon alone, had convinced Trace that something was wrong.

Laramie had covered less than half a mile when he saw the sheep grazing beside the water. As he approached the flock he found Ellen confronting him, her rifle cradled in her arms. Sight of her set his blood to pounding and for the moment he forgot his mission there.

"Reckon I didn't make myself plain," she greeted him coldly. "I warned you to keep out of this canyon. I don't know how you come to be here; Stony is on the rim with orders to let no one in. How does it come he didn't stop you?"

"He—he tried, ma'am." Laramie saw her face pale. "You needn't be alarmed," he went on hurriedly; "he ain't been harmed."

His concern was all for her and it was reflected in his face. It did not escape her, but her eyes hardened with suspicion. "I ran you out of here before," she said. "This time I'll run you out and you'll stay out. You turn your horse around."

"Ma'am, I'll go willin' enough, but there's somethin' I got to say to you first. It'll make you think less of me than you do now, but it's got to be said, and there ain't nothin' to be gained by tryin' to find an easy way of sayin' it. It's just this: we're takin' over this canyon.

"You won't be safe here but a few hours longer. You've got to take your sheep and get out as quickly as you can. There's goin' to be fightin' here—plenty of it—and I don't want to see you get mixed up in it."

Ellen's pallor deepened, but it was indignation rather than fear that left her cheeks bloodless. "So you *were* spying on us the other day," she charged. "Now you come to warn me, eh?" Her tone was mocking.

"Your time evidently means very little to you, but I daresay you'll be careful not to warn Father Isaiah." Her look was one of utter contempt. "Do you think we Marrs are afraid of Bliss Corbett and his tramp outfit? I say to you, we know how to treat thieves! Move in here if you dare! It will be your tomb!"

She was unconsciously magnificent in her wrath.

"Ma'am, you don't understand," Laramie pleaded. "We drove into Limestone Tanks this mornin' only to find the Marrs had plugged the springs. We've got to find water somewhere else in a hurry, and it's goin' to be here."

And now Ellen could not believe him at all. She had heard Father Marr's decision to waive his rights to the tanks. She knew he was too righteous a man to destroy the springs before giving them up. Her voice was so charged with emotion as she accused Laramie that it broke.

"I said only the truth," he insisted. "Think what you will, ma'am, but please go while there's time. If you find I lied to you, you can always come back."

His earnestness stilled the biting retort that trembled on her lips. He never would have guessed it, but he had seldom been out of her thoughts in the days just past. If the deep, searching glance she gave him now told her anything it was that he meant her well. And yet, perversely enough, it only emboldened her to taunt him further.

"I could understand you better if you tried to tie me up, as you no doubt have done with Stony," she murmured scornfully. "You must feel awfully sure of yourself, offering to let me go, knowing the first thing I would do would be to warn Father Marr. Or maybe you had not thought of that—"

Laramie's mouth tightened. "I'm thinkin' of it now," he said, "and I'm still askin' you to go. What you do after you leave here will be up to you. Another man rode into the canyon with me today. It'll be better if he doesn't know you're here. I'll get along now and pick him up. You keep back in the brush. In half an hour it'll be safe for you to get the sheep on their way."

Ellen was silent as distrust gave way to conviction that he was risking a great deal in her behalf.

"Promise me you'll go," he urged.

"All right," she murmured slowly, "I'll go—"

"No, you won't!" Morrell's voice broke in on them. "Just drop that rifle, sister. I'm goin' to have somethin' to say about this."

Laramie's hands flashed to his guns, ready to draw, as Trace stepped out from a clump of mahogany bush. Morrell had been there for minutes, overhearing every word that passed between them. He found it a tasty morsel, for he believed he had Laramie exactly where he wanted him now. Thumbs tucked carelessly under his gunbelt so that the slightest movement would enable him to fill his hand in a hurry, he swaggered up to the bank where they stood.

Ellen felt her throat tighten as the two men faced each other. Morrell's eyes were murderous; Laramie's held an icy glitter. She knew it needed only a word to provoke a tragedy. Any doubt that Laramie had sought to befriend her was gone from her mind.

"So you followed me, eh?" Laramie's tone cut like a knife. "I should have known you would; you've got sneak written all over you."

Morrell laughed harshly. "That comes well from you, don't it? I'll say I followed you, and I heard plenty! Did you think you were foolin' me, Johnson? Not for a minute! I knew there was somethin' here you didn't want me to see!" He paused to run his eyes over Ellen. "I hardly figured it would be anythin' as interestin' as this. I didn't know you was so romantically inclined—"

"Better be careful of your words, Morrell," Laramie warned. "If you want any satisfaction from me you sure can get it; but any difference of opinion between us concerns only us." Without shifting his gaze, he addressed himself to Ellen. "Ma'am, you round up your squaws and start movin' out of here."

"No, she won't!" Trace roared. "You cheap double-crosser, do you think I'm goin' to let her go so she can bring her whole damned Mormon outfit down on us? If you do, you got another guess comin', Johnson!"

"Don't pay any attention to him, ma'am," Laramie flung back. "Just go."

Before Ellen could take a step Morrell pounced on her, knocking the rifle out of her hands. Laramie leaped in between them and drove Morrell back, bringing his knee up into the big fellow's stomach with such force that it knocked the wind out of Trace. As he fumbled for his guns, Laramie's fist crashed into his jaw and he went over backwards to stretch his length on the ground.

"I warned you to go slow," Laramie panted as he stood over him.

There was no answer from Morrell; he was out cold. Laramie took his guns. He glanced at Ellen. Her lips were tremulous and her face pale.

"I should have taken your warning," she murmured contritely. "He'll make trouble for you. It will cost you your job—maybe a great deal more—"

"Don't worry about me, ma'am; I'll manage to take care of myself. You go now—as quickly as you can."

"Not before I thank you," she whispered. "I won't forget—"

Laramie stared after her as she hurried away.

"I seem to have cut myself off all the way around," he thought. "If I'm forced out of this fight now I'll lose everythin' that means anythin' to me."

Trace sat up, blinking his eyes. He felt for his guns and found them gone. "I'll get you for this, Johnson!" he threatened viciously. "I'll put a bug in Corbett's ear! Thanks to you, the Fryin'-pan's got a fight on its hands before it gets in here. I didn't think you'd be damn fool enough to try to get away with a double-cross like this!"

"If Bliss feels I double-crossed him in gettin' that girl out of here, he'll have to think so," Laramie told him. "I draw the line at fightin' women."

"It won't get you nothin' standin' up for this one," Morrell blurted out in his rage. "You ain't got a chance with her, Johnson. She belongs to—" He checked himself on the very brink of the abyss into which his hot words were about to plunge him. ". . . to some of them Marrs," he finished lamely.

"Why not say what you started to say?" Laramie whipped out.

"Meanin' what?"

"That Ellen Garth is Snap Marr's girl—"

"Well, maybe that is the case," Morrell growled.

"You would know, of course," Laramie drove on. "Snap must have told you when he met you in back of the hotel in Castro."

Trace could not dissemble his surprise and confusion. He sucked in his breath noisily and his hawklike face twisted into a snarl. "So, that's your game, eh?" He spat the words out. "You find yourself in a jam, so you're goin' to try to turn the tables on me. Well, you can't get away with it! I never met Snap Marr anywhere!"

"Is that so?" Laramie jeered. "Maybe I can refresh your memory. I may even be able to produce a witness or two."

It was a bluff, but a superb one. Morrell's eyes shifted uneasily.

"I tell you, you're mistaken!" he cried.

"Yeh?" Laramie made him meet him eye to eye. "Maybe I am at that—the same way you're going to be mistaken about what you overheard here this mornin'."

Morrell's look said that he understood him.

"I ain't askin' you to keep your mouth shut," Laramie went on. "You can talk if you want to; but keep a straight tongue in your mouth, Morrell, and keep Ellen Garth's name out of your conversation!"

Before leaving the canyon, Laramie looked for Stony. He was not to be found.

"Of course he ain't here," Morrell grumbled. "Use your head, Johnson. The first thing that girl did was to find him. That Injun may be old, but I'll bet he's dog-trottin' to Zion this minute, and he won't stop till he gets there. In three hours—four at the outside—the Marrs will be perched up there on the rimrocks. We won't drive any Fryin'-pan steers into this canyon today."

"Maybe we will," Laramie answered laconically.

"Yeh? You ain't got no idea we can show up here before evenin', have you?"

"We'll do better than that; we'll have to. We won't lose any time lookin' for the Marrs. The way is open through the sand hills. It's long, but Bliss can't ask for a better break."

"I'm thinkin' it won't be open two or three hours from now," Trace muttered pessimistically. He wore his guns again.

"Maybe not. It all depends on how long it'll take word to reach old Isaiah's young men. It ain't likely he kept them home today. If they're out rangin' the desert—lookin' for us—we've got a chance."

They were soon moving east, watching each other almost as intently as they scanned the rolling plains for sight of the Marrs.

Laramie thought of Ellen. Her promise not to forget the service he had done her was reward enough for him. Not for a moment did he delude himself into thinking that any sense of indebtedness to him would keep her from warning Isaiah. Her loyalty was to the Marrs, and he knew she would not fail them.

Corbett met them a mile from the tanks.

"You've been gone a long while," he exclaimed as he drew up. "Have any trouble?"

Laramie let Morrell answer.

"No," Trace said grimly. "We drifted through them sand hills and followed 'em all the way to the rim."

"How did you find things?"

"Just about the same as I did the other day," Laramie informed him. He felt it was an honest answer. "Nothin' to stop us from movin' in."

"Well, that's great!" Bliss glowed. "Did you locate that Bar 44 bunch?"

"I figured we were better off not to waste time huntin' them," said Laramie. "The way we took is open; all we've got to do is get movin'."

"Good enough!" Corbett declared. "I just wanted to be sure the Marrs wasn't in front of us. We can pull out of the tanks in the early evenin' and be in the canyon by the time the moon begins to show."

Laramie said no. "We've got to pull out right away—without wastin' a minute, Bliss. If we don't, we'll find them in our way."

"You sound pretty sure of that," Corbett countered. "Have you any reason for thinkin' it?"

To Laramie's surprise, Morrell came to his rescue.

"The Marrs can read signs," he said. "We left plenty."

"Right," Corbett admitted, perfectly satisfied with Trace's answer. "We'll get the stuff out of the tanks in a hurry. It won't take long with the men we've got."

"As soon as we get the herd movin' it might be a smart idea to make a bluff that we're interested in another direction," Laramie offered.

"For instance?"

"Well, give me two men and we'll strike to the southwest. We'll give the Marrs a chance to see us. Soon as they do, we'll drop back and try to give 'em the idea we're aimin' to swing around to the south of 'em. That'll draw them away from you and we can head back here if necessary. You can't do over three miles an hour with the herd, so we'll be up with you long before you reach the canyon."

"That's bein' cagy," Bliss exclaimed. "I ain't got no fault to find with that arrangement. You take Trace and Frenchy."

Laramie had the best of reasons for not wanting to find himself caught between Morrell and Le Brun.

"No," he demurred, "I want a cooler head than Le Brun. I'd like Sante Fé, if you can spare him."

"That's up to you," said Corbett, not entirely fooled. Frenchy Le Brun could be ice itself in a pinch. Laramie's unwillingness to take him along made Bliss wonder if he didn't have a more pertinent reason for putting thumbs down on him. His glance shifted from Laramie to Morrell. "Did you boys have a run-in?" he asked shrewdly.

"No," Laramie answered for himself and Trace. "We reached quite an understandin'."

Corbett found it hard to believe. "That right, Trace?" he prodded.

"Sure! Why not?" the big fellow answered.

With all hands assisting, the herd was finally started for the canyon, but they found it no easy task to haze the cattle off the best grass they had ever been on.

"I guess we'll pull away," Laramie announced to Morrell and Sante Fé. "We'll just take it easy and keep away from anythin' that looks like cover. We're liable to bump into these hombres most any place."

They reached the long arroyo, however, without sighting a Bar 44 man.

"Do we go across?" Sante Fé asked.

"We do not!" Laramie answered decisively. "We'll follow this bank. I reckon we'll flush 'em in the course of a mile or two."

They moved along cautiously for a few hundred yards, taking advantage of every clump of brush and ledge of rocks that offered protection from possible rifle fire from across the arroyo. In itself it made their movements furtive, which was exactly the impression they wished to convey.

"This wash is gettin' wider all the time," Sante Fé remarked. "Must be two hundred yards across there now."

"Just spittin' distance for a good rifle," Morrell complained. "If they spot us first, and it's a cinch they will, we're a good bet to get ventilated."

"The only way we can beat it is to keep our eyes peel—"

Laramie let the word go unfinished. "There they are!" he jerked out. "Just above that cut bank!"

The next instant a rifle barked across the arroyo. A slug slapped the dust out of Laramie's Stetson. Three or four other shots screamed harmlessly over their heads.

They fell back immediately.

"Let's see if they come after us," Laramie suggested as they pulled up their horses. "It's my guess they won't."

Minutes passed without bringing any sign of pursuit.

"They're standin' pat," Sante Fé declared. "They're goin' to do their fightin' on their side of the wash."

"That's exactly what we want," said Laramie. "We'll drop back a ways further and let 'em lose sight of us for a few minutes. When we move up again it'll be half a mile down the arroyo. It's my guess they'll drop down too and try to keep abreast us."

It was exactly what happened. Again Bar 44 rifles roared across the wash, and once more the three men fell back. When they made their third swing to the arroyo they were nearly a mile further south. They met with the same reception that had already greeted them twice.

"We've pulled 'em a long ways out of position," Laramie said. "This time when we drop back we'll keep on goin' and start our big swing to pick up Bliss and the boys."

The gelding was far from fresh, Morrell's horse had a jaded look.

"You'll have to push 'em a bit," Sante Fé remarked. "Be turnin' cool in another hour; that'll freshen 'em a little."

Laramie felt he had reason to congratulate himself, for his strategy had been eminently successful. He realized that the Marrs might have more than one war party out.

"Unlikely though," he thought. "Must have been seven or eight men in that bunch."

"Laramie, it's a good thing you ain't two or three inches taller," Sante Fé laughed as they rode along. "You'd sure have had your scalp lifted."

"Plenty of time for that yet," Laramie drawled. He rolled a cigarette deftly. "I'm thinkin' anyone in this outfit with a hankerin' for gunsmoke won't have to complain for lack of congenial employment."

It drew a grunt from Morrell. "I reckon we'll all find it interestin'," he muttered; "—some more so than others."

"No doubt of it," Laramie agreed, understanding him perfectly. "But every man to his game. I always watch the deal and play my cards as I get 'em."

This talk was over Sante Fé's head, but he sensed that a threat was being aired. With rare diplomacy, he said nothing.

The shadows were beginning to grow long by the time they came out of the sand hills. A moving smudge of dust several miles to the west told them where to look for the herd.

"They made good time," Sante Fé declared. "We'll have to move right along to overhaul 'em."

"We will for a fact," said Laramie. "I hate to ride a horse into the ground, but we've got to do it. Bliss is countin' on us to join up with him before he reaches that last of these hills."

"If he's smart, he'll wait for us," Morrell argued. "The bunch that was bangin' away at us has had plenty time to reach the canyon. It ain't in the cards to believe they're still waitin' for us along that wash."

"My thought exactly," Laramie exclaimed. "Let's go!"

When they reached the head of the drive they learned that Bliss had gone on alone to reconnoiter the entrance to the canyon. He returned a few minutes later.

"Wide open," he declared. "I was right up to the rim. Ain't a man there. Did you boys turn up anythin'?"

Laramie gave him a hurried account of what had occurred.

"It sure worked out all right for us," Bliss acknowledged. "It strikes me it's up to us to go through with our plans and shove these steers into the canyon as quick as we can."

"The quicker the better," Laramie agreed. "If the Marrs come at us they'll come a-shootin'."

"At least we know the direction in which to look for 'em." Corbett signaled his men to send the herd along. "Suppose the three of you ride on," he suggested, "and drop down below the entrance for a few hundred yards. You'll be able to cover us as we drive in."

The wisdom of such a move was apparent, and Laramie, Morrell and Sante Fé went ahead at once to take up a position close to the rim.

CHAPTER 10
Six-Gun Siege

THE THREE MEN FOUND WAITING A TEDIOUS JOB AFTER THE strenuous day they had put in. Their jaded horses stood with heads drooping, their eyes dull.

Another forty minutes passed, however, before the first Frying-pan steer entered the canyon. The others were soon pouring down the trail. The cattle had scented water, and they did not hang back. But Corbett had brought almost two thousand head of stock west with him, and it took time to handle them, however eager they were to reach the creek.

Minutes fled as the work continued. Laramie and the two men with him observed it from a distance.

"Takin' 'em long enough," Morrell muttered. "Why is Corbett holdin' 'em like that—sendin' in a little bunch at a time?"

"They'd be pushin' one another over the rim if he didn't," Laramie answered. "They'd reach the creek in a hurry, but they'd be practically useless for anythin' but coyote bait."

"What's the matter? You worryin' about that puff of dust off there to the south?" Sante Fé queried.

"I sure am," Trace growled. "It's movin' awful fast. Ain't nothin' but hard-ridden horses kickin' it up. In another two or three minutes you'll see I'm right."

"Reckon there ain't no chance of your bein' wrong," Laramie stated. "It's the Marrs, all right. They can't get here in less than a quarter of an hour. Bliss ought to be in the clear by then."

"Not the way he's goin' at it," Morrell insisted. "One of us better ride back and jack him up. There's goin' to be hell to pay here in a few minutes. I ain't foolish enough to believe the three of us can hold off that bunch very long."

"I'll say we can't, not if we have to fight it out here!" Laramie agreed tensely. "To have a chance, we've got to drop back to the entrance and get sprawled out on the rimrocks. That means gettin' our hosses into the canyon before the fireworks begin. You ride back and speak to Corbett, Morrell. Tell him he's got to be in the clear in fifteen minutes. Before you go, let's see how many there is in this bunch. We'll be able to tell directly."

"You can see 'em now," Sante Fé exclaimed. "They've strung out comin' over that low rise." He started to count them.

"Twelve of 'em," Laramie announced, clipping the words off sharply. "They've picked up some reinforcements since we saw 'em last. You better go now, Morrell. And don't let nothin' stop you from gettin' back in a hurry. We're goin' to start bangin' away when they cut the range down to about four hundred yards. It will give 'em somethin' to think about that will slow 'em up for a few minutes."

Trace managed to pull his horse into a gallop that quickly carried him the short distance to the entrance. Laramie and Sante Fé drew out their rifles and wiped the dust off them.

"Looks like the showdown is here," Sante Fé muttered. He was prepared to meet the situation calmly. "Goin' to be some old grudges squared."

"Yeh, and some that ain't so old," Laramie muttered with a preoccupied air. He was thinking of Ellen. He knew the presence of the Marrs in such number could be explained only by the fact that she had warned them. And yet, as things were turning out, he was glad he had urged her to leave the canyon. His decision had not worked any hardship on the Frying-pan. A fight had been inevitable.

Morrell was back presently. Oddie Dill came with him.

"Bliss says he'll have the stuff out of the way and the bunch will be ready to lend a hand," he announced. "He don't want us to stay here after they begin to close in."

"Good enough," Laramie observed, fingering his rifle.

"They see us now!" Sante Fé exclaimed. "Shall we open up on 'em?"

"Wait till they hit that bare spot," Laramie ordered. "We'll let 'em have it then."

Sante Fé fired first. In another second the others brought their rifles into action.

"They're pullin' up!" Oddie cried. "We must have dropped a slug or two pretty close to 'em!"

Laramie saw the Bar 44 men drop back fifty yards. They made no attempt to answer the fusillade. Suddenly they spurred their horses, but they were veering off sharply to the east.

"Goin' to make use of that outcroppin; to get within good shootin' distance." It was Morrell who spoke. In a second or two they saw he was right. Laramie turned to see how matters were going at the entrance. Corbett and the rest of the outfit were working feverishly to get the last of the steers into the canyon. He realized it would take them fully ten minutes more to finish.

"We got to stay here a while longer," he said. "If we let the Marrs come up behind that outcroppin' we're goin' to find this an awful hot spot."

"How you aimin' to stop 'em?" Morrell demanded gruffly.

"By movin' over to that outcroppin' ourselves. It'll serve us just as well as it will them if we get there first." The horses were a liability now. Laramie spoke to Oddie. "Gather up these broncs and get 'em into the canyon," he told him. "Don't bother to come back, Oddie; we'll make it alone."

"You know damn well you're apt to be cut off, don't yuh?" Oddie shot back. He didn't relish being put out of the fight, even temporarily.

"It'll be up to Bliss and the rest of you to open up the way for us if that happens," Laramie replied. "On your way!"

Sante Fé and Trace had taken up points of vantage and were firing already.

"I doubled up one of 'em!" Morrell growled, his eyes stained with excitement. "You want to be ready. They'll try to rush us directly." There was a desperate, reckless air about him that emphasized the hardness of his face, with its high cheekbones and hawklike nose.

Laramie flicked a glance at him. He professed to see nothing strange in the fact that the big fellow was throwing himself whole-heartedly into the fight, even though his position was an anomalous one and the outcome must affect his secret *entente* with Snap Marr.

"Bein' under fire is no new experience to him," Laramie told himself. "The smell of powder has a drag for him that he can't resist." He had seen more than one cowboy drift into outlawry for no better reason.

"Look out!" Sante Fé cried as the first volley from the Marrs began to spatter the rocks. It did not take them long to get the range. A spent bullet ricocheted off the ledge and brushed Sante Fé's right cheek, leaving a red trail.

"Glad I didn't meet that baby head on," he muttered as he wiped the blood away. He reloaded his rifle and began to pump it.

For five minutes the firing continued without a break. In the hail of lead that fell about them they marvelously escaped being hit.

"That's the break we've been waitin' for!" said Laramie. "They evidently don't figure we're just sparrin' for time. We'll just hold off for a second or two until they reach that open spot. It must be twelve to fifteen yards across. We'll give it to 'em good then."

They had recognized Snap Marr's horse, but they could not be sure that he was leading the fight for the Bar 44.

"It'll be Snap," Sante Fé declared. "The old man may be the head general, but he ain't in that bunch. When you get up against him you'll find somethin' smarter than this bein' pulled on you."

The Marrs made three or four attempts to cross the open space where the ledge was so low it offered no protection whatsoever.

"They don't like it a little bit," Morrell ground out.

"You think they're really tryin' to get across?" Laramie asked. "It don't seem so to me."

"What do you mean?" Trace demanded. Sante Fé echoed the question.

"I mean it looks like a bluff; that they're trickin' us some way."

"What's the use of borrowin' trouble?" Sante Fé questioned. He was about to go on when he saw him stiffen suddenly.

"I was right!" said Laramie. "Look off there toward the sand hills! There's another bunch comin' at us—five or six men!"

Sante Fé stared and said nothing. Trace cursed to himself. Laramie turned to flash a glance at the canyon entrance. Not a steer was to be seen.

"Come on!" he ordered. "We're gettin' away from here in a hurry!"

They fell back a hundred yards before they dropped to fire again. The Bar 44 men following the outcropping had regained their horses and were dashing at them, shooting as they rode. From the direction of the sand hills, the other horsemen closed in.

"All the way to the canyon this time!" Laramie told Trace and Sante Fé. "Don't bother to look back! Just keep on runnin'! It'll be mighty close—"

The Marrs came on fearlessly, although they knew by now that the Frying-pan was in the canyon in force. Laramie saw

Sante Fé pitch forward on his face. He had only stumbled. Before he could get up, Corbett's voice reached them.

"Stay down!" he yelled. "We're goin' to open up!"

The three men rolled into a slight hollow. Immediately, bullets began to whine over their heads.

"That's got 'em stopped!" Sante Fé ground out.

The Marrs held their ground for a minute, returning a withering fire. They outnumbered the Frying-pan, but the rimrocks gave Corbett a definite advantage.

The firing ceased abruptly. Laramie raised his head to see that the Mormons were retiring to the outcropping.

"It's safe to come in!" they heard Bliss shout. "Just step lively!"

They had about two hundred yards to go. They negotiated it without difficulty.

"You didn't open up any too soon," Laramie grinned as he faced Corbett.

"We had to hold off; you were right in the line of fire," Bliss replied. He was visibly relieved after looking them over. "When I saw you go down, I thought they'd fetched you," he said to Sante Fé. "I see they creased you at that."

"It don't amount to nothin'," Sante Fé answered. "We burned a few of them too."

"Reckon we'll have to put a lot of them out of commission before Isaiah Marr will admit we're here to stay." Bliss was a little awed by what he had accomplished. "Think of it!" he exclaimed. "We're here—in the promised land! The Marrs said it couldn't be done—Well, they'll grow old before they ever get me out of here."

It went without saying that the attack would be renewed. But evening came on without another gun being fired.

"Waitin' to move up after dark," Laramie suggested.

"I'll be ready for 'em," Bliss declared confidently. "We'll roll a few rocks across the entrance and block it up. That'll be as good as a couple more men to us."

It was a comparatively easy task to block the trail. Rifles were cleaned and fresh ammunition handed out. Oddie and Little Billy got the wagon down to the creek, cooked supper and carried it up to the rim. It took the edge off the men's weariness.

Finally the long twilight faded and black night fell. Cigarettes were pinched out and voices lowered to a whisper. Nerves began to get jumpy as the tension grew. Half an hour passed. Suddenly, then, the night was slashed with flame. Opposite the entrance, seven or eight rifles barked. They kept at it, the slugs *ping-g-ging* off the rocks.

"Don't answer 'em!" Corbett cautioned. "That's only a bluff! Every man they can muster will be in this attack, and they'll come at us from the right and left, not head on!"

"Somebody off there along the rim," Laramie whispered.

"Let 'em have it," Bliss ordered. "Just shoot blind and see what happens."

Off in the darkness a man groaned. The next moment there was an answering volley from four or five guns. As if by prearrangement, rifles began to spurt flame off to the other side of the entrance. It was a battle in earnest now.

Snuffy Rollins crumpled up beside Corbett. Bliss tried to arouse him, but got no answer. Little Billy cursed as a slug tore through his right shoulder.

"They got you too, eh!" Corbett groaned. "Don't let up for a second, boys!" he cried. "Give 'em hell! It's a cinch we're hittin' some of them!" He made his way over to Laramie. "We're holdin' our own," he said.

"They're gettin' in pretty close," Laramie answered. "Better set the sage afire and smoke 'em out. Break off a little dry stuff and get it goin' good before you toss it over. And keep your head down."

The dry sage brush broke into flame quickly, one clump igniting the next. Burning brightly, it was only a minute before the fire illumined the plain about the canyon entrance. Two of Isaiah's Indians had been within forty yards of the rim. They threw away their guns now and ran. Sante Fé and Frenchy fired at them, but the Piutes made good their escape. They were the only Bar 44 men to be caught flat-footed, the others scurrying to safety before the flames made any headway.

"I can see somebody stretched out over there," Sante Fé announced. "Ain't no Injun, either. Be terrible if it was Snap Marr, wouldn't it?"

Both sides continued to blaze away. The attack had been broken up, however. As soon as the glowing embers turned to ash, the Marrs charged again. They were repulsed rather easily this time, for their horses kicked up graying ashes that had enough fire left in them to give off a dull glow. They quickly realized that the flying sparks told the other side where to look for them, and they retired.

Thirty minutes later they tried it again. This time they fought savagely. The low, raking fire from the rimrocks was too much for them. Thoroughly defeated, they drew off.

Beyond the sand hills the moon gave evidence of its coming.

"Guess that puts an end to it for tonight," said Laramie. "I reckon they're pretty well banged up."

"Yes, sir, we've driven 'em off!" Corbett beamed. "I've waited five years for this minute! They're goin' home with some empty saddles—"

"I don't see no one out there now," Sante Fé muttered. "I suppose they picked him up."

"Yeh. They sure had some losses, all right," Morrell agreed. He asked Bliss about Snuffy.

"He's pretty bad off," said Corbett, his eyes clouding. "But Snuffy is as tough as bullhide. Oddie and I will carry him down to the wagon and see what we can do for him. You come along, Billy. We'll patch you up. The rest of you stay here.

"I figure we've proved to the Marrs that they can't budge us out of this canyon; that we're not only here, but here to stay. They'll do some snipin' at us whenever they get a chance. It won't change the decision none. We're west of the Grande Ronde—just as we said we'd be. And who knows? Maybe this is just the beginnin'!"

Morrell turned to Laramie, a sneer on his lips. "He better not get too ambitious," he muttered under his breath.

Day and night for the rest of the week, Corbett kept never less than three men on the rim. They did not have to fire a gun. There was some sniping, as he had foreseen, but it came from the opposite side of the canyon.

The Frying-pan cattle had settled down to a pleasant existence, spreading out over the canyon floor. Those that strayed too close to the southern wall were picked off. When ten or more had been shot down, Bliss determined to put a stop to the slaughter, and Laramie, Trace and Sante Fé were dispatched to drive the snipers off.

They were successful. The barking of rifles no longer shattered the desert silence. Several mornings later, at breakfast time, they rode in.

"Anythin' new?" Corbett asked.

"There sure is," Laramie grinned. "We ran into some wire.

It's about a mile south of this canyon. They've put up a lot of it."

"Well, what do you know about that!" Corbett laughed. He slapped his knee to express his satisfaction. "Isaiah is admittin' he's through here. That fence is to be the deadline, I take it. Can't mean anythin' else."

Bliss insisted on seeing the fence. In the afternoon, he and Laramie rode over. Sight of it affected Corbett strongly.

"This is the first," he muttered gloomily. "There'll be plenty more in the days just ahead. That means titles and taxes."

They stayed only a few minutes. Bliss threw off his moodiness.

"I'll sure have to bring Uncle Elmer over to have a look at this," he said. "He's never seen barbed wire."

Corbett had never put it into words, but he realized that his success in moving west was due largely to Laramie. He mentioned it now as they rode back to the canyon.

"No need to thank me," said Laramie. "It's all in the day's work as I see it."

"I'm goin' to do more than thank you," Bliss replied. "You've never opened up about yourself—who you are or where you come from—and I ain't the least bit curious. It's enough for me to look a man in the eye and feel that he's a square-shooter." He nodded to himself over something that softened the grimness of his mouth. "I gathered more than that when we banged head on in Castro. I did my best to keep you from suspectin' it but I knew right off that you couldn't be bluffed or bulldozed an inch."

"Say, you've got somethin' on your mind," Laramie laughed. "What is it?"

"I can tell you in a few words," Bliss replied. "If things work out as I figure they will, I'm goin' to give you a piece of this outfit."

His generosity embarrassed Laramie. He was grateful, but it was not easily voiced.

"Don't bother tryin' to thank me," Bliss went on. "I know I'm really doin' myself a favor. You can handle men and you always seem to be a jump ahead of the other fellow. That comes in mighty handy right now. I'm goin' to make you boss for a week or ten days."

"You headin' back east?" Laramie asked.

"Yeh, I'm pullin' out for Antelope this evenin'. I've got to know how things are shapin' up. I'll go on to the coulée and see how Uncle Elmer is makin' it. From there I expect to head for Castro. It's plain to me we're short-handed.

"Brent and Pete should be showin' up about the time I hit town. I'll take on two or three other good men too. Billy will be all right in a week or so. I don't know about Snuffy. I'm afraid he won't ride again."

This talk of reinforcements did not fool Laramie.

"Bliss," he said, "you're gettin' ready to make another move, ain't you? You're figurin' on cuttin' that wire some night."

"You're steppin' right on my toes now," Corbett laughed mirthlessly. "We're all right in the canyon for a month or so, but you know as well as I do that we haven't grass enough there for all the stuff we brought west. We've got to find more some-where or start movin' half of 'em back to the Grande Ronde. If we have to do that we won't be much better off than we were in the first place."

"That's true," Laramie was compelled to admit. "I'd do a lot of lookin' though before I tried to push the Marrs back any further."

"Suppose you do some while I'm gone," Corbett suggested.

"I've been doin' a little already."

"Yeh? Where?"

"Above the canyon. There's bunch grass enough in those draws to keep a small herd goin'."

"But not a drop of water, eh?" Bliss queried pessimistically.

"Why, I found two small springs," Laramie declared. "If we had some dynamite it would be my idea to blow down a little of the northern wall and make an entrance that would let us out thataway. It could be done easy enough, and it would give us a chance to use that country for whatever it's worth."

"You can try it if you want to," Corbett agreed. It plainly did not appeal to him. "There's plenty dynamite in the coulée. I'll send Shorty back with a case or two if you've got your mind set on tryin' it."

"Suppose you do then," Laramie said. "It may turn out bet-ter than you figure."

Bliss got away in the early evening. That night Snuffy took a turn for the worse. Oddie and Laramie were up with him until dawn. The sun was just peeking into the canyon when his eyes began to glaze. He was gone in a few minutes.

The others crowded around, their faces grim. Death was no novelty to them, but it tightened their throats.

They buried Snuffy that afternoon. The ceremony was confined to a few words by Oddie, and they were as strange as man ever uttered at such a moment. "God in heaven," he began, a hollow ring in his voice, "we're gathered here this afternoon to give our friend Snuffy Rollins a decent and proper buryin'. He was just a tumbleweed like us, and there ain't no denying he was powerful fond of raisin' hell. But he never went back on a friend or hurt a horse. He's ridin' Your range now, and after You git a chance to look him over, we hope You'll find room for him in Your outfit and put Your brand on him forever and ever, amen!"

Shorty came in two days later, leading a pack animal that carried three cases of dynamite. Some work had already been done on the wall, and Laramie now proceeded to complete the undertaking. A serviceable trail was made in a day. He had two hundred steers moved on to the new range at once. After the lush grass of the canyon, the cattle refused to forage for a living.

"They'll think better of it by tomorrow," Morrell assured Laramie. "We'll just keep 'em from driftin' back into the canyon for the present."

At the end of several days the experiment was working so successfully that Laramie drove another fifty head out of the canyon. He knew it did not solve Corbett's problem. It eased the situation however, and he had no hope to do more.

Although they saw nothing of the Marrs, Morrell suggested one evening that it might not be amiss to have someone cruise through the low hills directly north of the canyon. He offered to go, taking Frenchy with him.

Laramie appeared to be heartily in favor of such a move. Secretly, he was instantly suspicious. He had arranged the work up to now so that Trace and Le Brun had always been under observation by someone in the outfit. He did not propose to send them off together on this errand.

"You can pull out early in the mornin'," he said. "I'll send Sante Fé along with you so you can give the hills a good workout."

Morrell masked his displeasure, but the look of frustration that flitted across Le Brun's face left no doubt that they found some secret plan gone amiss.

"It'll leave you short-handed if anythin' goes wrong," Trace pointed out craftily.

"We'll get along all right," Laramie assured him. "You'll be back late in the evenin'."

They were gone from the canyon about fourteen hours. Frenchy and Trace were sullen and disgruntled when they returned. Sante Fé was not in much better mood, for they had seen nothing to justify the long ride.

Laramie began to look for Bliss. It was not until the following Friday that he returned. He brought with him not only Brent Taylor and Pete Bronson, who had gone to Omaha with the spring beef, but three new men, all of whom seemed to be more or less acquainted with Sante Fé and the others.

Corbett was duly informed of the success they had had north of the canyon.

"Fine," he said. His tone lacked enthusiasm. A question or two and he dismissed the subject. Obviously, he had other plans.

Laramie did not have to wait long for what he knew must come, for it was only two nights later that Corbett announced that they were going to cut the fence and push into Zion. Laramie said nothing, for he knew Bliss would not be dissuaded.

The attack was made, but they were stopped before they got through the wire. They had no rimrocks now on which to fall back to stem the Bar 44 charge. With Shorty and one of the new men seriously wounded and four others barely able to sit their saddles, they made their way back to the canyon.

Corbett took the lesson to heart and was quick to admit his foolhardiness.

"I should have listened to you," he said to Laramie. "I don't know what we're goin' to do now."

"You get these men patched up," Laramie told him. "I'm goin' to see what I can do at the tanks. It may be just a waste of time; but we've got some dynamite left, and I'll use it. We sure haven't anythin' to lose."

He took Sante Fé with him. Beyond cleaning out the springs and trying to move the rock cap back into its original position with a heavy charge of dynamite, he had no plan of action. At best it was a forlorn hope.

It took them a full day to remove the broken rock. Some of the pieces were so large that when they finally succeeded in getting a chain around them it was all their two horses could do to drag them out. The greater part of the second day was spent in placing the charge.

"If the cap will only slip instead of splittin' when we touch the shot off, we may get some water here," Laramie said as they rested from their labor.

"I'd hate to think we'd have to wait for a drink until we got it here," Sante Fé answered grumpily. "If you ask me, we're sweatin' the tallow out of our spines for nothin'. But you go in for these nice little jobs. Like sendin' me off with Trace and Frenchy."

"What was wrong with that?" Laramie asked dryly.

"You know what was wrong with it. Just a case of two's company and three's a crowd." He gave Laramie a keen, penetrating glance. "Maybe I'm too bright for this outfit, but if you ain't watchin' Morrell like he was a diamondback rattler I'm four kinds of a locoed jackrabbit. I'd sure admire to know what you've got on him."

"Yeh?" Laramie queried with a tell-nothing smile. "What makes you think I've got anythin' on him?"

"Oh, hell! I know Morrell, don't I?" Sante Fé flared back. "He used to be ace-high with Corbett. Now he seems to be in the discard. And he don't say a thing. That ain't Trace at all. So I ask myself what it means, and the only answer that makes sense is that somebody's puttin' the pressure on him awful hard."

Laramie put him off with a smile. "You notice anythin' else?"

"I noticed that him and Frenchy tried to give me the slip every chance they got that day. And as long as you're askin', I don't mind tellin' you I couldn't figger out any reason for it unless they was set on meetin' somebody they didn't want me to see."

"You wouldn't have any idea who that unknown party might be, would you?"

Sante Fé grinned impudently. "The same party you figger it might be," he said, purposely mysterious.

Laramie kept a poker face, but he found Sante Fé's unsuspected powers of observation rather disconcerting. Choice as much as circumstance had thrown them together a great deal in the last two weeks. Each had come to appreciate the other's worth, without giving expression to the fact.

"Might be a good idea if you just keep on noticin' things," he laughed. "If you're ready, we'll touch off this stuff and see what happens."

The dynamite was exploded. The rock cap did not split. Neither did the springs begin to flow.

"Guess that's the answer," Sante Fé grumbled. "We can start back to the canyon. If we move right along we'll be there in time for supper."

"We won't be in any hurry about gettin' away," Laramie demurred. "It may take a few minutes for the water to work to the surface."

They were picking up their tools when Sante Fé let a cry out of him that jerked Laramie around. He dropped the shovels he had been gathering up and stared at the springs. A trickle of water was seeping out of the limestone! Awed to tongue-tied silence, they stared at it as the flow increased.

In ten minutes the water was running clear. It meant the difference between defeat and victory for the Frying-pan.

"It's kinda like a miracle, ain't it?" Sante Fé got out huskily.

"Just about," Laramie sighed. "I'm goin' to send you to the canyon. Bliss will have to see this with his own eyes before he'll believe it."

"You're goin' to stay here?"

"You bet! I'm not goin' to give the Marrs a second chance to plug it."

Night fell before Bliss arrived. Morrell came with him. Laramie had been working steadily on the pool. It already held several inches of water.

Corbett took his hat off reverently as he gazed at the flowing tanks, sparkling in the light of the fire Laramie had kindled. He could not have been more humble had he found himself in some great cathedral. Trace was more practical; he stretched out and quenched his thirst.

"I couldn't believe Sante Fé," Bliss murmured incredulously, "and it's just about as hard to believe now. The flow is as steady and heavy as it was the day we first rode in here, Johnson."

"It's all of that," Laramie agreed. He had never seen Corbett so moved. "I reckon it was just luck or fate—whatever you want to call it."

Bliss shook his head.

"No, it wasn't luck alone, Johnson; it was you. You were the one who thought there was a chance. Left to myself, I wouldn't have bothered. Guess you realize what this means to us. We're sittin' on top of the world now."

"And all because of you, Johnson," Morrell murmured sarcastically. "What a lucky break it was for this outfit that you couldn't hit it off with the town board of Castro."

"You're dead right there!" Corbett burst out hotly. "Isaiah Marr didn't know what a favor he was doin' me when he asked Nat Washburn to have Snap released."

He turned to Laramie. "We understand each other. When I told you a piece of this outfit was yours if things worked out as I figured, I meant it. They've more than done it. Three months ago this was just a dream. It's real enough now. Limestone Tanks is goin' to be our home range from now on.

"When we go to town on the fall drive, we'll bring back men and material to build a house here. We'll get as civilized as the Marrs. In the meantime, I'll move enough stuff out of the canyon to give us breathin' room. That accomplished, we'll pull another bunch out of the Grande Ronde. We'll go very light on the coulée for a year and give it a chance to come back."

"When do we start all this?" Laramie inquired.

"Tomorrow! I'm goin' to leave you in the canyon and give you four or five men. I'll look after things here and to the east."

CHAPTER 11
The Telltale Iron

As THE DAYS PASSED, LARAMIE REALIZED THAT SANTE FÉ WAS watching him as closely as he in turn was watching Morrell and Le Brun. He said nothing about it, but it served as an ever present reminder of the fact that Sante Fé believed him to be in danger.

Corbett had shifted the Frying-pan cattle round so that Laramie had only a thousand head to worry about. A fourth of that number now ranged the hills to the north of the canyon, an arrangement which he calculated would permit him to save sufficient grass so that he could put up hay enough to carry the herd through the winter.

It addition to Trace, Frenchy and Sante Fé, he had Brent Taylor and Little Billy with him. Billy was still ailing, but he was able to do the cooking and tend camp. The others put in long, hard days, which included a regular reconnaissance as far south as the Bar 44 fence. The wire stretched eastward now almost to the long arroyo.

"Old Isaiah is pourin' a lot of money into that fence," Sante Fé remarked one evening as he and Laramie rode back to the canyon.

"It's the best thing that could have happened," Laramie argued. "I hope he turns south with it and follows the arroyo. It'll mark our boundary as well as his."

Laramie and his men often caught sight of some of the Marrs, for the Bar 44 patrolled its fence night and day. There had been no further hostilities however. He found it hard to believe it was anything more than an armed truce. And yet, there was the fence to contradict that argument. In any event, years would have to pass before the flame of hatred between the two outfits died down.

It made Laramie realize how wide was the gulf between Ellen and himself. He saw nothing of her, even though on several occasions he rode far to the west, hoping chance might lead him to her. Nothing came of it, and all he had to keep hope alive was her promise not to forget.

He had by no means lost sight of the mission that had brought him into Idaho. North of the canyon he had created a situation, without seeming to, that was baited for Morrell and the mysterious rustlers who had ravaged the Frying-pan herd on Squaw Creek. That the rustlers would prove to be Ike Mundy and his gang was as yet only a hope. He was convinced however, that whoever they were, Trace was in collusion with them.

But days passed without bringing any sign of them. He was beginning to wonder if he had been mistaken all the way around, when Sante Fé rode in to inform him that he had found unmistakable evidence of rustlers within three miles of the rim. Laramie heard him out with a feeling of grim satisfaction.

"They get away with anythin'?" he asked.

"No, they lit out as soon as they spotted me. There was four of 'em. I followed 'em for two hours, but they finally gave me the slip. They'll be back; you know that."

"Undoubtedly," Laramie agreed. "In the meantime, keep this quiet; don't say a word. I'll send Morrell and Frenchy up tomorrow."

Sante Fé snorted his disgust. "That'll be fine, won't it?" he muttered sarcastically. "You forgettin' what happened on Squaw Creek?"

"Not for a minute! There's an old sayin' and still a true one: give a rustler rope enough and he'll hang himself. I'm playin' this hand thataway."

Trace and Frenchy were sent out the following morning to cover the country to the north. An hour later, having proclaimed his intention to ride over to the tanks, Laramie set out after them.

It was not his plan to ride them down. He wanted them to have a free hand, even though it meant losing some steers. He was tracker enough to follow their trail. It led deep into the hills to the northeast, as he suspected it would.

"Lookin' for their friends, just as I thought," he told himself. "We ain't got a single steer up that far. Along in the late afternoon, providin' they meet up with the parties they're lookin' for, they'll be headin' back thisaway to get in among our stuff."

He followed them for four miles and then turned back, confident that on another day he could locate the rustlers' camp. The hills were piling up into the formidable peaks of the Salmon River Range. Rustled cattle would have to be driven through them, so it was in the passes he would have to look.

"Minin' camps beyond those peaks," he recalled. "That means a market for beef—and mighty few questions asked about where it comes from."

He dropped back several miles and took up a point of vantage from which he could watch a wide sweep of country. The sky was blue and cloudless as usual. A soft breeze fanned the sage. It was a day made for dreaming. And yet, so much impended that he found it difficult to think of the future. Bliss was offering an opportunity that might never come his way again. In five years it would make him a well-to-do man.

"It would be pretty hard to turn my back on that," he mused. "There's another reason why I'd hate to leave this country." He had reference to Ellen Garth now. "But first of all, I've got to square Kit's account, whether it means movin' on or not. I set out to do it, and I'll stick with it to the finish."

Noon came and the sun began to swing toward the west as the hours passed. From the crest of the ridge, where he lay stretched out, he could see the blue shadows creeping over the little valleys in which the cattle grazed. In all the time he had been there he had not caught a glimpse of a rider.

"Gettin' late," he sighed uneasily, wondering if Morrell and

Frenchy had not taken alarm and made the most of this opportunity to strike out for a new country. "No," he decided finally, "they would have pulled out days ago if that was the case. They'll show up."

Another hour passed before he thought he saw five horsemen making their way down a draw, off to the east. In a few minutes he knew he was not mistaken. To his dismay, they continued on south for half a mile instead of moving toward the ridge on which he waited.

At that distance, recognition was not only impossible, but he was in danger of losing sight of them altogether if they crossed over the hogback ahead of them. He decided to quit the ridge at once, even at the risk of being seen, cross the valley and follow the course they were taking.

Forty minutes later he stood on the hogback on which he had last seen them. He could not locate them now. Believing they were still ahead of him, he went on cautiously. At the end of another thirty minutes he had to admit he had lost them completely.

"They went off that hogback right into the valley," he grumbled to himself. "Be a miracle if they didn't see me."

Haste was more important than caution now, and he wheeled the gelding and started to retrace his way as rapidly as the footing would permit. He was thoroughly out of patience with himself.

"Had 'em and let 'em slip through my fingers," he muttered fiercely. "I'll be lucky if I see 'em again today."

The big black stumbled and almost went down. In another hundred yards the horse was so lame it slowed down to a walk.

"That ends it," Laramie groaned. "Might as well get down into the valley now."

As he suspected, no one was in sight. A thin wisp of smoke trailed against the sky. He made his way to it and found the smouldering ashes of a small fire. He knew they had heated an iron there. He studied the ground for sign.

"They split up here," he decided. "Two of them went on across the valley; the rest headed north, drivin' some stuff with 'em."

There was nothing he could do about it now. The gelding needed attention if the animal was to get him back to the canyon. He made a bandage and was binding it around the lamed leg when the bawling of a steer caught his attention. He looked up to see a yearling hightailing it down the valley. He surmised at once that it had broken away from the bunch the rustlers were driving off. That they would pursue it any distance was unlikely.

A great curiosity to examine the critter took possession of Laramie, and when he saw it turn into the little cove in the hills in which one of the springs was located, he got into the saddle and walked the gelding over to it.

The steer stood there, bawling frantically. A glance explained why. The Frying-pan brand had been cruelly obliterated, rather than vented, and a big Box Z burned just below it. The ears had been renotched too.

"You're a pretty sight," Laramie muttered grimly. "No matter where you go, scarred up like that, folks will know you was rustled; but once off your own range nobody can say who you belonged to. I reckon the ones they run off got the same dose."

The freshly burned Box Z made many things clear to him.

"It's written evidence, so to speak, that I've had the right slant on those two hombres from the first. Can't be no question now but what Morrell and Le Brun helped to rustle all that stuff on Squaw Creek.

"When Bliss sent them out this spring to brand calves, they did it, and a mighty thorough job they done, but they didn't use his iron. When they had no more calves to hand over to their friends, they began on the older stuff. And that's the game they're figurin' on playin' here."

Two men, working unmolested, could rebrand upwards of thirty-five steers a day. For the last five days they were alone on the creek, Trace and Le Brun had averaged higher than that. Altogether, according to Corbett's estimate, the Frying-pan had lost over six hundred head of stock since the snow went off.

"That's rustlin' on a scale to interest Mundy," Laramie murmured. "No doubt a lot of Bar 44 stuff has gone the same way as ours."

It was a problem to decide what to do with the steer. If he left it on the range, the men would find it, and such positive proof that the rustlers had moved in on them would call for redoubled vigilance on his part. Failure to resort to such action could not help but make Morrell and Frenchy suspicious.

"And I don't want to get in their way for a day or two," he argued. "If I get rid of this critter and keep them from gettin' in touch with their friends for the present, they won't have no reason to think they've stubbed their toe."

But before deciding to drive the steer into the malpais and shoot it, there was another angle to be considered. Certainly the rustlers knew the steer had turned back and that when it was discovered it must proclaim their presence in the hills.

"And that ain't no part of their game," Laramie thought. "If they didn't turn back now to pick it up it's only because they're figurin' on payin' us another visit about daylight. They'll be lookin' for this critter then. If they don't find it they'll know somethin' is up. The best thing I can do is to leave it here and gamble that it'll be gone before any of us get up tomorrow."

After scanning the hills for a few minutes, he made his way back to the smoking ashes of the little fire and picked up the trail that led across the valley. After following it for several hundred yards he slipped out of his saddle and went ahead on foot. The gelding limped along after him.

"Come on, you can't be that lame." Laramie pretended to scold. "That's just an Injun trick to get yourself turned out to grass for a week. I don't mind walkin' in, but I'm goin' to have need of you tomorrow."

The big black rolled its limpid eyes with almost human understanding.

The trail was easily followed, but Laramie glanced at the sun, wondering if he could reach the canyon before night fell. He knew he was better than three miles north of the rim.

"I'll just about make it," he thought. "It'll be up to me to go all the way around to the east entrance too, seein' I'm supposed to have been over visitin' Bliss."

The gelding, relieved of his weight, began to move faster. It was encouraging. "You wouldn't be doin' it if you'd pulled a tendon," Laramie remarked. "I reckon a twisted muscle is all that's wrong with you, old-timer."

Making better time than he had calculated, he found himself nearing the canyon, with daylight enough left to enable him to keep to the trail of the two men without any great difficulty.

It did not surprise him to find it taking him to the northern entrance, for he knew beyond the shadow of a doubt that he was trailing Morrell and Le Brun; but within less than a hundred yards of it, he saw where they had turned sharply aside into the rimrocks. It aroused Laramie's curiosity. After making sure that they had entered the canyon, he came back to discover, if possible, the reason for the abrupt detour.

"They either were lookin' for somethin' here or had somethin' to hide," he reasoned as he crawled over the rocks on hands and knees.

He was not left in doubt long, for when he reached under a little ledge of crumbling granite his hand closed on a pair of short-handled Box Z branding irons. He had to grin, so accurately had he called the turn.

"Gettin' ready to do just what they did over on Squaw Creek," he said to himself.

Replacing the irons, he continued on to the east entrance. It was night when he reached the canyon floor. He found the men stretched out around a fire.

"Didn't know whether you was comin' back tonight or not," Sante Fé called out.

"Got a lame horse," Laramie explained. "I've been hoofin' it for miles. Nothin' serious, but I was figurin' on usin' him tomorrow. I'm goin' over to the Grande Ronde for a day or two."

"Plenty of horses here," Morrell volunteered.

"Not like him," Laramie declared. "I'll put a poultice on that leg as soon as I have a bite to eat. The soreness may be gone by mornin'. How did you find things up above?"

"First rate!" Trace exclaimed without a moment's hesitation. "The stuff seems to be doin' well."

"Any sign of folks movin' in on us?"

"Nary a one."

"Glad to hear that," Laramie remarked thoughtfully as he poured himself a cup of coffee. "Reckon I've been worryin' over nothin'. No use sendin' two men a day up there. From now on one man will be enough. You go up tomorrow, Brent. Sante Fé can go the followin' day, and then you take a turn, Trace. I'll be back here by that time."

If this arrangement was to Morrell's liking, he gave no sign of it. That night as Laramie worked over the gelding he got Sante Fé's eye. A few minutes later he found a chance for a whispered word with him.

"Just pretend we're talkin' about the horse," he warned. "Morrell is watchin' us. I want you to keep that pair in sight tomorrow and the next day. Don't let 'em out of this canyon even if you have to throw a six-gun on 'em. Can I depend on you?"

"You sure can," Sante Fé murmured guardedly as he massaged the horse's leg. "Sounds like the blow-off is here."

"It won't be long now," Laramie answered laconically.

The next morning the big black seemed to be as good as ever. Laramie rode the horse up and down the creek for a mile.

"Guess he's all right," he told the others. "I'm gettin' a late start, but I'll pull out at that. You better get goin' yourself, Brent. Sante Fé will look after things until I return."

On reaching the rim, he headed directly for Limestone Tanks. He was not ready to take Corbett into his confidence, but something had to be said to him.

"I can't have him ridin' into the canyon lookin' for me when we're supposed to be on the way to the coulée. I'll just tell him I'm suspicious of things to the north and that I'm ridin' up that-away for a look around. I'll have to pick up a little grub too."

When he spoke to Bliss, the latter offered to go with him. Laramie refused to consider it.

"You needn't say anythin' about where I'm headin'," he advised. "On Thursday night you might ride over to the canyon. If I ain't there you'd better start lookin' for me."

On leaving the tanks he held almost due north and when he camped in the hills that evening he was between five and six miles east of the spot where he had seen the rustlers on the previous afternoon. Shortly after daylight, he continued on, climbing ever higher. Before long he found himself in a tangled, broken country, with little parks of aspen and scrub cedar fringing the mountain meadows.

He began to move to the west now, scrutinizing every little valley and side canyon. Miles of country unrolled below him, but in all of it he found no sign of a human being. Off to his right, the ragged peaks soared up into the sky. He knew the rustlers had found a way through them. Still, in all that long day, he found no pass that did not pinch out in a mile or two. He camped that night without a fire.

An hour before dawn, it began to rain. He pulled his tarp over his head and slept on, waiting for the shower to pass. When he awakened, the sun was shining and the mountainside blue with lupine.

He had better luck that morning, picking up the trail of five shod horses within an hour after he broke camp. The rain had rounded the edges of the tracks, but for all that, he knew they were less than ten days old.

"This undoubtedly is the way they came in," he reasoned. "Their wagon and what outfit they've got has been left on the other side of the peaks. Evidently they figure this is goin' to be a quick clean-up."

The fact that the trail showed they had not run a single steer over it suggested that they might have found an easier way out.

"That may be the case," he admitted. "More likely they're holdin' 'em in some pocket in these hills until they're ready to pull out for good."

He turned south, keeping to the high places and moving slowly, using all the caution at his command, for he knew the game he was stalking was desperate. The morning slipped away, however, without rewarding him with a glimpse of his quarry.

From the position of the sun, he judged it was almost noon when he came out above a deep, willow-clogged canyon. He was debating the wisdom of searching it when the acrid smell of wood smoke reached his nostrils. He stiffened to attention, and as he waited he caught the sharp ring of an ax.

After moving back so his horse could not be seen from below, he crawled forward again, intent on finding a way of getting into the canyon. He could see where it headed in a rocky saddle, half a mile back. By retracing his way and swinging off to the east, he believed he could work into it without being seen.

He reached the saddle easily enough, but it was immediately apparent that he would have to proceed on foot. Beneath him were tons of loose rock. A misstep would put it in motion, raising a din that would wake the dead.

In a patch of mahogany brush beyond the saddle, he hobbled the black. Ten minutes later he was picking his way over the loose rock. Every step had to be taken with care. At last the tops of the willows began to reach up to meet him and he soon found solid ground under his feet. Perfectly screened by the almost impenetrable willow brakes, he lay still for a few moments, trying to figure out the contour of the canyon and the location of the outlaw camp.

Convinced that he was some distance above it, he began to work down, keeping close to the eastern wall. In the course of several hundred yards it began to open up, patches of grass appearing between the clumps of willows that dotted the flat. He was presently aware that cattle were grazing in the canyon. It was difficult to estimate how many there were. Those he saw were all rebranded steers, wearing a freshly burned Box Z.

"At least a hundred head," he calculated. "Not all our stuff though. Those white-faced Herefords came from the Bar 44."

A tiny rill of water cut a course down the flat. He believed he would find the rustlers camped beside it. In this he was correct, but before he got his first glimpse of them, he came upon a crude brush corral into which they had turned their horses. One of the animals, a bald-face roan, looked strangely familiar.

A hundred yards away was the camp itself. Six men were to be seen. He had expected to find only five. He thought of the horse in the corral.

"They've got company," he concluded. "By the looks of 'em, they've been doin' a little celebratin'."

As he watched, he saw a bottle pass from one to the other. Drunken laughter reached him. It served his purpose to find them fuddled with liquor, and he wormed his way to within fifty yards of where they sat. A butt of beef, skewered on a green willow pole, hung over the fire, giving off an appetizing odor.

"Let's eat!" one of the gang called out. He staggered to his feet, a little, bandy-legged man. Laramie got a good look at his face. It left him breathless for a moment. Beyond any chance of mistake, he knew he was staring at Ike Mundy, the outlaw who for years had terrorized the Wind River Valley with his infamous Hole-in-the-Wall gang.

The others were lurching to their feet, a dirty, disheveled crew, with hard-bitten faces. One, however, was unable to arise. He tried it several times before Mundy jerked him to his feet. As the man swung around, Laramie saw it was Snap Marr.

"I knew that roan was his horse," Laramie reminded himself. Finding Snap in the rustlers' camp came as no surprise. "I've had the right line on that hombre ever since the night in Castro when I caught him with Morrell. He's been runnin' a crooked iron on his father's stuff just as Trace and Le Brun have been doin' with Corbett."

He continued to watch them. A battered, blackened coffee pot seemed to be the extent of their camp equipment. Mundy had got out a long-bladed knife. Whittling off chunks of the roasted meat, he tossed them to the men and they wolfed it down.

Anxious as he was to get away, Laramie remained where he was, knowing that when they had gorged themselves they would sprawl out on the grass and drowse off into stupefied sleep.

Although they seemed to take forever about it, he finally found himself back at the corral. Snap had pulled his saddle off the roan and draped it over the gate. His rope and branding bag hung from the horn. It was the latter that interested Laramie.

Crawling up to the gate, he managed to lift the bag so that the loop by which it hung slipped over the horn. Making his way into the willows, he opened the bag and brought out two irons. One of them was a Bar 44 iron; the other, a Box Z.

"I'll take this stuff along with me," he decided. "I'm sure ready to put my cards on the table now!"

CHAPTER 12
Rope Justice

THE LONG DESERT TWILIGHT WAS FADING INTO NIGHT AS LARamie approached the eastern entrance to the canyon. He was anxious to talk to Corbett, and but for the latter's promise to ride over this night, he would have gone to the tanks at once. It was also in his mind to make an attempt to see old Isaiah early in the morning.

He realized that Bliss would undoubtedly be opposed to making any overture to the Bar 44 that might be construed as an invitation to assist in rounding up the rustlers. To acquaint the old Mormon with the facts would not be easy.

"It's just one of those situations that can't be improved by refusin' to face the facts," he told himself. "It'll be a bitter pill for Isaiah to swallow, but I don't believe he'll hang back after he knows the truth. The two outfits have got to live here. If there's any chance of reachin' a better understandin' through wipin' out Mundy and the rest of 'em, I'm for makin' the effort."

He was so deeply engrossed in his thoughts that he was not aware at once that the gelding was eyeing with suspicion a black blur that moved along the rim. When the fact finally dawned on him he was within a few hundred yards of the entrance. He pulled up at once, thinking someone was stalking him.

Whoever the person was, he was afoot and moving stealthily. In the few minutes that Laramie waited, the scurrying figure went on, drawing slowly away.

"That don't look as though he was gunnin' for me," he

thought. "He's stickin' close to the rim, but walkin' right away from the entrance."

He decided to cut the distance between them in two and order the skulker to stand. The maneuver brought surprising results, for he saw it was a girl who was fleeing from him.

"Ellen—is that you?" he called out in sudden consternation as he found something familiar about the shadowy figure.

A glad cry answered him, and in a moment he saw that it was indeed Ellen Garth. She had obviously been trying to avoid being seen. He could only wonder how she came to be there, alone and afoot after nightfall. He slid out of his saddle and rushed to her side.

"I—I thought you were Snap," she exclaimed breathlessly. "I know Father Marr must have the men out looking for me. They must not find me—"

Her voice trailed off to a weary whisper.

"Ma'am, I can't pretend to understand the meanin' of this," he said, "but I can see you're pretty excited. Let me help you over to the rocks where you can sit down and rest."

She permitted him to put an arm about her and half carry her to the rim.

"I'll be all right in a minute," she murmured as he bent over her anxiously. "You needn't be alarmed; I'm not the least bit hysterical." She gave him a faint, tremulous smile.

"You just take it easy," he urged tenderly. "And don't worry about any of the Marrs findin' you. It wouldn't do 'em no good, unless you wanted to go with 'em, ma'am. Maybe I'm takin' a lot for granted, but I can't help thinkin' that Snap is responsible in some way for your bein' so upset."

"You don't know how true that is," Ellen sighed. "For two years he has been asking Father Marr for permission to marry me. And now he has consented."

"Do you mean to say Isaiah Marr intends to hand you over to Snap whether you'll have it thataway or not?" Laramie's tone was charged with a mighty indignation.

"Don't be angry with Father Marr," said Ellen. "He believes through me he can save Snap. He's an old man, and very proud. These past few weeks have been the cruelest of his life. It was against his orders that Snap blew up the springs. For that alone, we thought Father Marr would banish him forever from Zion.

"You will not believe it, but it was almost as hard a blow as losing this canyon, which he claims is only the wrath of heaven being visited on him for Snap's act. And the fighting—two men killed and Zack, Brig and Heber Marr wounded so seriously they are still bedridden.'' Ellen shook her head sadly. "I pity Father Marr—''

"I reckon he is to be pitied—more than you have any reason to suspect," Laramie murmured soberly, "but that's no reason why you should carry his load. What did he say to Snap?''

"As a Mormon and the head of his clan there was only one answer he could give. Tomorrow, Father Marr plans to start with us for Blackfoot—there is no bishop any nearer." She choked back a sob. "I owe Father Marr so much. He's always been so kind to me. I don't want to hurt him, but I can't marry Snap.

"This evening, I stole away from the house, and got out of Zion. I didn't dare to take a horse. Just after I reached the rim, I heard them sounding the horn, calling the men in, and I knew it meant they'd be looking for me in a few minutes. I ran until I was exhausted. When night fell, I began to realize I had no place to go. So I just kept on. Anything seemed better than going back to marry Snap—''

'You don't have to worry about him, ma'am,' Laramie assured her. "Snap won't bother you no more. He'll reach the end of his rope tomorrow, and he'll pull up with a jerk that'll take him a lot further than Blackfoot, I'm thinkin'.''

Ellen stared at him wondering if she understood him correctly.

"Maybe you'll understand me better if I speak a little plainer," he said, "I've got Snap's brandin' bag on my saddle this minute. There's two irons in it and one of 'em is a rustler's iron.''

"No!" Ellen gasped. "You don't mean that Snap has been rustling Father Marr's yearlings—''

"That's exactly what I mean! I've suspected it for a long time. I can prove it now.''

Ellen sat spellbound as he explained himself. Incidents, about which Laramie knew nothing, recurred to her and confirmed Snap's guilt.

"Poor Father Marr," she murmured chokingly. "He doesn't deserve this—''

"And yet, he ought to be told. I don't know how he'll take it. He may try to save Snap. Certainly, ma'am, you can't go back to Zion until this matter is settled. You'll be safe enough if I hide you in the hills. You wouldn't be frightened alone there for a night or two?''

"Of course not. I've often been alone in the open. But you have too much to do now to bother with me—"

"So you think so slight a favor as that would be a bother to me?" he asked, shaking his head reprovingly. "I was hopin' you knew different.''

"I do," Ellen admitted, a queer little catch in her voice. "I haven't forgotten that last morning in the canyon. Many times I've thought of you—"

In truth, he had never been out of her thoughts. Times without number she had drawn comparisons between Snap and him, and always in his favor.

"Reckon I've done my share of thinking," Laramie admitted. "Twice I almost circled Zion, hopin' chance might bring us together for a minute. With all this bad feeling between the Fryin'-pan and the Marrs, I was beginnin' to think I never would see you again. Certainly I never expected to find you here on this rim, under such circumstances.

"I feel it kinda gives me the right to take charge of you, and I'm goin' to do it. We've made a new entrance to the canyon. I'll take you there and hide you in the rocks for an hour. You'll be perfectly safe until I get back with blankets and some grub. We can ride double then until we find a good place above one of the springs, where no one will bother you.''

Ellen had so completely recovered her poise that she was conscious of her disheveled hair. She began to tuck it into place deftly. As for Laramie, he found her presence as intoxicating as wine.

"I never knew how pleasant it could be to have someone take charge of you," she said. "I'm not the least bit afraid now."

Laramie was summoning courage to say he longed to take charge of her forever, when the thudding of hoofs broke in on his musing. He listened a moment and knew he was not mistaken.

"Four or five horses comin'," he said. "Maybe more—"

"It'll be Father Marr," Ellen exclaimed.

Laramie was not so sure. It well might be Corbett and some of the men riding over from the tanks. In either case, he was not minded to have Ellen's presence discovered. Lifting her to his saddle, he got up behind her and began to move away, following the rim.

It took them fully half an hour to reach the vicinity of the northern entrance. There, Laramie left her and entered the canyon at once. He found Sante Fé and the others backing away from the fire, their guns drawn.

"Somebody coming down the old trail," Sante Fé explained. "They ain't losin' no time either!"

"It may be Corbett and some of our own crowd," Laramie told them. "Whoever it is, don't go bangin' away until I say so."

In a few minutes, they saw it was Isaiah Marr, Nephi and four other Bar 44 men. Laramie stepped out to confront them as they drew up in the circle of firelight. They were heavily armed, their faces grimly hostile.

"You're the man I want to speak to!" the old Mormon blazed at him. "I do not propose to choose my words. You know why I'm here! When your outfit took possession of this basin, I wondered why the girl and the sheep and Indians you found here were not molested. Well, I know the reason now!"

This was the first intimation Sante Fé and the others, save Morrell, had had of Ellen's presence in the canyon. Laramie felt their suprise.

"I figured the incident explained itself," he answered Isaiah. "I did it even though I was reminded that you would be warned at once that we're movin' in. I presume you were told."

"I was," Isaiah admitted, "but I never knew until this evening that you had a personal reason for doing it. I had to get that from one of my Indians."

"Whatever you learned—if it was the truth—it was not to my discredit," Laramie declared.

"Perhaps you do not consider it to your discredit that you are hiding Ellen in this canyon, knowing she is pledged to wed my son Snap. We've scoured the desert; there's no place she could be but here!"

"Say, what is all this talk?" Sante Fé burst out wrathfully. "There's ain't no girl in this canyon!"

"Why don't you let Johnson answer for himself?" Morrell queried with a sneering grin.

"That's exactly what I intend to do!" Laramie drawled ominously. "You'll have to look elsewhere for Ellen," he told the old Mormon. "I know where she is, but handin' her over to you is the last thing in the world I've got any intention of doin'."

Nephi and the other Bar 44 men were in no mood to hear

Father Marr defied. They muttered among themselves and shifted about in their saddles in a way that told Laramie what was running through their minds. The situation was pregnant with danger, and he realized it.

"I advise you not to go too far, Johnson!" Isaiah warned. He was an impressive figure, astride his white horse. "You've stolen my range and rustled my steers, but don't let that deceive you into believing you can interfere with my women-folk!"

Brent's jaw clicked together angrily. Sante Fé bristled like a mad dog. Morrell and Le Brun remained wooden faced. Little Billy pushed them aside and stepped up to Laramie.

"That's fightin' talk with me!" he whipped out. "I don't know nothin' about this girl, but when any man rides in here and accuses us of bein' a pack of range thieves and rustlers, I stand ready to make him eat his words!"

"Don't you go for your guns!" Laramie cautioned him. "I'll handle this situation. I ain't nowheres near done yet." He focused his attention on Isaiah once more. "The little I've seen of you hasn't led me to expect loose talk from you. I know you claimed this range, but in a free-grass country that don't necessarily mean you owned it.

"I admit your right to disagree with us on that; I'll even admit I'm refusin' to hand Ellen over to you. But when you accuse us of rustlin' your stuff, you don't leave yourself a leg to stand on. I know you've been losin' stock—very mysteriously too. You could have solved the riddle if you had looked to home."

Isaiah drew in his breath sharply and his eyes struck fire.

"So that's how you would save yourself, eh?" he demanded furiously. "You would cast suspicion on my own people—" He shook his head pityingly. "That will not serve your purpose, Johnson! You forget the blood ties that bind my men to me!"

"That *should* bind them to you," Laramie amended. "It is not easy for me to say this, but it is the truth—the provable truth—and it must be said. Every steer you've lost has been rustled by a Bar 44 man. If I refuse to hand Ellen over to you it's partly because I'll not see her married to a rustler, even though he's your own flesh and blood!"

The old Mormon stiffened in his saddle, the blood draining away from his face and leaving it waxlike in the bright glow of the fire. He glanced at Nephi and his men. Something in their cold, stony eyes told him they did not find the accusation against Snap incredible.

"No!" he cried aghast, fleeing now from suspicions of his own that he had fought down for days. "Whatever Snap's faults may be, he's not a rustler! Your charge is baseless, Johnson!"

"For your sake, I could wish that was so," Laramie replied. "But I can only repeat that you've heard the truth. If you'll not believe me, perhaps you'll believe your own eyes."

He walked over to the gelding and got Snap's bag, every man watching him tensely. Isaiah recognized it even before Laramie held it up for his inspection. It wrung a groan from him.

"You'll find two irons in it," said Laramie, offering him the bag. "You better have a look at 'em."

The old Mormon sat slouched over in his saddle, a look of agony transfixing his bloodless face.

"I'll take it," Nephi offered. Twelve pair of eyes on him, he drew out the two irons. Isaiah stared at them in helpless horror. "Box Z—" said Nephi. "You know any such outfit, Johnson?"

"Box Z!" Sante Fé exclaimed excitedly before Laramie could answer. "Does this mean that Snap Marr is one of the gang that cleaned us out on Squaw Creek?"

"Well, Snap has been turnin' over to 'em the stuff he rustles, so I guess you might say he's one of 'em."

Men on both sides crowded close to have a look at the iron. As they surrounded Laramie, Morrell and Frenchy exchanged a frightened glance. There was a harried look in their eyes that was far more eloquent than words. Flight was all that remained for them. The jig was up, and they recognized the fact.

Their own horses were in the corral, unsaddled, but the two ponies which Sante Fé and Brent had been using that evening stood at the corral gate, reins dangling. Morrell jerked his head in their direction. Frenchy nodded.

At once they began to move out of the crowd. The horses were thirty yards away. Every yard became a mile. But they did not dare to run. Expecting to be stopped every step, they went on, ready to dash for the animals at an instant's notice. At last they had the corral between themselves and the fire.

In the charged excitement of the moment, Laramie and Sante Fé failed to notice that Trace and Frenchy had slipped away.

"I want you to tell me how you came into possession of this branding bag," Isaiah requested, his voice cold and lifeless.

Realizing that any answer approximating the truth must tell Morrell and Le Brun that they were found out, Laramie was hard put to make any reply that would satisfy Isaiah. As he hesitated, he tried to locate the two men. With a start of surprise, he realized they were gone.

"Santa Fé—where are they?" he jerked out.

A tattoo of flying hoofs answered him. For a moment the firelight revealed Morrell and Le Brun racing toward the northern entrance. Sante Fé emptied his guns at them.

"Let 'em go," Laramie said. "I know where to look for 'em." He turned to the old Mormon. "I can give you an honest answer now. If I hesitated a moment ago it was because I didn't want that pair to know how much I had on 'em. Evidently they tumbled. They've been doin' to us exactly what Snap's been doin' to you. This gang is holed up in the hills about ten miles north of here. I saw Snap in their camp this noon."

He was about to proceed with his story when Nephi stopped him.

"Is this a trap, Johnson?" he demanded. "There's three or four men ridin' down that eastern trail."

"It'll be Corbett and some of the men from the tanks," Laramie answered. "They're comin' to find out if I got back safely. There won't be any trouble with you folks."

It was only a few minutes before Bliss and three of his men rode in among them. Corbett's surprise at finding the Marrs in the canyon left him speechless for a moment.

"It's all right," Laramie informed him. "Everything's peaceable here." He proceeded to explain the Mormons' presence and enlighten Bliss about the events leading up to the flight of Morrell and Le Brun. Corbett's surprise grew rather than abated as he heard him out. He had no comment to make concerning Ellen, the disclosures regarding the rustling clamoring for attention.

"Morrell and Frenchy!" he gasped. "I never suspected 'em! I gave them every chance to clean me out, and they made the most of it. Trace was always so suspicious of other outfits—so afraid we wouldn't do well. It was all a bluff to cover up his thievin'."

Bliss couldn't get over it.

"Corbett, if you find this a bitter moment, you should be in my place," said Isaiah. "It remained for my own son to shame me. Not only did he steal from me, but he always went to great length to deceive me into believing that whatever he did, whether I approved or not—and often I couldn't—was done in my behalf. I believed him—against my better judgment. Looking back over the years, I can recall a hundred things that should have warned me.

"When he embroiled me with you in Castro, I should have called a halt. But he went on to defy me and blow up the tanks—to poison me into believing you were rustling my cattle." He shook his head sadly. "He flouted his religion, and I tell you that a man who does that is no man at all. Liquor—the riffraff of Castro—that was what he wanted! Well, he's had his way. Now he'll pay for it. In my eyes he is no longer a Marr! No more a son of mine! We're ready to ride whenever you are!"

"Brad and the others must be somewhere west of the canyon by now," Nephi said to his father. "We should get word to them. We may need every man."

"True," Isaiah agreed. He turned to Laramie. "Before we go, let me send Ellen back to Zion, where she will be safe. No obstacle will be put in your way, should you ever care to see her there."

"I know she'll be glad to go back," Laramie said. "I'll take you to her." He spoke to Santa Fé and Brent, advising them to saddle up at once. "We don't want to lose too much time. That bunch will be movin' soon after Morrell and Frenchy hit their camp, 'cause they sure will know we're comin' after 'em."

"That's a fact," Corbett muttered. He had not yet overcome his amazement. "I've been turnin' some things over in my mind. Knowin' what I do now, it's easy to see how I was taken in. I can't understand, Johnson, why you didn't say anythin' to me about catchin' Snap and Morrell together in back of the hotel."

Laramie did not answer at once.

"I don't mind tellin' you," he said finally. "Fact is, I owe you an explanation. You once reminded me that I'd never said anythin' about myself. Maybe this is the time to do it. I certainly feel all of you ought to know what you're goin' up against before we pull out of here. I know you've all heard of Ike Mundy's old Hole-in-the-Wall gang. That's the crowd—or what's left of it—that we're goin' after."

In a dozen different ways they expressed their surprise.

"Don't think that bunch will fold up when you shove a gun at 'em. They'll fight as long as they can work a trigger. They're all wanted—dead or alive. I've been huntin' them for over a year."

He told them why; how he had trailed them through Wyoming and Montana and finally into Idaho.

"When I first saw Morrell in Castro, I figured I was gettin' close," he continued. "Nothin' else tempted me to take the job of marshal. If he was the man I thought he was, I didn't want him wiped out. I knew he would lead me to the others. That's why I didn't say anythin' to you, Bliss; I didn't want you to break with him.

"It wasn't long before I knew I was on the right track. When we moved in here and I suggested puttin' a little stock north of the canyon, I was just baitin' the trap for 'em. We've lost a few steers, but we'll get 'em back. Some Bar 44 Herefords too in the bunch they're holdin'."

"They interest me only as evidence," said Isaiah. His voice was steady. "Whenever you're ready, Corbett, we'll go."

"Right," Bliss answered. "I guess we can go now. You lead the way, Johnson."

In single file they climbed out of the canyon by way of the northern entrance. When they reached the top, Laramie turned to Isaiah.

"Have you decided who you'll send back with Ellen?"

"Yes." He motioned to one of his men. "I'll send you back, Jeptha."

The young Mormon nodded, but he was obviously none too well pleased at being ordered home.

"Come with me," said Laramie. Father Marr and young Jeptha swung their horses over to follow him.

"We'll wait here," Corbett called out.

Laramie had the place where he had left Ellen well marked in his mind. As soon as he came abreast it, he got down from his saddle and made his way across the rocks.

"Ellen!" he called out, not seeing her at once. He got no answer. Raising his voice, he called again. When still she did not answer, he shouted. Isaiah hurried up to him.

"Are you sure this is where you left her?" he demanded anxiously.

"I'm positive of it!" Laramie struck a light. "You can see the sand is packed down, can't you?" Fear tightened his throat.

Father Marr broke off a piece of dead sage, and lighting it, saw where Ellen had crossed the rocks, her footprints easily discernible in the sand pockets.

Corbett rode up. "What is it?" he demanded.

"She's gone—we can't find her!" Laramie answered. He was

about to ask Bliss to have the men spread out and search the rim when he saw the old Mormon bend down and pick up something. "What have you got?" he asked excitedly.

"One of Ellen's moccasins," Isaiah answered. "There's been a struggle here. Somebody has carried her off."

"Morrell and Frenchy! No doubt of it!" Laramie burst out fiercely. "I suppose she heard them comin', and thinkin' it was me, walked right into their arms!" With an oath, he flung himself into his saddle. "I'll see them in hell for this!" he cried. "Follow me! You'll ride those broncs into the ground tonight!"

"What about Brad's party?" Nephi asked his father.

"Give them a yell," Isaiah advised. "It'll carry a long way. They may be near enough to catch it."

Nephi sent a weird hallo echoing across the desert. From off to the west came an answering cry.

"You wait here for them," said Father Marr. "When they come up, take after us."

"Let's go!" Laramie cried. He touched the big black with the spurs. The animal leaped away. Corbett and Isaiah fell into place behind him. In a few moments they were stretched out, a thin line of silent, grim-faced men as they headed for the hills.

They covered the first seven miles in record time. It took them out of the valley. But the footing steadily became more precarious and they were compelled to move slower and slower, until at times they could do no better than walk their horses.

Nephi and Moroni Marr, with Brad Nash and Reb Taney, overhauled them, their mounts badly winded.

The moon was riding high by now, touching the ridges with silver and enabling them to see a long way. The side canyons, however, were patches of inky blackness.

"Do we stay on this ridge?" Corbett called out.

"No, we'll have to cross to the next one," Laramie answered. "Got better than two miles to go yet. Most of it's pretty tough goin'. Be midnight and after before we get there."

He knew they had made better time than Morrell and Le Brun, for whichever one of them carried Ellen had certainly not been able to let his horse out. But allowing for the start the pair had, he calculated they must already be in the deep canyon in which the gang was camped. His hope was to reach the mouth of the canyon and bottle them up before they could get out.

Crossing to the next ridge, they continued to climb ever higher. To the north, the peaks began to loom dark and forbidding.

Midnight passed. Corbett moved up abreast Laramie.

"We must be gettin' close," he suggested.

"That black slash over there to the northeast is where we're headin'," Laramie answered. "Better send word back to close up a little. We'll get off this ridge in a few minutes and hunt some cover as we close in. They could pick us off pretty easy up here."

Corbett relayed the order to the others, and quitting the ridge, they hugged the shadows and made their way across the sandy flat that stretched up to the portal. Laramie deployed the men and dropped back to confer with Bliss and Isaiah.

"If they haven't slipped out already," he said, "I reckon we've got 'em in a jug. As far as I could see this afternoon, this is the only way you can get a horse out of here. Of course, when they find we've got 'em cornered and have men enough to stand them off, they'll likely try anythin'."

"I'm not unfamiliar with this country," the old Mormon remarked. "It is possible to get above this canyon and turn them back if they decide to abandon their horses. You better let me send Nephi and some of my men up to guard against that."

"I was just goin' to suggest it," Laramie replied. "I'd have them get started."

Nephi, Brad Nash, and two others left at once.

"Is it your idea to wait here till dawn before findin' out whether we've got 'em trapped or not?" Bliss asked Laramie. "If they've given us the slip already, they'll be mighty hard to find by the time it grows light."

"Ain't no denyin' that," Laramie answered gravely. "But I won't ask the men to go chargin' blind into this canyon. I'll go in myself."

"You'll have a swell chance in there by yourself with the odds eight to one against you," Bliss grumbled.

"If I find they're in there, I'll drop back in a hurry. Just be sure you don't pick me off by mistake if you hear me comin'."

"Better let me go with you," Santa Fé pleaded.

Laramie said no and faded away into the shadows.

Corbett was prepared to see the night slashed with gunfire. Minutes dragged on, however, without bringing any sound to disturb the tranquillity of the desert night.

An hour passed. Nerves had begun to snarl.

"I can't understand it," Bliss said to Isaiah. "He's been gone long enough to cover this canyon from end to end. If he's all right, why don't he come back?"

"I can't say, other than that he appears to be a man of rare judgment," Isaiah remarked. "I have no doubt he will be back."

A few minutes later, they heard Laramie call. It was just to identify himself as he hurried toward them.

"They're gone," he announced. "Nothin' in there but cattle! They led their horses over the loose rock at the upper end of the canyon before Nephi was in position to stop 'em!"

Corbett cursed his luck. His men did likewise.

"Did you talk to Nephi?" Isaiah asked.

"Yeh, I called up to him," Laramie answered. "He found the place where they crawled out. He's headin' back here now."

"Did he say which way their trail led?"

"North. They're makin' for the peaks, sure as fate!"

"I thought they might make that mistake!" the old Mormon exclaimed. "They are not familiar with this country or they wouldn't head north. The peaks are nearer in that direction, but they cannot get through. They would have to turn east to find a pass. They're heading for the palisades, and the man doesn't live who can scale them!"

"That's a break!" Corbett cried. "They've trapped themselves, eh?"

They began to move back to the ridge and skirt the canyon, looking for Nephi and his party. Half an hour later they joined forces. Nephi reined in his horse sharply at Isaiah's side.

"Father—Brad's gone!" he got out excitedly.

"Gone? What do you mean by that?" the old Mormon asked.

"I mean he has run out on us—that he slipped away the first chance he got. I guess there's only one answer to that. Brad and Snap have been pretty thick."

"Another one!" Isaiah groaned. "Afraid lest he be found out, he flees." He shook his head sadly. "Fool—all of them fools! The wrath of the Lord is on them and they cannot escape! Amen!" He turned to Laramie. "I know this country far better than you. Let me lead the way!"

Without protest, they fell in behind him. Dawn was less than two hours away. With only the creaking of saddle leather, the champing of bits and an occasional whispered word, passing down the line from man to man, breaking the silence, they rode on. When the first hint of coming day began to tinge the eastern sky, they found themselves among the weird monuments and fantastic, wind-carved out-croppings beneath the frowning granite walls that old Isaiah called the palisades.

"You see, I was right," he said, pointing to the sheer walls. "From here there can be no escape. This is a canyon of the dead." His voice was suddenly prophetic. "Nothing lives here. Nothing shall."

As it grew lighter, Laramie looked for tracks. In the first little drift of sand he found them.

"They're here," he exclaimed.

"They are here," Isaiah repeated tonelessly. "Just beyond this shoulder there is a blind pass that leads nowhere. In their ignorance, they will be tempted to try it. We'll sight them from this slope."

"We better pile off these broncs if that's the case," Laramie advised.

"We'll leave the horses here," Isaiah said.

On hands and knees they crawled up the shoulder. Laramie saw Sante Fé freeze to attention. "Look out!" he cautioned. "Get your head down if they're there!"

"They're just comin' out of that blind pass," said Sante Fé. "Safe enough to take a look."

Laramie and Corbett climbed up beside him.

"It's sure them!" Bliss exclaimed. "We'll settle this business right here!"

"We won't finish it here unless we have to," Laramie corrected. "I want Morrell and Mundy to know why I was out to get 'em before their account is closed. How many do you see down there?"

"Eight, as I make it," Bliss replied.

"There ought to be nine—not countin' Ellen—if Brad Nash is with 'em! I'd know Nash if I saw him; he ain't there!"

Nephi joined them. His jaws clicked together as he saw his brother. "This is goin' to be awful hard on father."

"Do you see Nash down there?" Laramie demanded harshly, his eyes bleak.

"No—nor Ellen! What do you suppose they've done with her, Johnson?"

"I wish I knew! If I was sure that Nash met 'em last night, I'd think Snap had turned Ellen over to him and that he's hidin' out somewheres with her."

"That's just about what they've done," said Nephi. "Brad knows the Camas Prairie country, west of here. He'd head for there. Thank heaven she won't be mixed up in what's goin' to take place here!"

"I guess that's somethin' to be thankful for at that," Laramie muttered.

Isaiah and the others crawled up alongside them. Laramie felt the old man wince as he recognized Snap.

"Maybe you'd better go back to the horses," he said to him.

"No," Isaiah answered, "I will not shirk my duty. He is no longer my son."

They could see Snap arguing with Morrell and Mundy and pointing to the palisades.

"They're beginnin' to realize they've made an awful mistake," thought Laramie. As yet they had not the slightest suspicion that they were being watched.

"No sense wastin' any more time," Corbett rasped. "Better call on 'em to throw up their hands. If they don't—let 'em have it!"

"Wait a moment!" Laramie argued. "Let's see what they do now. If they start movin' away it will be proof enough that Ellen isn't down there anywhere."

With Mundy leading, the rustlers drew away from the blind pass. Laramie thought they were going to cross to the opposite wall, but after swinging wide around the shoulder, they suddenly dashed directly for it.

"What do you make of that?" Bliss asked, clipping his words off breathlessly. "They can't climb up from that side!"

"They saw our horses when they swung out there!" Laramie jerked out. "Drop back and be ready for 'em! They'll work around us if they can!"

The words were not out of his mouth before a rifle barked. In another moment a dozen guns were spitting flame.

"Don't let 'em get below us!" Corbett shouted. "They'll stampede our horses and pot us before we get off this slope!"

After two repulses, Mundy herded his followers in close to the face of the shoulder. In that position they could not be reached from above. It was only a temporary respite. Realizing it, he divided his forces and attacked on two sides simultaneously.

It caught Laramie and the others by surprise. Intent on driving the rustlers back on one side, they succeeded only to be fired on from the other direction.

Isaiah swung around to see Snap ride into view. He was an easy target. Father Marr raised his rifle, but he could not shoot down his own son.

Snap fired. The bullet was intended for Laramie. It missed him and struck young Jeptha.

"Don't hold your fire!" Isaiah commanded as he saw Laramie hesitate. That instant Corbett's rifle spoke. Snap pitched out of his saddle.

"I got him!" Bliss cried.

"Amen!" Father Marr sobbed.

Sante Fé was firing steadily, first on one side and then the other. A rustler bullet had shot away the lobe of his right ear. His face was a red smear, but there was an unholy grin on it, and every time he thought a shot went home, he gave a grunt of satisfaction.

"I got one of 'em!" he grinned as the rustlers retreated. "If I didn't wing a couple others, I'm a dog-eatin' Injun!"

Jeptha was seriously wounded. Aside from him, they had come off without a man being put out of the fight.

"That was a smart trick Mundy pulled on us," said Laramie. "Suppose we try it. I'll take four men and go over the right side. You take four more and go the other way, Nephi. The rest of you can stay here. If they make a break for the blind pass, throw all the lead you can at 'em. If we can keep 'em out in the open this thing will be over directly."

A few minutes later, they made the counterattack. The rustlers fought desperately, but they were driven back from the shoulder. Quitting their horses, they threw themselves behind the crumbling monuments and boulders and continued to blaze away.

Laramie saw Mundy toss his rifle aside as he ran out of cartridges. He knew the others could not be much better off for ammunition. Mundy began to use his six guns.

"Keep on crowdin' 'em!" he ordered. "We got 'em on the run!"

Le Brun dropped back first, dragging his right leg. Morrell and Mundy had had the clothes literally shot off their backs, but they alone of their outfit had come through without being wounded. The fight had moved out far enough to permit Corbett and those who had remained with him to take a hand. It forced a decision on the rustlers.

"We've had enough!" Mundy yelled. "You can come and get us!"

"Throw away your guns!" Laramie shouted back.

He had them lined up in a few minutes. Morrell was the only one who had anything to say.

"Looks like it's your deal, Johnson," he sneered as insolently as ever. "You got us, all right, but you're still lookin' for Ellen Garth, ain't you?"

Laramie refused to reward him with a reply. He saw that Bliss and those who had been left on the slope were getting into their saddles.

"We'll wait here for 'em," he said to Nephi. "They're bringin' our horses."

Corbett rode up in a few moments. Grim-visaged, relentless, he scowled at Morrell and Le Brun.

"Put these gents on their horses," he ordered. "Tie their hands and loop their stirrups over their saddle-bows. We're movin' down to the cottonwoods on the last creek we crossed."

Isaiah joined them as they finished trussing up the prisoners.

"Will you be able to get that boy Jeptha back to Zion?" Bliss asked.

"I'll have to get him back if he is to live," the Mormon answered. "I'm sending two of my men with him. They'll take turns carrying him."

"What about Snap, father?" Nephi inquired.

"The men are burying him here," Isaiah answered sternly. "I'll have no grave of his in Zion to always remind me that I begot a thief. When Reb and the others have done what they can, we will be ready to leave." He called Laramie aside. "Have these men said aught of Ellen?"

Laramie repeated Morrell's taunt.

"We'll find a way to make them talk when we reach the creek," Isaiah observed. "As soon as we ha3e finished with them, we'll comb these mountains until we find her."

Twenty minutes later they began the downhill journey to the creek. The rustlers knew what awaited them, but they accepted it stolidly, with the exception of Le Brun. Frenchy cursed and whimpered by turn.

"That breed don't want to die," Laramie said to Isaiah. "If

he knows anythin' about Ellen, he'll sell the information awfully cheap.''

Corbett was the first to reach the creek. He continued along it until he came to a grassy flat among the cottonwoods.

"This will do," he announced as the men formed a circle about the prisoners. "This jackrabbit court is now in session. Isaiah Marr will be the judge; I'll be prosecutor. If the jury will come to order, we'll proceed." He waited for the men to quiet down. "These skunks are rustlers. You all know what the evidence is against 'em, so we won't waste no time on that. Let the court take the case."

Father Marr leveled his frosty eyes on the six men. "Have you anything to say for yourselves?" he asked.

Mundy shook his head.

"You got nothin' on us!" Morrell blazed.

"We got enough on you to hang you a dozen times," Laramie ground out. "I've trailed you and Mundy ever since you left the Hole-in-the-Wall."

There was no masking their surprise at this information.

"Your gang killed my kid brother on the Diamond J ranch—shot him down without a chance," Laramie continued. "You're guilty of a hundred crimes."

"Men," Father Marr exclaimed, "what's your answer?"

"Guilty!" they chorused. "String 'em up!"

"So be it!" said Isaiah. "Let the decision of this court be carried out!"

The ropes were made ready. Laramie approached Le Brun.

"Come on, Frenchy," he ordered. "You'll be the first!"

"No!" the breed screamed, his face working convulsively. "No, don't make me go first! I had nothin' to do with killin' your brother."

"Who did?" Laramie whipped out.

"Ike, Morrell, Spade and Shiney—they did it!" He pointed them out.

"So, I got them all," Laramie muttered. He was not through with Le Brun. He caught Frenchy's bridle rein and started to lead the condemned man across the flat to the tree where a noose already dangled. Sight of it finished Frenchy. He raised his bound hands to his eyes that he might not see it.

"Give me a few minutes," he wailed. "That girl—I tell you where to find her—"

"Keep your mouth shut, you yellow belly!" Morrell screamed
at him. It had no effect on Le Brun.

"I tell you everythin'," he gasped.

"You have my promise," said Laramie. "Where is she?"

"Nash has her. He's headin' for the North Fork of Camas
Creek."

"He's supposed to wait there for the rest of you?"

"Yeh—"

"All right, Frenchy," Laramie sighed with relief, "you go
last."

The grisly task they had set themselves became an ordeal that
left them silent and white of face. They went about it dispassionately, sustained by the knowledge that justice, grim though
it might be, was being done. At last, Frenchy—blindfolded at
his request—was led forward to share the fate of Morrell and the
others. It was all over in a few minutes.

"We'll leave them here," Corbett got out soberly. "We have
done our duty."

"That we have," Father Marr agreed. "It means the end of
rustling in this country. In a few years there'll be law and order
in these wild hills."

With the old Mormon leading the way, they crossed the creek
and followed one ridge after another until they found themselves
in the lower foothills. The way west to the North Fork of Camas
Creek lay before them.

"We have a long ride facing us," said Isaiah. "It is not less
than forty miles from here to the North Fork. It will be slow
going; our horses are weary now."

"It's not necessary for all of us to go," Laramie declared.
"Five or six will be enough. We'll save our horses as much as
we can. When the sun gets high we'll pull up and rest 'em for
an hour."

"Six men can spread out across this valley and work it thoroughly," Isaiah admitted. He insisted on being one of those to
go. He selected Nephi and Mormoni to accompany him.

"I won't drop out now," Corbett stated. "Sante Fé will ride
with us. That'll give us six, countin' you, Johnson."

It was so decided and they started immediately. As the valley
widened, they spread out until Sante Fé and Laramie, who were
following the hills, could catch only occasional glimpses of the
rest.

"Ain't no ideas in your mind that Le Brun was lyin' about this, is there?" Sante Fé asked.

"No, I figure he was tellin' the truth," Laramie replied. "He was too scared to lie."

The big gelding's head began to droop as the sun climbed higher. Three or four times Laramie pulled up for a few minutes.

"I'm goin' to yank the saddle off him and let him roll in the dust once or twice," he told Sante Fé. "It will freshen him up. We seem to be ahead of the others at that."

He was about to loosen the cinch when Sante Fé pointed out a horseman moving toward them from the west.

"He's seen us, I reckon," he said. "He's headin' right this way."

"Sit tight," Laramie advised. "It may be Brad Nash."

The oncoming rider rode at a comfortable lope. They watched him for four or five minutes, positive by now that the horseman was making for them.

"Good Lord!" Laramie cried out to Sante Fé's utter surprise. "That's no man! It's Ellen!"

The big black responded gamely to his urging, and leaving Sante Fé to signal the others, Laramie hurried off to meet her.

"Ellen—are you all right?" he cried as he lifted her down and drew her into his arms.

"I knew it must be you," she sighed. "I recognized your horse. I was sure you'd be looking for me—"

"And you're all right?"

"I'm all right now," she murmured softly, nestling closer to him. "I brought all this on myself. I should have stayed on the rim where you left me."

"I know," he told her. "It wasn't until this mornin' that we discovered you and Nash wa'n't with the others. How did you get away from him?"

"I held him up," she smiled, "if you must know the truth. We reached a little creek about daylight. We'd had no water all night. Brad stretched out to drink as you did that first morning in the canyon. There was a rifle under his saddle. I jerked it out and covered him. He had a forty-five on his belt. I got that too and rode off. When I told Brad I'd shoot if he followed me, he knew I meant it. He'll never be seen in this country again. But what of those men and Snap? I was so afraid there would be a terrible fight—that something dreadful would happen to you."

Laramie softened the account he gave her. And yet, the fight at the palisades and the fate that had overtaken the rustlers could not be robbed of all their grimness. But Ellen's life had been lived in a wild, lawless country. It had taught her fortitude and a ready acceptance of the fact that frontier justice, to be effective, often had to be swift and grim. However, her eyes misted as she thought of Father Marr.

"I wish he could have been spared this," she said. "As long as he had faith in Snap he was ready to do anything to save him—even to sacrificing me. I hope he understands why I ran away—"

"I'm sure he does," Laramie told her. "He's been as anxious to find you as I." He paused to smile at her fondly. "He's even gone so far as to tell me the road to Zion is open—that if I should ever care to see you, I will be made welcome—"

Ellen gazed into his eyes for a moment. What she found in their blue depths seemed to satisfy her.

"If you should care to see me—" she repeated, her voice barely a whisper. "Laramie—you *will* come to Zion?"

His arms tightened about her.

"I'll come, Ellen," he promised as she raised her lips to his. "Havin' seen you once, I must see you forever—"

The seconds fled as they stood there in silent communion. They were finally aware that Father Marr and Corbett were moving across the sage toward them. Sight of the two men, riding stirrup to stirrup, came to her as a propitious omen.

"Father Marr and Bliss Corbett riding together!" she rejoiced. "Surely it is a promise of kinder days to come."

"It is, Ellen, although it ain't likely either of 'em realize it yet," Laramie replied. "In a way, you might find it hard to believe that what we've been through today could bring two outfits together that have felt so bitter toward each other. But it did that, and more too, for it squared my brother's account. I can hang up my guns now. It won't be long before Bliss and Father Marr do the same. The old grudges will be forgoten, and we'll live here in peace on this desert."

MORE PRECIOUS THAN GOLD

CHAPTER 1

IT WAS EVENING. DOWN THE LENGTH OF THE MAIN STREET OF Las Animas moved a little cavalcade of men and burros. It was quite the usual thing—or so it seemed.

For forty years men had been slipping out of Las Animas in the cool of the evening with their faces pointed toward that wide land of mystery and silence to the south where even the lean coyote and the worm-bitten jackrabbit are not to be found. Many set out never to return. Many returned only to set out again and again—and still again!

Some found that for which they searched—Nils Jorgensen, for instance. Jorgensen was a rich man now. After twenty years of roaming the barren lands he had struck it and returned with the yellow metal of his dreams.

At regular intervals he disappeared, only to return with his jack heavily laden with almost virgin gold. No one knew where his "find" was located; the wise ones did not ask.

One rash individual had tried to trail him into the wastes. He was among the missing now—and no one asked questions concerning his demise.

But Jorgensen was one of the lucky ones; others had only tales to tell. Las Animas had heard them all—stories of death, of the great thirst that kills, of lost ledges, of terrific sand storms that changed the floor of the desert over night, burying a fortune for one and uncovering wealth for another.

Perhaps it was because of this that Las Animas tried so desperately to contrive an air of hospitality. It gilded its saloons, made its gambling attractive, and did its municipal best to prove that wine, women, and song were not the bitter medicine they were so often painted as being.

This spirit had proved to be a lodestone that drew together a strange crew. Men and women came from fading camps and "busted" boom towns all over the State. They were the floaters, the birds of passage, and often of prey, who follow the rising and falling tides of every mining town's prosperity.

Not that Las Animas was new or unduly prosperous. It was neither, in fact. As mining towns go, it was old, and yet it had the air and license of a boom town—and without being one. That gave it stability in the eyes of many, and for those who from choice gravitate to the regions of last restraint it became a haven, a place to which they returned between flights.

Their stays were often of short duration. Likewise, they were often violent, for certain old customs still were current in Las Animas. For one thing, men still wore deadly weapons; they minded their own business, for another.

A man's property rights were respected too; and, in certain quarters, that included his wife. There were those, however, who did not subscribe to this clause of the covenant. Kid Morales, the Frisco Flash, to give him his ring name, was one.

Two men, half asleep under the wooden awning in front of the El Dorado café, brought their chairs down on all fours with grotesque care as the jacks and men came nearer. They whistled their surprise when they recognized the approaching men.

"Jorgensen!" one muttered under his breath, his eyes popping.

"And Morales," the other added incredulously.

Jorgensen, nearing fifty, and looking sixty, his eyes and hair colorless, and his face screwed up into the perpetual squint of the desert breed, walked ahead. He nodded to the men under the awning.

Behind him followed three burros, the first two heavily laden. Morales walked beside the third animal. And now the men saw that the burden it bore was not a pack, but a woman!

They nudged each other and stared at her in tongue-tied surprise.

"Great guns!" one of them gasped at last. "That's Jorgensen's wife. He's taking her in with him this time! He must be mad!"

Even the rough clothes she wore could not conceal her beauty. She was young and prettier than one would have expected to find in Las Animas, for it was only a colorless little one-street town on the rim of the desert.

It boasted a railroad. Indeed, but for the railroad Las Animas would have long since ceased to exist. That the railroad was a dinky, broken-down, impoverished affair, passing eternally from one receiver's hands to the next, mattered little, for Las Animas's dreams were not of express trains and palatial Pullmans, but of those white wastes and naked mountains to the south where one found that precious thing called gold.

There are certain events which cast the shadow of their impending drama before them. It was so now. Both of the men staring after the little party which had passed and which was already growing indistinct against the graying sage sensed it.

They found their throats dry as they speculated in their own ways. A cold night breeze sprang up and licked the corners of the building. They shivered unconsciously, although the air was still warm.

"Well, what do you make of it?" one asked finally, his throat tight. "That Toyabe country is no place for a woman."

The other shook his head and sighed heavily.

"One of them ain't comin' back," he muttered. "Maybe two of 'em ain't comin' back."

His friend look at him deeply for a moment.

"Meaning the Kid—and her?" he asked. "Nils must know about them."

"He knows, all right. Do you think he'd be takin' her in if he wasn't? But personally I don't think that affair has gone as far as some people hint. As for Jorgensen—you know what he thinks of her."

"And he wasn't leaving her behind for the Kid to run away with."

"That ain't the way I figure it out. He's out to get Morales. She's just a decoy to get him where this business can be settled without any outside interference.

"I know Jorgensen; he goes straight ahead from a given point when he finally gets his mind made up. He'll find out in his own way just where matters stand with her and the Kid.

"If it ain't gone no farther than holdin' hands or maybe a kiss or two—and I don't think it has, for she's no fool—she'll come back, and she'll be cured, I'm tellin' you.

"As for the Kid—well, don't be surprised if you've seen him for the last time. Some folks would give their right arm to see Nils's mine. No one but him has had a peek at it up to now. If Morales sees it it won't be because old Nils is gettin' careless, but because he's got it figured out that it ain't goin' to do the Kid no good."

The taller of the two pushed back his Stetson and lighted his pipe with extravagant care.

"Shucks!" he exclaimed when he had it lighted to his satisfaction. "Don't think the Kid is that simple. I been observing him quite awhile. Maybe it's her that he wants, and maybe it's the mine. That may make a whale of a difference before this string is played out.

"If she's in love with him, Jorgensen may find himself looking into the wrong end of a gun when he least expects it. Women have tripped up wiser men than him. I tell you the Kid knows what he's doing. He's playing a long shot, and playing it to win. I know his game."

CHAPTER 2

IT LACKED AN HOUR OF DAWN WHEN JORGENSEN TOLD THEM IT was time to make camp. The night had been cold, as is the rule in the Toyabe Basin. The woman sighed wearily as he helped her out of the saddle.

"You're stiff, eh?" he queried bluntly, but with as great solicitude as he had ever shown her. It was the first time he had spoken in hours. She shook her head. Her teeth were chattering.

"I'm cold and tired," she managed to say.

"I'll make a fire," Jorgensen answered. He often camped there on his trips. In a few minutes he returned with a great pile of dry sage. It flamed as soon as the match struck it.

His wife, her name was Sigrid, held her hands to the fire. Somehow it failed to warm her blood. The cold which chilled her was in the very marrow of her bones—and it had nothing to do with the weather.

She glanced from Nils to the Kid, as she had done a thousand times that night. Not a word had been said to awaken the least suspicion that anything untoward was afoot. And yet she knew— knew that Nils had lied to her.

This was not the innocent trip to his secret mine that he tried to make it appear to be. He had wanted her to know where the property was located, if anything should happen to him. There was still a great fortune there: he didn't want her to be cheated out of it.

At the time she had tried to laugh down his fears, but he insisted. She'd have to have someone to work the mine for her if he turned up missing. Whom could they trust? Why, who better than the Kid? They both liked Morales, didn't they?

She remembered how his eyes had searched hers with this seemingly innocent question.

If the Kid would go in with them they would cut him in for a small share. It was worth something to keep a secret of that sort.

He wanted to do the square thing by Morales. Between them they'd bring out all they could carry this trip. No one could tell when a storm would come along and cover up the property so that no one could find it.

She smiled bitterly to herself, wondering how she had ever believed anything so absurd. But the Kid had been taken in too, and he was no fool. Why hadn't he suspected anything?

She looked around for him. He was off gathering more sage. Nils was bending over the fire, cooking breakfast. What was he thinking about Morales and her? If he would only speak—accuse her of anything—she could stand it better than this terrible silence which said everything yet said nothing.

She reviewed her life with him. Jorgensen was a good husband. She had been fairly happy since marrying him. But he should never have left her alone for months at a time, not in such a place as Las Animas. It was his fault if she had noticed Morales. What had he expected her to do? Act the recluse?

She took down her hair—great tawny masses of it—and ran her fingers through it. She trembled as she recalled how the Kid had done just that one night now a week gone. Jorgensen had been off in the desert. She caught her breath at the memory, and yet she was glad she had locked the door in Morales's face that night.

Nils brought her meal to her. She brushed the hair back from her cheeks and, lifting her big blue eyes, smiled warmly at him. The firelight danced on her velvety skin, as soft and pink as a child's. Even now, tired and worn as she was, she was beautiful, a deep-bosomed, full-throated goddess out of some old Norse legend.

She had a seductive way of throwing back her head and parting her lips when she smiled at him. In the past, Jorgensen had never failed to melt when she looked at him so. "Look out for that tin cup; it's hot," was all he said now.

Morales came back presently. Nils told him to eat. The Kid was not hungry; a cup of coffee sufficed for him. That finished, he lit a cigarette and stretched out on his blanket in luxurious ease.

The spot Nils had chosen for the camp was at the base of one of two great shafts of crumbling granite which rose sheer for nearly a hundred feet, not improperly called the Toyabe Needles.

"Going to be hot here, all right," Morales mused. It was their intention to remain there through the heat of the day.

"The Needles ain't a bad place to camp," Jorgensen came back; "we can move around with the sun and keep in the shade. If the sand blows, we're sheltered a little here. Better turn in; it'll be too hot to sleep after awhile."

Morales was in no hurry. He lit another cigarette and drew on it contentedly. He was a bizarre figure here even as he had been in town. And yet, knowing the Kid, you would have understood why such a place had suited him so well.

His career as a fighter was over, except for "sure thing" battles with second-rate "set-ups." At his best he had never been better than a good preliminary boxer. In that capacity he had fought in San Francisco and the Bay towns.

There it was that someone had dubbed him the "Frisco Flash"; Morales clung tenaciously to that ring "monniker." It was about all he had been able to salvage from his better days, not that he believed he was anything else but a great fighter even now.

He had won the fight, which originally brought him to town, in impressive fashion. Some there were who could have explained that; but he had managed to find a number of people in Las Animas willing to sustain him in his good opinion of himself.

And yet it was not to appease his vanity that he had lingered there fully three months. The Kid was still young—about thirty—and darkly handsome. His enemies called him a greaser. He referred to himself as a Spaniard. He was really a Portuguese.

Women, good and bad, liked the Kid. He had come through his ring battles unmarked. His eyes were large and smoldering. They invited trouble and attention; and yet they rarely flamed. When he smiled, which was seldom, his teeth flashed white and even. But it was something beyond physical attractiveness that made him interesting.

It may have been his detachment, his utter indifference to what went on about him, that carried a challenge to most women. One wondered just how deep he was. He never gambled, and seldom took a drink. When he spoke, he drawled his words as though weighing them carefully, if not cunningly.

Las Animas had seen little of him by day, for the Kid was a night flower. Late in the afternoon, when the sun had dropped behind the Toyabe Range, he would appear, always well dressed, and lounge about the hotel or take a chair out under the poplar trees which stood just to the right of the hotel porch, where he would sit with eyes half closed and dream for an hour.

Apparently he had no plans, no worries. One would never have guessed that he was waiting for something—something that he had seen and wanted and had determined to have.

His staying on involved more than waiting, however. His funds were running low, not that you would have guessed it. The problem he was trying to solve had to do with money, in a way; that is, he meant it to concern money before he was through with it.

There was the rub! By nature he was impatient of delay, and he waited now only because he had two purposes keeping him in Las Animas and he wanted those two made one.

He had first seen Sigrid on one of his evening strolls about town. She was sitting on the porch of the spick and span little house Nils had built for her. If not a rich man's home, it at least was better than its neighbors.

That first appraising glance had deepened into one of appreciation and approval on the instant. Sigrid had not paused in her rocking back and forth. But he looked at her again, and in such a way that he knew she was aware of him.

He went on, to the end of the street. She saw him returning and went inside. He knew he had driven her indoors. The Kid needed no further whip to his desire. Easy conquests did not appeal to him. He was something of a faun; he wanted to hunt, not to be hunted.

He was back the next night. She was sitting in her rocker again, better dressed, too. She had waved her hair. Morales smiled at her, but she pretended not to see him. But he knew and was satisfied.

A day later he ran into her down town. He spoke, and she cut him. That made her more desirable than ever in his eyes. It didn't take him long to find out that she was Jorgensen's wife. He knew Nils.

Rumor had it that some of Jorgensen's money was in his wife's name. He had no difficulty finding someone to introduce him. He was often on the porch with her.

Her throaty voice thrilled him. Her speech was strange; she was not American born. He found it fascinating. He sounded her out about Nils. Jorgensen was a "goot man," she said.

The situation was not a new one for the Kid. He made her talk about herself. He saw that she was lonely, that she wanted the luxuries and easy living that every woman wants, and which Jorgensen could have given her had he been anything but the desert rat that he was.

She had never been west of Reno. The Kid told her about San Francisco, painted glowing pictures of the good times he had had there. It was his purpose to make her hate Las Animas, and he succeeded easily enough; she was innocent as could be.

One night when he was leaving, he kissed her. She fought him off. The next night she only protested. It was dark on the porch. He noticed that she forgot to leave a light burning inside as she had done at first. That and other things told the Kid he was winning. And he was, of course; all he needed was time. Sigrid never had a chance; life had seen to that.

He met Jorgensen's friends around town. There was something in their attitude which warned him that they knew where he was spending his evenings. He didn't care; it made him bolder, if anything.

The Fourth came along. The town celebrated. There was noise and laughter everywhere. It got into Morales's blood. Sigrid wore a new dress that evening. He couldn't take his eyes away from her white arms and swelling bosom.

She caught her breath as she read the thought in his eyes. She tried to get to her feet, but he caught her and kissed her madly. She shook herself out of his arms and ran to the door. He was after her in a flash, and blocked the door with his foot.

"I'm coming in too, Sigrid," he gasped.

"No, no, *no!*" she cried.

He tried to brush past her, but she hurled him back; she was strong. He came at her again. She scratched him and slammed the door in his face.

He heard the key turn in the lock and knew she was standing there panting.

He sat down and waited. Minutes passed. Finally he heard her walk away. He got up then and strolled down town, cursing himself for a fool. He knew he had overplayed his hand; why hadn't he waited?

And all the while, across the street, Lars Jensen, Jorgensen's cousin, watched from his darkened window.

Jorgensen returned a day or two later. Lars Jensen spoke to him before he reached home. That evening Nils invited the Kid to supper. Morales spent a bad hour thinking over the invitation, and then, strapping on the gun he wore under his shoulder, he left the hotel, his dark, complacent self.

He was waiting for Nils to accuse him, but Jorgensen said nothing. He was just a man home from the desert, a genial, and, for him, a generous host. If either Sigrid or the Kid looked up to find his eyes on them, and found them cold and hard, it was only because they realized their guilt.

When the dishes had been cleared away, Nils made his proposition. He had a showman's instinct for effect. He didn't wait for the Kid to decide, but, with his help, lifted a heavy sack and poured out upon the table a golden flood—forty to fifty thousand dollars' worth of the fascinating yellow stuff.

Morales's eyes dilated. He drew in his breath and held it until it rushed out noisily. Putting his hand on the table he ran it through the ore as he had seen Sigrid run her fingers through her hair. For the moment he was afraid to trust his voice.

But there was small need of words! Nils had his answer; he knew the Kid would not say no.

A week had passed. They were alone in the open desert now—where most of the laws are unwritten ones—two men and a woman! And Morales dared not close his eyes.

Every mile he had put between himself and Las Animas had found him more watchful. He glanced across the fire at Sigrid, asleep now. Nils had tucked an extra blanket around her.

Jorgensen was just finishing cleaning his pots and pans, scouring them with sand and the tops of green sage. Water was too precious to waste on dishes.

His work done, he got out his pipe and smoked for a quarter of an hour, staring into the fire, his eyes untroubled. He knew he was in no danger until they reached the mine. At last he pulled off his boots and rolled up in his blanket as simply as though he were home in bed.

The Kid's eyes were half closed, but he was not asleep. Several times he caught himself dozing off. Once something stirred out in the sage. He sat up nervously, trying to peer beyond the diminishing circle of light that the dying fire still gave.

Nils heard him.

"Only a gopher or a rabbit after the stuff I threw out," he murmured without moving.

Morales crawled back into his blanket, but not until Nils's snoring and regular breathing told him that Jorgensen slept did the Kid close his eyes. Tired as he was, sleep proved almost impossible, and when the dawn marched up the world he sat up wearily, gazing at its wonders with unseeing eyes. Far off in the tangled *malpais* a coyote barked his obeisance to the oncoming sun.

The Kid shivered. He looked at the sleeping Sigrid and wondered if the stake was worth the cost.

CHAPTER 3

THE SUN SWUNG HIGH; THE FURNACE DOORS OF HELL SEEMED to open, and in the glaring white heat of the desert noon ghostly specters danced a grisly masque upon the drifting sands. Only the jacks and Jorgensen seemed unaffected.

The Kid sulked silently; Sigrid drooped. They looked at each other and wondered how Nils could remain so calm, so cold and unconcerned.

Little did they suspect that of all of them he was the most harried. Asleep and awake, his mind knew no peace. He gave no sign of the turmoil raging within him; but that was his way, armor welded out of his long years of loneliness and solitude.

He had left Las Animas with a decision unmade. The town had weighed on him. Here, in the desert, which he no longer feared, and which, in a way, he had overcome, he had hoped to find himself able to think; but such thought as he had managed had left him as much at sea as ever.

He was not worried about Morales. He had a score to settle with the Kid, and it would be settled before ever they left the Toyabe Basin. He surmised that Morales suspected as much. But this was Jorgensen's country; he was the master here, and it never occurred to him to fear the other man.

His first intention had been to kill the Kid; even now he did not intend that Morales should ever leave the Toyabe country alive. But he had resolved to use his gun only as a last resort. Experience told him that the desert has a little way of giving up its secrets.

There were other and better ways of accomplishing his purpose. Just what that should resolve itself into, he didn't know; but somewhere on the trip in or out something would present itself—something that he would take advantage of—something possibly that Sigrid might witness, and failing to see that his hand was in it, be able, ever after, therefore, to swear to his innocence. For Jorgensen did not intend to pay, not even in part, for ridding the world of Morales.

But Morales was not his great concern; he was satisfied to wait for time to present an opportunity for settling that affair. It was thought of Sigrid that pursued him night and day. He had loved her—more than he had realized.

Out of the tangled morass in which his mind wandered he reached the dry land of at least one conviction: he loved her still! She was the gold of his life even as the gold of the desert was the gold of his dreams; one without the other was meaningless. For her he had wanted wealth; for himself, finding it had been enough.

Jorgensen was not harassed by any blinding sense of outraged honor. He managed to look at the matter dispassionately enough to see that he was to blame himself, in part, if Sigrid had made a mistake. He realized that he was old for her; that he should not have left her alone for weeks at a time. And had not Lars Jensen said that she had slammed the door in Morales's face that night?

Nils put great faith in that and chose to believe he had returned home in time.

It did not make him hate the Kid any the less; Morales was still the thief. Jorgensen understood his game, and knew him well enough to realize what the end must have been had it been played out to the finish. Where Morales was concerned such a conclusion was inevitable.

He knew the Kid was not in love with his wife, nor ever had been, for the matter of that, just as he could not blink the fact that Sigrid was in love with the Kid, or had believed she was.

The truth ate like acid in Jorgensen; but the bitterness it brewed in his soul was all against the Kid, not her. He knew she had been his, implicitly his, until Morales had come along with his smoldering eyes and white teeth. He fancied he knew how the Kid had stolen her.

Well, he would pay for that. But that was not all. Had it been, Jorgensen would undoubtedly have thrown caution to the winds and killed Morales where he lay, sprawled out in the shadow of the great rock.

But that would not give him back the love that had once been his—and Jorgensen intended to have it back. It was not part of his plan to have Sigrid left secretly pining after a dead man. If he had any plan, it was that Sigrid must come to see the Kid for what he was; come to hate him even as he hated him.

How that was to be accomplished, Jorgensen could not have told. All the while that he watched the Kid, without seeming to watch him, he fumbled for an idea.

By nature he was a simple man. All his life had been given to straightforward dealing, and now, in his extremity, he found it difficult to plot and scheme, and it left him almost as impotent to take action as he was inarticulate.

The Kid's eyes had widened at the sight of yellow gold. Maybe that would provide a way. Jorgensen hoped so, even if it meant losing the mine. He could find another ledge somewhere, but there was only one Sigrid!

She was sitting beside Morales now, combing her hair. The Kid had got out a pack of cards and was playing solitaire. The game barely held his interest. Nils got to thinking that Sigrid was more interested in the turn of the cards than Morales was himself.

The shadows grew longer as the sun edged nearer the western Toyabe peaks. Jorgensen watched and watched. Suddenly his muscles tensed. Twenty feet in back of the Kid his faded eyes had come to rest on something slipping along noiselessly, its head raised and its forked tongue darting in and out.

Straight toward the Kid it came. Nils reached for his gun, but his hand stopped midway to his holster and he stiffened perceptibly. The snake was within four or five feet of Morales now. Sweat broke on Jorgensen's forehead.

Was this the thing he had been waiting for? Here was death, silent, sure. He alone of the three knew how to treat snake bite. He could disclaim that knowledge. Another devil whispered in his ear that he could hold the cure over the Kid's head—and make him confess what had been between Sigrid and him.

But in the second that he waited, the snake circled around in back of Sigrid. She saw it that instant and screamed wildly. The snake coiled and rattled. The Kid leaped to his feet as badly frightened as she; but he had caught a glimpse of the gun in Jorgensen's hand. He reached for his own as Nils rushed between them, but Nils's gun spat fire and the rattler's head sailed off into the sage.

Morales tried to catch Sigrid as her knees gave way, but she steadied herself and turned to Jorgensen. She caught his arm and clung to him. "Oh, it was goot you was so queeck, Nils, my man," she gasped. "I was so scare-ed I couldn't move."

Morales smiled to himself as Jorgensen put his arm around her.

"He was coming down for his evening meal," Nils told her. "Been sunning himself up there on the rocks."

"We go, eh, from here?" she asked.

"Yeh. I'll shake up a bite to eat first." He turned to Morales. "You bring in the jacks, Kid; I'll gather the stuff for a fire."

Jorgensen's heart was strangely light. It had been a little thing, but she had turned to him, not the Kid, in her fear.

They ate a short while later, and were under way before the sun dropped behind the western ranges.

Before long, purple shadows began to float across the flats. The high rim rocks were still splashed with vermilion and ocher. Nils puffed his pipe as he trudged along. Maybe this thing would work out all right after all! He would wait.

CHAPTER 4

THE PACE WAS FASTER TONIGHT. JORGENSEN HAD NOT DIS-closed his plans to either, but it was his intention to push on to the mine without stopping to camp a second time. The country which lay ahead of them was open and, by desert men, considered easy going.

About daylight they should strike the bad lands, too broken

and dangerous for night traveling by tenderfeet. It was a twisted, tortuous country, with the trail dropping lower and lower.

The danger of sand storms there was great. The winds seemed forever to be sucking down into the depths of that cavernous strip. Four or five hours would be consumed in the crossing. When they had again reached the level floor of the desert, the mine would be only a few miles distant.

It was not yet midnight when the Kid rebelled at the pace Jorgensen was setting. Nils was watching him, as ever, quick to see that the man's softness was beginning to tell on him. He smiled inscrutably to himself.

"What's the rush?" Morales demanded sulkily.

Nils explained. "I'd like to strike that country by daylight. It's going to be hot getting across; the earlier we make it the easier it's going to be on you and Sigrid. We ought to reach the mine by the middle of the afternoon, if we're lucky."

"What do you mean, if we're lucky?"

"If the sand ain't blowing. We'll rest for a spell, come breakfast time."

The Kid nodded and lifted his canteen to his lips. It was the second time in ten minutes that he had drunk.

"Better go easy on the water, Kid," Nils warned.

Morales glanced at him sharply.

"Why, we've got plenty of water, ain't we?" he asked, and his eyebrows arched into strange little question marks.

"We got enough—not plenty; and that makes quite a difference in the way we've got to use it. Every mouthful we save now will let us stay that much longer at the mine."

The Kid's eyes wandered to the jack which moved along beside him. The burro carried two kegs of water fitted upon a pack saddle of Jorgensen's own making. In addition to the two kegs, each carried his own canteen. They were large.

Jorgensen's was still half full; the Kid's was nearly empty. It marked the difference between them, and marked it with a deep significance.

In the months which Morales had spent in Las Animas he had heard great tales of the thirst that kills, and had believed them only in part. He had felt that there must be water somewhere; in a country as large as the Toyabe Basin there just *had* to be.

He was in the basin now—and he had changed his mind. For if his life had depended on it he would not have been foolhardy enough to have tried to find water in places as unpromising as those which he had seen in the last twenty-four hours.

The load which the burro carried took on new importance. His eyes came back to the water kegs. What if something should happen to these kegs? He shivered at the thought and smiled grimly to himself. Nothing would happen to them. He'd see to that!

Suddenly the care and fussing which, from the first, Jorgensen had lavished on them, and at which the Kid had smiled a little pityingly, became the greatest good sense. They loomed as importantly in his eyes now as they had from the beginning with Jorgensen.

The more he thought of it the surer he was that it didn't matter so much what either he or Nils did; the decision did not really rest with them, but with those kegs of water, swaying back and forth on the plodding burro's back. They spelled the difference between life and death. To possess them meant victory.

That started a new and engaging train of thought in Morales's mind. He mused over the matter for more than an hour, and still it intrigued his attention.

He caught up with Jorgensen and fell into step beside him.

"Didn't anyone ever find water in the basin?" he ventured in connection with what he was thinking.

Jorgensen shook his head.

"No water in the basin," said he. "I'd know if there was; I've been over every foot of it. Early in the spring, just after the snow has gone off in the mountains, you might find a pool here and there on the flats. But it begins to draw alkali before it has stood an hour. Even a jack wouldn't drink it, being too sensible by a long ways."

"Kill you, huh?"

Nils grunted contemptuously. "Killing ain't no name for it."

"I guess sucking the juice out of cactus roots would be better than that," the Kid went on, still fishing for facts.

"You ain't seen no cactus, have you?" Jorgensen demanded. "The cactus country is more than a hundred miles south of here. After tonight we won't see even much sage, just a little dwarfed stuff and maybe a sprinkling of *manzanita*. What makes you so curious, Kid?" he queried shrewdly.

Morales was caught without an answer.

"Oh, nothing—just wonderin'," he muttered finally.

Half an hour later he attacked Nils again.

"When we get to the mine we'll be about three days from water, won't we?" he queried lazily, as though the matter was but of trifling importance to him.

Jorgensen had been waiting for his question. It told him a great deal.

"Not so far as that," he replied casually. "If we were coming out this way it would be about three days—being loaded down and going slow; but we won't come out this way."

"No?" Morales prompted. His voice was almost too eager. Jorgensen's lips twitched in what was meant for a smile. He was enjoying this immensely.

"No!" he answered just as briefly.

He waited for Morales to prod him, but the Kid held his tongue; and then, afraid that the game was more wary than he supposed, and not wanting to be cheated of it, Jorgensen went on:

"We'll strike east when we leave the mine. We'll hold that course for nigh onto fifty miles. We'll head north, then, and travel for two days. We'll be going due west when we finally line out for Las Animas."

"Sounds like it's going to add fifty to a hundred miles to the trip," the Kid said.

"All of that. But we'll get water. Distance don't count if your kegs are full."

"Where you going to find water going out that way?" Morales fought hard to keep his voice steady.

"Piute Wells! Reckon you heard of the wells."

"Some folks call it Piute Tanks. Is that the same place?"

"That's it! Ain't no well or tank at all, as far as that goes. I guess it's no more than a little spring working up through the rocks, with sort of a basin in the outcropping catching some of the water. If you didn't know the place, you'd go right by it, never suspecting it was there."

"Water's always there, eh?"

"Well, it's *usually* there."

"Oh!" The Kid's tone was one of disappointment. "It's usually there, but you can't count on it, huh?"

"I been counting on it a long while," Nils rejoined.

"How many times you been there?"

"Oh, maybe twenty-five times in the last five years."

"Always found water there?"

"Always found water there," Jorgensen answered, and from his tone one would have gathered that he was terribly bored.

The Kid was silent for a minute or two.

"Well, you might say you *could* count on it, then," he argued.

"Well, yes and no." Nils drawled his reply. "You never can tell much about desert water, tanks like that, especially. I knew a fool once who ruined a better well than that one.

"He didn't find water enough there to suit him once, and believing where a little water seeped through a small crack there must be more that couldn't get out, he stuck in a stick of dynamite and blew the damned thing to hell. They ain't never been no water there since.

"Other times, springs like that just disappear, and no one knows what happened to them."

The Kid finished his cigarette in silence, regarding Jorgensen out of the corner of his eye the while.

"I suppose a party'd find himself pretty much up against it if he counted on finding water there and they wasn't none," he mused aloud at last.

The drift of all this was almost too plain. And yet Jorgensen dissembled admirably. Despite appearances, this talk of the Kid's bored him less and less. An idea had been born in his mind— *the* idea for which he had searched. He wondered that it hadn't occurred to him before. No preparation was necessary; no scheming had to be done. It seemed almost to have been ordained.

But the Kid was waiting for his answer.

"Up against it, eh?" he echoed. "God help him! I found all that was left of three or four who couldn't locate the wells. Poor devils! Still, a man's got to take chances. But why borrow trouble? I reckon we won't have any."

The Kid laughed.

"No, I don't expect any trouble," said he, and his tone was ominous with double meaning. Jorgensen stiffened a little at the boldness of his words. Morales was not bluffing. The thing he had in mind was definite enough already to promise success.

He had to know more about Piute Wells—everything would depend on that—but he could wait; time enough for it after they reached the mine.

Jorgensen was satisfied too. Piute Wells figured in his plans also. But he had no information to gather; he knew.

So they went on, each busy with his own thoughts—and strangely enough they were surprisingly alike in their reasoning.

CHAPTER 5

IN ANOTHER HOUR THE COUNTRY BEGAN TO CHANGE. GRADU-ally the level floor of the desert gave way to shallow *arroyos* and broken terrain, the first signs of what lay beyond.

Jorgensen glanced at his watch. It was a little after three o'clock. He dropped back to Sigrid. She was half awake. In a vague way she sensed that she was the stake for which Nils and the Kid played. She had heard most of what had passed between them this night. However, its *double entendre* had quite escaped her, for she had been too busily engaged comparing them.

Somehow, the Kid was no longer the romantic figure he had seemed, back in Las Animas. She had never liked the desert, and her dislike for it had grown to fear since evening. She imagined she saw strange figures slipping over the sage in the moonlight.

Several times she was at the point of calling out to Nils. But the things that frightened her proved to be no more than optical delusions. The snake had been real, however. How easily Jorgensen had disposed of it!

Unconsciously she bowed to his efficiency. Compared to him, the Kid seemed immature.

"It's a little after three," Nils informed her. "We'll stop in an hour. Maybe you'd better get down and walk for awhile; it'll rest you."

She shook her head emphatically. "I'm afraid, Nils."

"Snakes?"

She nodded.

"Naw! You couldn't find one with a telescope! They don't move around much at night—not when it's as cold as this."

Thus assured, she got down. The three of them walked side by side. Once her fingers touched the Kid's. It was quite by accident. Morales caught her hand and pressed it warmly. She drew it away as though she had touched hot metal. And it was not because she was afraid that Jorgensen might see!

They slept before they ate. At daylight they were on their way again. Jorgensen scanned the horizon time after time. Morales saw him lift his nose as though he were trying to smell out the weather.

"Well, what do you make of it?" he asked.

"It may blow a little after awhile. But we'll go on."

They entered a land of the dead. Nothing moved; nothing lived. The trail dropped and dropped. Great walls of crumbling sandstone closed in. At times they passed through narrow defiles where two could not walk abreast.

Morales lost all sense of direction. The sun was still low. For minutes at a time they could not see it, so sheer and high were the barrier walls.

Jorgensen went on, turning this way and that, never stopping, it seemed, to give a second thought to the way he took. When they came to places where the drifting sand had piled up higher than their heads, completely blocking their way, they got out their shovels and attacked it.

The Kid suggested circling around these places. Jorgensen shook his head; he knew but one way across.

Whenever the trail opened a little, crumbling walls and frowning rim rocks scowled down on them. The winds of many centuries had carved strange grotesques on those ancient ramparts. At their feet, ghostly fingers had left queer arabesques in the sand, patterns of winds and shadows.

Not a wing flecked the blue sky. Nils glanced up at it apprehensively at regular intervals. No one spoke much. That land was too forbidding for speech. The heat became stifling as the sun climbed higher. If the speed at which they progressed was slow, it was steady.

Sigrid clung close to Jorgensen. Once she looked back to see if she could tell which way they had come. It might have been one of a dozen ways. She caught her breath nervously. The place became a prison.

She sighed so heavily that Nils glanced at her anxiously. She shuddered at thought of the fate which awaited anyone unfortunate enough to be lost there. With startling vividness she pictured the blind groping, the mad frenzy, the growing despair, and finally the cruel death of the victim. It made her realize just how dependent they were on Jorgensen.

She caught herself watching him—watching him as the Kid had been watching him for hours.

Once Jorgensen hesitated as if uncertain which way to take. Sigrid's throat went dry.

"You wait here a minute," Nils advised. "I'll go ahead a ways and come back. This wall has fallen since I was here last. I think I'm right, but I want to be sure."

"I'll go along," Morales exclaimed instantly.

"You wait with Sigrid," Nils ordered sternly. "If I shout, come ahead."

He was gone, and into Sigrid's mind flashed the terrifying thought that maybe Jorgensen knew about those nights on the porch—that he had lured them there only to leave them.

"Nils! Nils!" she cried. "Come back!"

Jorgensen came running.

"What's the matter, Sigrid?" he cried anxiously.

"Nils, I go with you! Don't leave me here; I'm 'fraid!" Her voice broke, and she began to cry.

"You get so scared already?" he laughed. "Don't cry; we're not lost."

She threw her arms around his neck and clung to him.

The Kid was glad enough that Jorgensen had returned, but his lips curled scornfully, and, shrugging his shoulders, he turned his back on the sight of Sigrid in Nils's arms.

"We turn to the left, as I thought," Jorgensen announced a few seconds later. He glanced at the sky. It was no longer the deep blue it had been. "Maybe we do well to hurry a little," he advised. "The wind's beginning to blow up there."

They moved off in single file, Nils leading the way.

Morales fell into Jorgensen's habit of glancing at the heavens. He saw nothing to be alarmed at. Not until he noticed the dirty yellow tinge which had been creeping into the sky for half an hour was he convinced that all was not well.

Jorgensen called a halt. They adjusted their kerchiefs to cover mouth and nostrils. Nils got out a length of rope and tied one end of it about him.

"It maybe not be a bad blow," said he. "It's hard to tell. We'll be prepared, anyhow. Hang on to the rope; we'll stay together that way if the sand slips down and buries us."

It was not long before the stinging blast swooped down on them. Sand poured over the towering rim rocks in blinding sheets. The wind up above was scouring the floor of the desert clean and depositing the sweepings on their heads.

The sand seemed to run with the wind. It piled up in great

drifts quite as quickly as does dry snow before a stinging wintry blast.

It was unpleasant and uncomfortable—Jorgensen would admit no more. The experience was an old one with him. He made them hug the lee wall; held them back now; urged them ahead a moment later.

But, if under his guidance they avoided the deluge that poured down from above, it was impossible to escape the consequences of those tumbling streams of sand. The air was heavy with it.

It worked into their clothing and crept into their nostrils and eyes and mouths. They were no longer able to see ahead for more than a few feet at a time.

The Kid was in the rear. Once he moved almost too slowly. The rope was wrenched from his hands. The sand poured around him up to his knees. He climbed out of it with a furious burst of energy.

He stuck out his hand and touched the wall at his right. Keeping close to it, he ran ahead until the dim figures of Jorgensen and Sigrid and the plodding burros loomed before him.

They had stopped. Not because he had dropped behind; they had not missed him yet. Sand blocked the way once more.

The Kid's eyes flashed fire.

"Too bad you couldn't go on," he snapped sarcastically. "That last fall got me. Why didn't you wait?"

This was the first time he had been openly hostile. Jorgensen stared at him coldly.

"Because I expect you to look out for yourself," said he. "I can't see two ways at once. I told you to tie the rope around you. But you knew better. Don't make that mistake again. Grab a shovel, now, and let's get the stuff out of the way."

The Kid's sullenness deepened. "I've done all the shoveling I intend to do," he grumbled. "Ain't no sense in pushing on like this. Why can't we hole up somewhere and wait until this blow is over?"

"Do *you* know when it's going to be over?" Nils came back hotly, fast losing patience. "I don't, and I know this country pretty well.

"If you really want to shovel sand, wait here till this thing's over. You'll be wondering where your next drink is coming from before you reach the top. This ain't bad at all. Why, even Sigrid seems to be standing it all right."

Jorgensen leaned on his shovel, waiting for the Kid to decide what he wanted to do. In those few minutes the drift rose perceptibly. It brought Morales to his senses.

"How far have we come?" he asked grudgingly.

" 'Bout two-thirds of the way."

"All right," he muttered, catching up his shovel.

So they went on again. Once a burro floundered in the loose sand. Jorgensen lifted the animal to its feet as though it were a kitten. An hour passed. The storm continued. The country began to change, then. Jorgensen noticed it many minutes before the Kid began to appreciate the fact.

The defile widened. The cañon walls fell back. The driving sand bit deeper, but the drifts were fewer. Nils increased the pace. At the end of another mile they began to climb, the trail clinging precariously to the dangerously smooth shoulder of a great block of basalt.

Jorgensen swept the surrounding country with his red-rimmed eyes. "We'll reach the top in less than an hour. Ain't so much sand, now."

The Kid found that breathing was easier. He nodded to himself over the fact and, wetting his parched lips with his tongue, went on without a backward glance.

Finally they came to the last ascent. They paused to rest before taking it. The wind seemed to have dropped. Sigrid leaned wearily against her burro.

"This is the last climb," Nils encouraged her. "It's a little steep; watch out for it."

They reached the top without further mishap.

"We'll shake out our clothes now and rest a minute," Jorgensen announced. "Soon as we strike some sage I'll cook a bite to eat."

It was so calm there that it fooled the Kid into saying the storm was over.

Jorgensen shook his head.

"No, it's still blowing down there. Look back!"

Spread out below them was the country through which they had just passed. Great clouds of sand hung over it.

Jorgensen wasted but little time over the noonday meal. As afternoon waned they gradually approached a range of mountains, the Toquima Range.

The mountains ran northeast and southwest. They towered high and inhospitable. Morales looked in vain for sight of tree or human habitation. Both he and Sigrid knew that the journey's end lay in one of those deep cañons which slashed the range just ahead of them.

"It isn't far now, Nils?" Sigrid ventured.

"Not far now," he replied. She thought he had become singularly uncommunicative for one whose avowed purpose in bringing them there was to acquaint them with the location of the mine. The Kid had the same thought. Not that either deluded himself that such was the reason for their presence; they knew better.

But had they not long since come to realize as much, this, and other contradictions of the same sort, would have warned them of their mistake.

A great flat, half a mile wide, stretched away before them, its surface as smooth as polished marble. Water had stood there in the spring. After it had evaporated, the sun had drawn the remaining moisture out of the crust. The crust had cracked until it resembled an intricate mosaic.

Jorgensen scanned it minutely. To him it was as a sheet of paper on which he could read the story of what had transpired in his absence; for the crust was so dry that it went to powder under the least weight, and to set foot upon it was to leave a telltale trail that would not be erased for months.

Sigrid and Morales pressed forward. He waved them back. "We'll skirt this flat," said he. He was not leaving any sign there to lead some chance desert rover to his find.

Once around the flat, a cañon opened immediately ahead. Jorgensen studied every inch of it. Sigrid thought she saw him nod to himself as though he found all was well.

Morales's eyes were everywhere. He would have sworn that they were the first human beings to set foot there. Surely this cañon must run back farther than this. There was no sign of a mine.

Jorgensen was a few yards ahead. They saw him stop. "Well," he drawled, "we're here!"

"Where?" the Kid gasped.

"There!" and Nils pointed to an overhanging ledge ten yards away.

The Kid and Sigrid could see nothing—no dump, no tailings. Indeed there was nothing to see; Jorgensen had taken care of that.

He got out a shovel. They followed him. In a few minutes he had unearthed the tools and supplies he had cached. He continued to ply his shovel. Ten minutes more and the ledge of rotten quartz that held his fortune lay exposed.

The Kid's eyes popped, and the blood ran from his face. He saw the wide stringers of solid gold that streaked the ledge. He didn't know how deep they might go before pinching out. He didn't care, particularly; there was enough in sight; enough to make him rich beyond his wildest dreams.

"Think of it," he groaned, "all this stuff layin' here for somebody to come along and find! No shafts to sink, no tunnels to dig! Nothing! Just waiting to be picked up!"

He shook his head incredulously, unable even now to believe his eyes.

"It's a freak, all right," Jorgensen muttered. "You couldn't find a color anywhere else in the whole cañon."

The Kid didn't even hear him. Why talk of finding a color? Here was fortune enough for any man. All that remained to be done was to make it his. Money would mean something to a man like him.

Already in fancy he saw Sigrid and himself moving eastward—Chicago—New York! It was the Big Time for them from now on—Broadway—hobnobbing with the swells at Palm Beach—maybe Paris! He'd show this woman how to live!

CHAPTER 6

SIGRID BECAME THE COOK NOW. JORGENSEN DID THE MINING. The Kid carted away the broken rock after Nils had extracted the values. This was so that when they left no sign should remain of their having been there.

It was tedious work for Morales. By the end of the second day it was difficult for him to dissemble longer. He had no intention of ever returning there. Let someone find the ledge if they could, he'd be satisfied with what they took out this trip.

Jorgensen had warned them that they could not stay there more than three days. They didn't have water enough to warrant remaining longer. Morales promised himself that he would be the one to say when they left. Jorgensen's pick had uncovered a veritable jewelry shop. An extra day there would mean thousands of dollars. The Kid had no intention of being cheated out of that.

He had spoken to Nils about Piute Wells, but had not been able to pin him down. He intended to press the matter again tonight. It was late already. He moved across the cañon in the deepening twilight. From the opposite side came the sound of Nils's sledge. The camp was below the mine.

Morales left his jack there and went on. Without intending to, he moved stealthily. He was within a yard or two of Jorgensen before his foot dislodged a piece of rock and announced his presence.

Jorgensen whirled, gun in hand. The Kid stiffened.

"Oh, it's you, eh?" Nils laughed. "I didn't know who it was. Better sing out the next time, Kid."

The Kid made light of the incident, but he knew it was a warning.

"Guess we'd better call it a day, eh?"

"Yeh. I'm tired," Jorgensen answered.

They sat around the fire after they had eaten, and always Sigrid combed her hair.

"How much did you take out today?" the Kid asked.

"More than I ever dreamed one man could," Nils replied. "By tomorrow evening it won't total less than two hundred thousand. The jacks won't carry much more. It's going to be slow work getting out this time."

Two hundred thousand! Another day would make it a quarter of a million. The Kid swore they'd stay or he'd know why. He said nothing of this, but his greed warned Jorgensen of what was passing in his mind.

Nils turned to Sigrid.

"Do you think you could find this place again?" he asked.

"Never do I want to come here again, Nils."

"How about you, Kid? Could you make it?"

"Reckon I could if I had a map!"

"Maps are bad things to have around when gold is at the other end of them," Nils smiled grimly. "But shucks! Here," and he caught up a piece of brush and began to make lines in the sand at his feet.

In a few seconds he had sketched out the route they had come. "You know the points we made," he went on; "the Needles, the camp at the rim, the big flat, and so forth. Do you follow me?"

Morales nodded.

"You'd have trouble in the Bad Lands, no doubt, but you'd get on to that in time."

He started to smooth away the lines he had made.

"Wait!" the Kid exclaimed, catching his arm. He put his finger on the spot that indicated the mine. "You said we'd strike east from here," he queried; "does that mean we'll cross the range?"

"No, not here! When I said east maybe I should have said northeast. Still, we go east a ways."

"Just where *do* we cross?" Morales drove on.

Jorgensen did not have to search for his answers; they had been ready and waiting three days now. With the seeming innocence of a child he marked out the line of the Toquima Range.

"We'll cut across right there," he murmured without looking up. "There's water on the other side—Wild Horse Creek they call it; it's quite a stream. But we'll be lucky to get across in two days this time, being loaded so heavy. No night camps on the way out; we'll keep moving most of the time, night and day."

The Kid was silently calculating distances.

"Ought to be about fifty miles from here to where we begin crossing," he declared.

" 'Bout fifty mile," Nils answered. "We'll stay out on the flats; it's shorter thataway. The Toquimas swing pretty far to the west about there"—he indicated the spot on his crude map—"we'll strike for that point.

"There'd be no sense in hugging the mountains and making that long swing around the big bend. Piute Wells will be our first water, and we'll sure be needing it long before we reach it."

"Then we'll strike the wells before we take to the mountains," Morales deduced gravely.

"That's right," Nils muttered.

"Just where will that be?"

The Kid's voice was velvety. Jorgensen brushed the sand from his hands and got to his feet. With a sweep of his boot he erased the map.

"Well, Kid," he drawled, "I could tell you, and then again I couldn't. I could say it was here or there, and be lying to you or telling you the truth, but if I *was* telling you straight, it wouldn't mean nothing to you.

"This country's too big to put your finger down on a speck fifty mile away and say 'There it is!' You hear lots of talk about the wells, but I reckon there's mighty few that's ever seen it."

"I don't know about that," Morales cut in.

"Well, I do! My old pardner, Lief Holmquist, showed me the way. Seemed as simple as finding your boots. But it wasn't. I never saw the wells until Lief took me there—and I wasn't any tenderfoot at the time, either. That's what I'm going to do with you—take you there.

"The way I got it figured out, the wells is the key to this mine. The Bad Lands block the way on the west, and if a man can't locate the wells, he ain't going to try the east. I reckon you'll agree to that, Kid."

"What do you mean?" Morales demanded.

"I mean when you've seen the country," Jorgensen replied deeply.

"Oh!"

Nils imagined he caught a note of relief in the Kid's voice.

The fire was low. Jorgensen built it up, and then sat down again. Morales noticed that Nils wore his gun tonight. Sigrid remarked it too.

"You know," Nils continued after awhile, "it may seem to you, Kid, that life is being pretty good to me—all this money and a wife like Sigrid to look after me. I want you to remember that it wasn't always that way.

"I been pretty near a lifetime finding this ledge. I used to wonder where I was going to get money enough to be able to just keep on looking. That's all over, but I ain't forgetting it. If I was to lose out now, maybe I could strike it again, and maybe I couldn't; I ain't so young as I was."

Morales fidgeted nervously. What was all this talk leading up to?

"At first I thought I'd never let any man set eyes on this property," Nils went on. "But the time came when I had to tell: used to scare me to think of carrying this secret around. It wasn't being fair to Sigrid. That's why you're here, Kid.

"You've seen the mine, and day after tomorrow I'll show you the wells. You'll be able to come and go just about as easy as I have.

"I'm putting myself in your hands. If you want to double cross me, I won't be able to stop you. But I ain't afraid of that.

When I spoke to you I knew I had picked out a man who'd play square with me and do the right thing by Sigrid.''

Morales knew that Jorgensen was lying. But it was such admirable lying that the Kid had to pretend to believe him. Just an honest, guileless, confiding old prospector, eh? Bah! What sort of fool did Jorgensen take him for?

The Kid realized that Nils had played with him, that the information he had gathered so laboriously since they left the Needles had not been filched from Jorgensen. He saw now that he had learned only that which it had pleased Jorgensen to let him learn, that he had never had the slightest chance of surprising the man into telling him about Piute Wells.

How easily he had thought to gain the knowledge!

Murder flamed in Morales's eyes. Only the promise of revenge enabled him to contain himself. For the first time he hated Jorgensen with venom enough to find a savage pleasure in his plot.

All along, it had been his plan to bring things to a climax here at the mine. With Nils out of the way he believed he could soon bring Sigrid to terms. Then the flight to the wells and, in some way, escape across the Toquimas. Never by any chance did he dream of returning to Las Animas.

The thing he had in mind could be accomplished just as easily at the wells as here; and yet, because he was what he was, and because he had so often rehearsed in his mind the most minute details of what he proposed doing as taking place at the mine, he was loath to change his plans.

He looked at Jorgensen and laughed, and left it to Nils to decide just what he found so amusing.

"You prospectors are all alike," he declared contemptuously. "You like to make mystery where there is no mystery at all. Talk about not being able to find this well! I'll find it!

"Give me those jacks; they been here as often as you have, and I'll bank on it that they know this country better than you do. Get them within five miles of Piute Wells and you couldn't keep them from taking you there!"

Plainly he thought he had dropped a bombshell, and he waited defiantly, daring Nils to deny its truth. Somehow it failed to go off. Jorgensen seemed only mildly amused.

"There's the jacks, Kid," he replied. "Take your pick! Load him up with as much as he'll carry, and start tonight or in the morning. If you're there at the wells when we come along, I'll make you a present of every ounce of gold your jack is carrying!"

"I may take you up," Morales shot back sullenly, wondering if Jorgensen was bluffing.

"You won't if you're half as cagy as I think you are," Nils argued. "These jacks haven't been here often enough to savvy this country thataway. A jack will find water where a man won't if he gets near enough to scent it, but he ain't smelling it five miles off.

"If he can't scent it, he ain't worth a damn. I been watching my jacks for some sign of second sight like that. I ain't noticed any yet. If I ever do, they'll be on their way to jackass heaven in a hurry."

To be dismissed as though he were a schoolboy further infuriated Morales. His eyes narrowed, and into them crept the steely glitter of the killer.

Sigrid yawned. Jorgensen smiled at her. "Better turn in," said he. "You'll have to walk same as us going out. We'll pull out about sundown tomorrow. Get all the sleep you can; you'll need it."

Without glancing at the Kid he got up and went over to the kegs to measure the water they had left. Morales's fingers crept toward his gun.

Jorgensen voiced a grunt of surprise on discovering how little water they had left. "You gave the jacks too much today, Kid," he grumbled. "We ought to pull out in the morning."

His censuring tone proved too much for Morales. His mounting rage swept away the last vestige of restraint. He actually trembled in the sheer physical relief of being done with dissembling and playing the rôle that had been his since leaving town.

Jorgensen had crossed him for the last time! This was the show-down, right now! On the instant there blossomed full blown in his mind a fitting revenge for every indignity he had suffered.

So eager was he to see Jorgensen's cold contempt turn to bewildered surprise that his fingers trembled, and he fumbled his gun.

Sigrid screamed.

Jorgensen was still bending over the water keg. He turned in a crouch.

"Come on, stick 'em up!" the Kid droned. "I'll give the orders now!"

Jorgensen nodded slowly. "All right," he muttered, drawing himself erect. He moved too slowly to suit the Kid.

"*Climb,*" Morales prompted, "or I'll bust you!"

Sigrid leaped in between them. "No! *No!*" she cried wildly. "You're crazy, Kid!"

"Get back!" he roared. "You keep out of this. I'm running things now. Come on, Jorgensen, *walk!*"

Nils had taken only three or four steps when Sigrid screamed again. "*Look!* The water—it's running out!"

Jorgensen had opened the spigot as he stood over the keg.

"Great guns!" Morales groaned, taking in the situation at a glance. He leaped for the keg. It was too late to save the water; only a tiny trickle flowed out now.

Like a panther he whirled to kill Jorgensen on the spot. But the horrible oath that rumbled in his throat never left it. Paralysis seemed to grip him. Something was boring into his stomach. He dropped his hand to feel it. It was Jorgensen's big forty-five!

"Drop that gun!"

There was a dreadful insistence in Nils's voice. He had come to life with a vengeance. He, too, had lowered his mask. The blood froze in Morales's veins as he glimpsed Jorgensen's fighting face. He knew he was gazing into eternity. His stiffening fingers relaxed and his gun dropped to the ground.

Jorgensen kicked it out of the Kid's reach. "You want to grow up before you try anything like that on me," he ground out savagely. "You must have lost your head!"

The Kid began to breathe again. His nerve came back to him. "Shoot!" he dared. "Or quit treating me like a fool. You're driving me crazy!"

Jorgensen recovered the Kid's gun and emptied it. He put his own away next. "I didn't know I was riding you so hard," he declared more gently. "Still, two can't be boss.

"I only hope there wasn't anything more serious on your mind—like double crossing me, for instance. I reckon I'd have to shoot, then. I'm going to keep your gun, though.

"If you want to forget this, and mean it, I'll give it back to you when we strike the wells. Think it over; there's no hard feeling on my part."

"But what are we going to do for water now?" the Kid blazed. "My canteen ain't a third full."

"I know where water is, and you think you can find it," Nils answered. "Between the two of us we ought to locate it without trouble. We'll pull out as soon as we can after daybreak. There's *some* water in my canteen. I'll share it with you. How about yours, Sigrid?''

Examination proved it to be over half full.

"Maybe if we split it even we can make the wells," the Kid suggested. Nils shook his head.

"You and I'll split, Kid, but Sigrid keeps what she's got. She'll need it.''

CHAPTER 7

THEY BREAKFASTED IN THE DAWN. JORGENSEN GAVE THE ORders, and Morales worked harder than he had since coming in. Before the sun popped above the range, they were ready to leave.

Jorgensen was the last to go. When he had satisfied himself that they were leaving little or no evidence of having been there, he turned to follow Sigrid and the Kid. His pace was slow until he left the cañon, for he stopped time after time to blot out their tracks.

The day was still cool. Jorgensen knew they must take advantage of those early morning hours. In the past, when necessity had demanded it, he had covered the entire distance to the wells without pausing to rest. Never had he made it in less than fourteen hours.

He knew they would have to stop many times this trip. Neither would they make the wells in anything like fourteen hours. It well might be morning before they arrived there. It all depended on Sigrid and Morales.

Jorgensen believed Sigrid's vitality was greater than the Kid's. He knew she had the greater courage, too. And yet the advantage lay with the Kid, for the long trip in, and the work he had done at the mine had toughened his feet, and with a broken country to traverse, wading through deep sand and climbing in and out of countless arroyos, that would be an all-important factor.

As for himself, Jorgensen was not worried. He had often been in like predicament, and through accident, not by design, as was the case now. Sigrid was his only worry. What happened to the Kid mattered not at all to him.

Nils dismissed the gun play at the mine for the bungling work of a would-be bad man whose nerves were shaky. Neither had it come as a surprise nor as proving anything he had not already known. Morales had lost every trick so far.

But all this was only skirmishing. Jorgensen realized that. The ace remained to be played. It would be turned up when they reached the wells, and Nils intended that he, not fate, should be the dealer.

This was a game of winner take all. He had schemed with that in mind. Jorgensen not only wanted to win, but to prove to Morales that, in losing, he not only lost, but had never had a chance of winning. To keep him from taking Sigrid was not enough. Jorgensen had to know that she didn't want him—and the proof must come from her.

It takes rope to hang a man. Nils intended to give the Kid plenty—even to returning his gun. His was a desperate plan, entailing, as it did, the risk of losing both Sigrid and the mine. And yet he could not do differently; he had to know—and only Sigrid, placed so that the decision was squarely up to her, and unaware that the cards were stacked, could answer.

By ten o'clock the desert was a furnace. They moved along steadily. Sigrid and the Kid were ahead of the burros and out of the dust the animals kicked up. Nils, in the rear, enjoyed no such advantage.

The jacks were in no need of water yet, and they gave no trouble. It was possibly half an hour later that Nils glanced ahead to discover that Sigrid and the Kid had stopped. He joined them a few moments later. Morales's lips were swelling. It was Sigrid, however, who had been forced to call a halt.

"I yust have to have a drink, Nils," she sighed.

"All right, take one," Jorgensen urged. "We've come a ways already. We can't travel any faster or farther than you can. If you stand up, we'll make it. Your feet all right?"

Sigrid nodded, and Nils was immensely relieved. He turned to the Kid. "Your lips are puffing out, Kid," he said. "Keep 'em wet. You had a drink yet?"

"Don't bother about me," Morales answered crossly.

Nils said no more.

At noon time they halted. No one was hungry. There was no shade; so they stretched out in the blinding sun with their hats over their faces.

Jorgensen lit his pipe. The Kid moved away. The acrid smoke

was too much for his dry throat, inveterate smoker that he was. As he moved, his eyes encountered the three canteens reposing in the doubtful shadow of a clump of sage. The three canteens were identical. The Kid had been careful to note where Sigrid placed hers.

He glanced over his shoulder at Jorgensen. Nils was not watching him. In the turn of a second he had exchanged his own canteen for Sigrid's. He drank his fill soon after they started once more. It was the middle of the afternoon before Sigrid discovered that the canteen she carried was almost empty.

Jorgensen's eyes narrowed, and he singled out the Kid.

"Let me heft your canteen," he drawled ominously.

It was nearly empty too. Nils gave it back to Morales.

"Guess Sigrid's been drinking oftener than she thought," the Kid declared virtuously.

"Yeh?" Jorgensen's tone was coldly challenging. He knew what had happened. "There's some things a man forgets," he muttered. "I aim to remember this one!" He turned to Sigrid. "Drink! When yours is gone you can have mine."

The hours between three and six proved the worst of the day. Sigrid began to limp. The Kid, for all the water he had had, began to suffer. His lips were twice their natural size. Jorgensen seemed strangely unaffected.

"Can you go on until dark?" he asked Sigrid. "It's getting cooler now."

Sigrid said yes, but in another hour they had to stop. Her feet were terribly swollen.

Jorgensen surveyed the country before them in the deepening afterglow. "Been a bad storm here since I saw it last," he said to the Kid. "Don't worry Sigrid with that," he added as he gathered brush for a fire.

Beans and a can of tomatoes—both food and drink—made up their supper. Only Jorgensen ate what was on his plate. Having eaten, he massaged Sigrid's feet for almost an hour.

"Maybe I go on now, Nils," she volunteered bravely.

He shook his head. "Better to get a good rest. It'll beat going on now and having to stop a little while later. You got any water left at all?"

Sigrid said no. Nils asked the Kid the same question.

"I ain't had any since four o'clock," said he.

"Well, I got a little. Sigrid gets it; you and I'll have to get along without any."

"When will we hit the wells?" he asked thickly.

"Not later than daylight. Better sleep an hour now." He hobbled the jacks, and lay down himself.

"There'll surely be water at the wells, eh?" the Kid whispered.

"Sure!"

"But the storm—maybe things will be covered up."

"Better quit talking," Nils advised. In a few minutes he was asleep. When he awoke it was nine o'clock. Sigrid was sleeping soundly. He waited a quarter of an hour before he called her. She seemed refreshed. Even the Kid was able to talk clearly. The night air was bracing, and carried some degree of moisture to his parched lips.

They went on presently. Nils told Sigrid to make the pace. She moved off resolutely. It was a rarely beautiful night. The great desert moon hung low over the Toquimas.

Nils had never doubted that they would reach the wells. Several times during the afternoon, however, he had feared that Sigrid would arrive there in such condition that his hand would be forced, and all his scheming go for nothing.

That thought no longer worried him. As midnight neared, his confidence grew. But just when he was assuring himself that all danger was passed, Sigrid toppled over. Morales was the first to reach her.

"Just fainted!" he exclaimed, as Jorgensen hurried up to them.

Nils pushed him back, and put his canteen to Sigrid's lips. It held only a tablespoonful or two of water. He began to rub her hands, then. In a few moments she opened her eyes and stared uncomprehendingly about her for a second.

"Why didn't you say we were going too fast?" Nils chided her.

She smiled at him wanly. "We were going so goot I like not to stop, Nils," she murmured.

In another half hour she had recovered sufficiently to warrant their pressing forward. Nils moved in front now, and the Kid brought up the rear. Of necessity their pace was slower, so that when daylight came they had not reached the wells.

The question in the Kid's eyes had no need of articulation to make itself understood. There was no sympathy for him in Jorgensen's heart. Indeed, he turned away to hide his grim smile of triumph. Wait until this day was over, he whispered to himself. Morales's punishment would have fairly begun by sunset.

Nils turned to glance at Sigrid, then, and his heart smote him, and all his resolves almost went for nothing. She did not complain, but he could see that she was suffering, and he read in her eyes the bitter disappointment that the morning brought her.

"We'll be there soon," he told her. "Only a mile or so, now."

There was no sight of tree or green thing; no hint of water anywhere. Gradually in Morales's mind there grew the suspicion that Jorgensen had no destination in view, that he was only leading them on until they dropped. For the thousandth time the Kid regretted that he had not killed him when he had the chance.

Implausible schemes of revenge in which he tortured Jorgensen with fiendish glee and took a double toll for every fancied wrong flitted through Morales's head. In the midst of his bitter musing he was thrilled to hear Nils saying: "There's the wells! Maybe I carry you the rest of the way, Sigrid?"

The Kid saw the outcropping, low and unpromising, that Jorgensen said was the wells.

Sigrid refused to be carried. The promise of water gave her new strength even as it did the Kid. In his eagerness Morales forgot to notice if their excitement had been communicated to the jacks.

"You'd hardly think of looking here for water, eh, Kid?" Jorgensen laughed mirthlessly.

The Kid did not wait to answer, but ran ahead. He had only a few yards to go. Jorgensen's face froze into a mask of ice. He could not look at Sigrid.

Suddenly the Kid's voice broke in a shrill scream. He was staring at something in the ground. They saw him fall to his knees and dig in the sand with his hands. The next moment he fell back, clasping his head, his lips seared with a cry of horror.

Sigrid was but a step away. She saw what the Kid saw. Her eyes widened and widened, and her hands flew to her mouth to crush back the cry of utter despair that rushed to her lips.

The well was dry!

A little wet sand was all that the pool held!

Jorgensen shook his head, as if he, too, were stunned. Morales was speechless. For minutes no one spoke. Jorgensen trembled as Sigrid began to cry.

The Kid found his tongue. "She's dry!" he gasped miserably.

"Not a spoonful," Nils mumbled. "Don't cry, Sigrid," he begged. "We've got two cans of tomatoes left."

"No, Nils," she sobbed, "that only puts it off maybe a little while. This is the end."

"You're right, Sigrid," the Kid exclaimed. "What are we going to do now?"

This was the moment that Jorgensen had long foreseen.

"Those two cans of tomatoes hold enough juice to keep a man going two days. There is the way over the range." He lifted his arm and pointed out the great horseshoe cañon abreast of where they stood. "Two days from here is Wild Horse Creek. Maybe we can make it. I can get along with just a sip now and then. Maybe you and the Kid could pull through on the rest."

Sigrid raised her eyes and gazed off at the mountains, more than a mile away. Here, as at the mine, they rose to a tremendous height. They promised sheer ascents and deep abysses. It made her wince even to contemplate crossing them. From where was the strength to come for such an undertaking?

"Climb and climb," she murmured. "No, Nils, I never make it. Better I stay here."

"It ain't so bad! Mighty little climbing. Just hug that cañon wall on the right—just keep close to it and you can't get lost. It twists and turns a lot, but it gets you up—and without your realizing it. We can make it."

"We got to do something," the Kid urged. "Every hour counts."

"You're right, Kid," said Nils. "We can't stay here."

"Please no, Nils," Sigrid entreated. "I'm so tired."

"But it's our only chance!" Morales declared.

Jorgensen scratched his head in deep meditation. "No—no, it ain't our only chance!" he exclaimed gravely. "It's our best chance, but it ain't our only one. There's another."

He did not have to look at them to know that they were hanging on every word that fell from his lips.

"Look right over the top of this outcropping—do you see that other one, 'way off about three mile? Well, I've heard they was water there. Holmquist told me, and he knew this country better than anyone else who ever roamed it.

"That well may be dry, too, but it's a chance. I could make it there and back in three or four hours. You and the Kid could stay here. I'll take just the canteens. What do you say?"

The Kid's mind was working fast. He knew the way out—two cans of tomatoes! They loomed large in his eyes.

"You think maybe there's water there, Nils?" Sigrid asked eagerly. "Yust a little?"

"I can only find out, Sigrid." He answered gruffly, that she might not suspect what her suffering cost him.

"Why argue?" Morales demanded. "If there's a chance, take it! We're desperate!"

"All right, I go," Nils muttered. "You hobble the jacks so they don't stray off, Kid. And here's your gun. You may need it."

He slung the canteens over his shoulder. No other preparation was necessary, save a last word with Sigrid. "Don't lose your nerve," he smiled. "I'll be back soon."

They watched him draw away. In half an hour he was only a tiny speck bobbing up and down on the heat waves.

Morales waited no longer. He was armed, now. Here was Sigrid, and here was the gold for which he had suffered. Almost as equally precious was the food in Jorgensen's pack: flour, and the food that was food and drink—tomatoes! It was all his now.

If Piute Wells was dry, what reason was there to believe that some unheard-of well, that Jorgensen remembered only in his desperation, was not?

Jorgensen had said he would not be back for three or four hours. He'd come back tired, too.

The Kid thought of all these things and found them to his advantage. In three hours he'd be high up in the Toquimas. Let Jorgensen follow if he dared or could! There'd be no argument, no warning, this time! It would be a killing.

CHAPTER 8

JORGENSEN WAS NOT LOOKING FOR WATER. WHY LOOK WHERE none was to be had? Not much more than a mile from the wells, he came to an *arroyo*. It was deep enough to offer some protection from the sun until noon. He crawled into it without bothering to look back, knowing he was too far from the wells for the Kid to be certain of his whereabouts.

The trap had been set—almost as he had foreseen—and there

was no need of his going farther. His throat was parched, but that weighed lightly on him. His thought was of Sigrid.

"Everything would have worked out as I planned if the Kid hadn't stolen her canteen," he mused. "She'd have come through without any trouble, then. I sure didn't figure to make her suffer the way she is."

He knew she was in worse condition than Morales. Nils surmised that the Kid's exhaustion was feigned in part. Surely he had had twice his share of water.

No such thought occurred to Jorgensen in regard to Sigrid. His eyes told him too much. Not that he believed she had reached the limit of her endurance. Her vitality was too great for that.

As long as she had believed they would find water at the wells, she had been able to go on. He knew she would go on again if hope were rekindled in her breast.

Jorgensen fancied the Kid would attempt that. Strangely enough, it worried him little. He did not doubt but what Morales already appreciated the advantage that was his now. He held every card—as Nils had intended he should—and he believed the Kid would play them but one way.

He felt almost as certain of what Sigrid would do; but because she meant so much to him, was so necessary, his torture grew with every passing minute.

Time had never passed so slowly for him. He fumed and fretted and effectively proved himself anything but the phlegmatic, unemotional being he so often appeared to be.

He had said he might return in three hours. Three hours passed eventually. He wondered, then, if it was too soon to return. In utter agony he allowed another half an hour to pass before he climbed out of the *arroyo* and pointed his steps toward the wells.

What was he to find there? Now that he was soon to know, he found the confidence that had sustained him all along, and had led him to what he had done, was wavering. As he neared the wells he was afraid to glance ahead.

If the jacks were still there they would be discernible at a distance. If he could not see them, it meant they were not there. If they were gone, who had gone with them? Not to know was greater torture than he could bear.

He was tired; for the mental anguish of the past hours had affected him more than all the miles he had trod. And yet he increased his pace until he was almost running.

He maneuvered so as to keep the highest point of the outcropping between himself and the spot where he had left Sigrid and the Kid. Thus he approached to within a hundred yards of the wells before he raised his eyes and stared ahead defiantly to see what awaited him.

A savage cry, almost inhuman in its utter ferocity, was wrung from his lips—there was no one there!

The burros were gone! The Kid! Sigrid!

Jorgensen began to crumple. His legs wabbled. He was like a fighter who has been knocked out but is still on his feet. Just when it seemed he would crash down to earth, he stiffened perceptibly. The steel of him had not melted; it had become malleable.

He staggered on to the spot where he had left Sigrid. As he stared at the ground and saw the unmistakable marks of a violent struggle, he shook his head as if to clear it, quite as a boxer often does after a deadly blow.

"How she must have fought him!" he groaned. "He had to drag her along to make her go."

He could follow the trail the jacks had left. It was very distinct. Straight for the horseshoe cañon it pointed—ten yards—twenty—thirty——

He let his eyes run off into distance with it. Suddenly he caught his breath. His mouth fell open in terror. Surprise passed, but he could not move. A great choking groan burst from his tightened throat.

"Heaven help us!" was all he could say.

There was something lying out there on the desert—something that did not move—something that he realized was Sigrid!

He threw up his arms and flailed the air as though to break the shackles that held him chained there. His mind functioned again. His muscles and body responded, and he ran, actually *ran* to where she lay.

What had happened? Had Morales killed her because she refused to flee with him? Jorgensen could not answer. He knew only that had he not left her alone with the Kid, nothing would have happened.

"Sigrid! Sigrid!" he cried as he picked her up. "What have I done?"

She lay in his arms without moving, her hair disheveled, her clothes torn. Jorgensen saw that the sun had been at work in the hours she had lain where he found her. His heart sank. Surely she must be dead! She was so still. With heart sinking he felt for her pulse. It was beating faintly. He raised his eyes to heaven in gratitude.

Hope surged in him again. Perhaps she had only fainted, or was her unconsciousness due to a blow or fall? He was not skilled enough to determine. Perhaps it was no more than the comatose condition induced by utter exhaustion that gripped her. What did it matter? She lived, and if water would save her, he had it to offer.

He carried her back to the wells and laid her gently on the sand. Whipping off his shirt, he contrived a crude awning out of it. He began to dig then, not in the pool itself, but just beyond its lower end.

He had gone only a foot or so when the sand began to show traces of moisture. He kept on. Before long his shovel struck wood. He worked faster then. In another ten minutes he had uncovered and brought to the surface just such a keg as those which they had carried to the mine.

It was heavy. The keg was cool. It began to sweat at once. Jorgensen patted its fat side tenderly. "Now we got water!" he grinned.

He had cached the keg there on his last trip out, knowing from bitter experience that the wells always went dry in July.

He filled a canteen and let the water trickle down Sigrid's parched throat. She stirred restlessly in his arms. He bathed her face and hands. She sighed tremulously.

A few minutes later he gave her another sip. Her eyelids fluttered open. She gazed at Jorgensen for long seconds before recognition crept into her eyes. "You, Nils?" she whispered softly. "You found the water, eh?"

He nodded. He could not speak. Sigrid's eyed closed once more. Jorgensen saw that she slept now. He got to his feet after making her as comfortable as he could, and filled the three canteens. "I'll put the keg back in the ground," he said shrewdly. "Maybe it's better she never knows where I got the water."

He drank his fill first, smacking his lips over every mouthful. The distant cañon came under his gaze. "I guess you'd sell your soul for a swig of this, Kid," he chuckled. "It beats tomatoes—especially when they ain't any!"

He knew Morales had discovered that hoax before now. Nils shook his head. What a moment that must have been! And yet it was as nothing compared to a moment yet to come—coming as surely as evening came.

Sigrid had yet to tell her story of what had occurred at the wells, but Jorgensen almost knew without her telling, and he gloated over the fate that was soon to engulf Morales.

The Kid had placed himself beyond any hope of mercy. He had much for which to atone, but for what he thought he was doing that morning, as well as for what he had done, there could be no expiation short of being left to die on the very desert and in the very way in which he thought to leave them, while he stole away with the precious juice that might have saved them. That he had opened the pack, only to find it empty, made him no less guilty.

And such was the fate that Jorgensen had good reason to believe was even then staring the Kid in the face. He knew Morales was not many miles away; but had it been a matter of yards rather than miles, Jorgensen would not have stirred a step to succor him. The cañon, which Nils had told Sigrid—for the Kid's benefit—led across the Toquimas, led nowhere at all.

It was a blind cañon, a gigantic horseshoe so wide that a tenderfoot would follow its wall for miles without realizing that he was making a great circle that must bring him back eventually almost to the point from which he started.

Jorgensen believed that the Kid would never leave it alive. In his days on the desert he had felt the thirst that kills; he knew the symptoms, the delusions, the bitter agony of it. It was not difficult for him to travel in fancy at the Kid's elbow now.

He was cleaning his gun when Sigrid sat up without warning. She looked about uncertainly for a moment, and even when she saw Nils, recognition did not dawn in her eyes at once.

"Sigrid!" he called, and rushed to her side. His voice seemed to fully awaken her.

"Oh, Nils!" she managed to gasp before he crushed her in his arms.

"You all right, Sigrid?" he demanded loudly.

She had more important things to discuss than her own condition. "The Kid stole all the ore, Nils!" she declared excitedly. "He took the jacks and everything—he even try to take me!"

"And you wouldn't go, eh?"

She shook her head pityingly. "Look at me, Nils," she commanded. "You think I trade one like you for ten of him? No! I been a fool, Nils," she went on contritely. "You know; you didn't have to tell me.

"Seem like you never come back, last time. I get so lonesome. He comes along, and I—I flirt with him. I must have been crazy, I guess. I—oh, don't look at me like that, Nils! You always been my man—yust you, Nils!''

Jorgensen winced before her tear-dimmed eyes.

''Say you believe me,'' she begged. ''Never I do such thing again, Nils! Never! How I hate him! He's bad!'' She broke down completely then.

Jorgensen stroked her hair. ''Don't cry,'' he murmured. ''I know you're speaking the truth. Did he try to make you go with him?''

''He asked me, and I scratch him goot! He's bigger fool than me to think I go with him.''

''But I found you a hundred yards from here!''

''Oh, when I see what he is trying to do, I hang onto him. The food, the ore—everything he is taking. He drag me along. I won't let go. So he hit me.'' She paused to shake her head sadly. ''All that ore, Nils——''

''Don't worry about that; we'll find him. We got plenty water now. We'll take our time.''

He carried her the better part of the way to the cañon. He found a spot that was out of the sun but still commanded a view up the valley.

''We'll stay here until it gets cool,'' he told her. ''Sleep if you can.''

Sigrid had no thought of sleep now. She had Nils back! She found confession good for the mind as well as the soul. It removed the restraint and tension that had kept them apart for days.

The singsong of her voice proved too much for Jorgensen. His nodding head drooped lower and lower until he was sound asleep. He had never done that before. It made her realize how tired he was.

She made him more comfortable, and then sat down at his side to watch over him, although her own eyes were heavy. There was something primitive and strangely affecting about her vigil.

As the afternoon wore away and the sun edged toward the horizon, it became almost impossible for her to keep awake. Indeed, she suspected that she was dozing off now and then for minutes at a time. So it happened that when she first became aware of someone moving down the cañon, she thought it only a trick of her imagination.

She blinked her eyes owlishly. The staggering figure and

swaying burros did not disappear! They were moving very slowly, the man clutching one of the jacks to keep himself on his feet.

He was too far away for recognition. But that was hardly necessary. She counted the burros—three of them! Who else could this be but the Kid?

She nudged Nils. "Someone coming," she whispered, although there was no need for guarding her voice.

Jorgensen got up and scanned the cañon.

"It's him!" he exclaimed, his amazement genuine. "How's he stood it?" Nils glanced at the sun; Morales should have dropped hours back. "He's fighting hard, now! There he goes! He's down!"

"But why is he coming back?" Sigrid gasped.

"He must have lost the way. There, he's up again! He'll hardly get this far, though. See him stagger!"

The Kid fell again, but he got up. Jorgensen knew he didn't want to die. He could appreciate the fight Morales was making. The Kid had discarded his pack. His hat was gone. His clothes were in tatters.

Sigrid clutched Jorgensen's arm. The Kid was only a hundred yards away. "He'll be here soon," she whispered.

Jorgensen began to think so, too. He got out his gun. Sigrid questioned him with her eyes. "He's armed," Nils said simply. "Just keep back out of sight."

Slowly the distance dwindled between them. Not the slightest suspicion of their presence reached the Kid. He was more dead than alive.

An hour back he had discovered that he was returning to the mouth of the cañon. He understood fully what had happened. He lived only in the ever-dwindling hope that he might find Jorgensen before his gun fell from his lifeless fingers.

Of his own misdeeds and the sublime justice of his travail, he was unconscious. Every time he fell it became harder for him to get on his feet. He knew that soon he would go down never to get up again.

Jorgensen waited until only ten yards separated them.

"Hello, Kid!" he grinned.

Morales screamed. Words were beyond him. For seconds they faced each other without speaking, the Kid swaying groggily and Jorgensen watching him like a cat. Suddenly the Kid remembered. He brought up his gun. He could not hold it steady. It waved like wheat in the wind. He moved his feet to brace himself.

"He'll kill you!" Sigrid shouted to Nils. "Take his gun away!"

Nils shook his head and waited. The Kid's knees were giving way, his eyes were filming. His gun fell out of his hand. The next instant he pitched to his face at Jorgensen's feet. Nils did not bother to pick up Morales's gun. There was something horribly significant in his failure to do so. Sigrid thought she understood.

"He's dead?" she cried.

"Almost," he answered. "He won't get up again. It's all come to this, Kid, ain't it—all the scheming and crookedness? I knew you for what you were; I wanted Sigrid to know. I reckon she does now."

The Kid's eyes remained open in a glassy stare.

"I guess we can go," Jorgensen said.

"No, no, Nils!" Sigrid cried. "He's not dead. We can't leave him like this."

Jorgensen wheeled on her almost savagely. "What?" he exclaimed. "After all he has done to me and to you, you still would have mercy on him?"

"It's not him, Nils; it's us—you and me! I don't want to see those eyes staring over your shoulder at me every time you go away. We got plenty water. If we can save him, please do. Do it for me, Nils!"

Jorgensen shook his head dumbfoundedly. "I don't understand you; you're beyond me," he grumbled. "He leaves us to die, he gets trapped himself, and now you ask me to save him. You know what that means? It means I got to carry him on my back for miles. We got water, but no food. We must keep moving."

"But how could we go home and leave him here like this? No, no! Maybe he deserve to die, but not at our hands. If we leave him it be yust like murder! If he lives, he never come back here, Nils!"

"All right! Hand me your canteen," Jorgensen ordered. "I do this for you!"